AND

TIME'S ARROW
BOOK 3: THE FUTURE

AND

TIME'S ARROW
BOOK 3: THE FUTURE

Tom DeFalco & eluki bes shahar

ILLUSTRATIONS BY
TOM GRUMMETT & DOUG HAZLEWOOD

BYRON PREISS MULTIMEDIA COMPANY, INC.

NEW YORK

BERKLEY BOULEVARD BOOKS, NEW YORK

Special thanks to Ginjer Buchanan, Steve Roman, Howard Zimmerman, Michelle LaMarca, Emily Epstein, Ursula Ward, Mike Thomas, and Steve Behling.

X-MEN & SPIDER-MAN: TIME'S ARROW Book 3: THE FUTURE

A Berkley Boulevard Book
A Byron Preiss Multimedia Company, Inc. Book

PRINTING HISTORY
Berkley Boulevard paperback edition / September 1998

All rights reserved.
Copyright © 1998 Marvel Characters, Inc.
Edited by Keith R. A. DeCandido.
Cover design by Claude Goodwin.
Cover art by Jim Burns, based on a sketch by Tom Grummett.
Book design by Michael Mendelsohn.
This book may not be reproduced in whole or in part,
by mimeograph or any other means, without permission.
For information address: Byron Preiss Multimedia Company, Inc.,
24 West 25th Street, New York, New York 10010.

The Penguin Putnam Inc. World Wide Web site
address is http://www.penguinputnam.com

Check out the Byron Preiss Multimedia Co., Inc. site on the
World Wide Web:
http://www.byronpreiss.com

Check out the Ace Science Fiction/Fantasy newsletter,
and much more, at Club PPI!

ISBN: 0-425-16500-0

BERKLEY BOULEVARD
Berkley Boulevard Books are published by The Berkley Publishing
Group, a member of Penguin Putnam Inc.,
375 Hudson Street, New York, New York 10014.
BERKLEY BOULEVARD and its logo
are trademarks belonging to Berkley Publishing Corporation.

PRINTED IN THE UNITED STATES OF AMERICA

10 9 8 7 6 5 4 3 2 1

This one's for Ron Frenz. Keep the faith, bud! The good guys always win in the end—at least in *our* stories!

—TD

To Dave Lawson, who did the spreadsheets that helped me keep track of everything; to charming Keith R. A. DeCandido, who invited me to come and play in the first place; and to the X-Men and Spidey: you're a great bunch of folks to work with.

—ebs

PROLOGUE

MAINLINE +1, THE PRESENT

O nce upon a time, there was a law. . . .
The Super-Powers Registration Act of 1991 made it illegal to wield or possess super-powers without government approval. A lot of people spoke out against it. You don't see them anymore.

The skies of Manhattan are empty these days. No Daredevil. No Iron Man. Avengers Mansion is closed. The Baxter Building is on the market. The world is a very ordinary place.

Today, all that will change.

Lehnsherr's Law: All bunkers look alike. Case in point, the archival facilities of Project: Pegasus. It was a system of three interconnected silos, set in the earth within an ordinary-looking, fenced-in compound. Only the symbol of the project on the nearest silo revealed anything extraordinary about this place: the winged stallion, tamed to humanity's use by an enchanted bridle—an apt image for a vile policy.

All around him the hopeless fighting raged. The labs and stasis grid that were the target of his strike force were in the southernmost silo, the stasis prison in the central one. Somewhere in Silo South his fate, and the fate of all the men and women imprisoned under the Super-Powers Registration Act and condemned to the living death of stasis, were being decided by Aliya and her team, with the help of two interlopers who came, not from the future, but from the universe next door: Bishop and Spider-Man.

Spider-Man. How ironic that this gaudily garbed double of a brave man they knew so well should come to succor them in their darkest hour.

Or die with them.

The man born Eric Magnus Lehnsherr smiled bitterly

to himself as he made a sweeping gesture that sent a hail of debris to explode like shrapnel against the bodies of the advancing Mandroids. His opponents might be non-metallic—in a deliberate attempt to balk his mutant powers of magnetism—but Project: Pegasus itself could not have been built without metal—at least not cost consciously—and the tall white-haired man in the flowing metal cape had plenty of ammunition.

"Pack it in, Magneto!" a hated voice shouted from behind the Mandroid horde. "Surrender and you will not be harmed! I give you my word!"

"Your word, Cyclops?" Magneto shouted back. He'd succeeded in whipping a length of copper wire around one of the Mandroids—it gave him sufficient purchase to use the creature as a bludgeon with which to mow down its fellows. "Word such as you gave to Charles Xavier, boy, when you betrayed and imprisoned him to pursue your twisted ambitions?"

An optic blast was his only reply, exploding from among the massed ranks of Mandroids to spray against the magnetic shield Magneto raised only just in time. At his command, the wreckage, the very earth itself, awoke to savage life, sweeping toward the hated X-Men like a giant's open-handed slap.

Magneto saw Marvel Girl rise into the air, only to fall to earth again as he twisted the magnetic fields of the air against her. Powerful as he was, he would inevitably fall to his enemies, for in this battle the master of magnetism stood alone.

Scant hours before, there had been three teams—thirteen people—dispatched to breach the project's perimeter, destroy the stasis generator, and release the prisoners. The members of his Power Liberation Front cell who had fought beside him only a short time before—Titania, the Sandman, Volcana—were already dead.

He wondered how many members of the other two

teams were still alive—but while Magneto lived, *Homo sapiens superior* would not bow its neck to the pawns of petty tyrants.

Not that he'd be alive much longer.

Covering his retreat with a hail of projectiles and sparkling electromagnetic displays, Magneto retired across slagged and broken rubble in the direction of Silo South, knowing as he did that he was only delaying the inevitable. The Mandroids were not advancing, which meant that the X-Men were about to mount a serious attack.

And then a miracle occurred.

They burst from the top of the silo like strange sentient lava. Women dressed as rabbits and hawks and canaries and dominatrixes. Men dressed as frogs and flying rodents and insects and football players. In armor and flying under their own power, borne aloft by magic rings and enchanted hammers, carried by teammates and former enemies. Cyborgs and robots and aliens who had made the Earth their home, mutants of every possible form and function. Vigilantes and team players, pacifists and war hawks, capitalists and communists, kings and high school students.

Captain America, the Black Bee, Dominic Fortune. Daredevil, Hawkeye, Mockingbird, Moon Knight, Tigra, Hellcat, the Black Panther, the Black Widow, the Black Cat, Iron Man, the Ghost Rider . . .

They had nothing in common. They had everything in common. They'd been enemies and saints, traitors and martyrs. Children. Some of them hadn't even called themselves super heroes. But in this moment they were united by one thought that blazed through every mind, human and alien, mutant and metal.

Fabian Stankowicz—the Mechano-Marauder. Black Goliath. Iron Fist. Shang-Chi. Luke Cage, Hero for Hire. Prince Namor, the Sub-Mariner, here with his old Avengers teammates Yellowjacket and the Wasp.

Names that would live forever, names that would be forgotten. Firebird and the Texas Twister. Cloak and Dagger. She-Hulk. Doc Samson. Nova, the Falcon, Nighthawk, the Gargoyle, the Torpedo . . .

They'd been freed from a sleep that many of them were only now dimly beginning to comprehend had stretched for years—long enough to cut them off from their friends, their families, their missions. To destroy their lives.

It was time for payback.

And still they came, legends enough to bring the world back to life. And among them all, the brightly costumed form of the youngster known as the Air-Skater, who had been the last to fall to the X-Men's evil plans and the first to be released, now took his place among the champions of the world.

"Eric!" Aliya shouted.

A brief thanksgiving filled Magneto—he'd thought the valiant freedom-fighter from the future was dead, perhaps the most sorrowful loss in a day of losses.

"Flame on!" a voice shouted from behind her.

There was no time even for Magneto to register his joy that the tide of battle had turned—only a wash of heat, and then the first wave of heroes reached his position. The blazing body of the Human Torch flew past Magneto, shining like an earthbound sun.

"You're safe!" Magneto said, as Aliya skidded to a stop in front of him and swung her ion gun to mow down a pack of flanking Mandroids. Her face was smudged with soot, but there was a feral light of triumph in her eyes.

"We've won," she shouted over the din of battle. "The stasis grid is down!"

He'd allowed himself to be distracted from the confrontation for only a moment. When Magneto looked

back toward the X-Men's line, the imprisoned paranor-
mals whom Aliya had freed had moved to the attack in
waves.

The weathermongers among them seized control of the
elements by means technological and holy. In moments
the battle scene before Magneto's eyes was filled with a
fine haze of mist.

The ground trembled as Benjamin J. Grimm pounded
toward the attack, at his side the commanding red-white-
and-blue figure of America's conscience, Captain America.

Overhead, silhouetted against the gathering clouds in
the sky, angels and devils fought—the X-Man known as
the Angel battled furiously against the red-clad Daredevil, who clung to his foe even as he tried to bring him
down.

There was a crack of gunfire; a chilling laugh that
made Magneto's blood run cold even in the heat of battle.
He reached for the iron in Angel's blood, but before he
could grasp it there was a flash of light, bright as a bomb
flare, followed by a crash of thunder that was the howl
of a mad demon. When he could see again, both Angel
and Daredevil had vanished.

The black-and-yellow-garbed X-Men began to retreat,
protected by their endless horde of Mandroid servants.
Even the X-Men could not hope to defeat all of Project:
Pegasus's captives by themselves, but they did not have
to. Not with the power of the Mandroids to call upon—
and worse. Not all the mutants who had come to light
since the Act had been passed had gone into the darkness
of the bunkers. The X-Men had been busy, training their
successors . . . and their allies.

"This is a temporary victory—once they've assessed
our allies, the X-Men will regroup and attack again,"
Magneto told Aliya.

"Then they can make formation in hell," Aliya said, shifting the ion cannon in her arms. "With the stasis grid out of operation, it's only a matter of time now before all of Project: Pegasus's victims are loosed."

"How many of us are left?" Magneto asked, referring to the members of the Power Liberation Front.

Aliya's expression hardened. "Just you and me," she said gruffly. "Speedball betrayed us; his latest betrayal was his last. The Park and Razorback are dead, and Spider-Man and Bishop have gone back to their own universe," Aliya added reluctantly.

Spider-Man and Bishop were from a parallel "now"—a universe where Aliya's dead love, the man called Cable, still lived. Their arrival had sparked a dangerous hope in the time warrior, one that Magneto could understand. He recognized why Aliya grieved over the adventurers' departure, but losing the Park, the NBA star and secret agent for the Power Liberation Front, was a harder loss for the Front's leader to bear. Magneto only hoped that the Park had somehow known before his death that his years of dangerous masquerade had brought his allies the tools to achieve victory. He glanced around, assessing his new compatriots.

The fragmented remnants of the super-teams and lone heroes who had once been Earth's proudest warriors milled about the area, regrouping, looking for friends and teammates, repairing equipment that had been challenged by their long incarcerations, seeking explanations. None of them left the field. All realized that if they were to gain freedom for themselves and those they had sworn to protect, it must be here and now.

Today hero and villain were here to fight at the side of the loyal opposition—Magneto—for the honor that once they had all shared.

But of all those gathered on this battlefield, one stood

out by dint of his deceptive normalcy: a tall, confident
bald man who strode throughout all this exploding chaos
with the determination of a born leader who knew he had
an appointment to keep. Quickly he strode across the battered landscape, like many others, seeking absent friends.

"Magnus?" It was a voice Magneto had never thought
to hear again, the voice of Professor Charles Xavier, who,
after years of imprisonment by the super hero team he'd
been instrumental in founding, was free at last to repair
the error he had so unwittingly and disastrously caused.

"Charles!" Magneto's genuine smile of greeting was
bittersweet with the memory of past contention. They had
been the best of enemies, always divided upon the best
way to shelter the burgeoning mutant population from the
persecution both men saw as its future. For years Magneto had thought Xavier's chosen "guardians" of mutantkind had killed him to expedite their own search for
power long ago, and was more relieved than he'd expected to know he'd been wrong.

"So they spared you after all?"

The slender bald mutant with the piercing blue eyes
stepped cautiously over the rubble as he made his way
to Magneto's side.

"I am not dead—but spared? I think not," Xavier said
bleakly. "I have lived to see the death of my dream."

"It is not your dream that was false, Charles, but its
standard bearers," Magneto said quietly. "Your X-Men
were greedy children with no cause but themselves.
When the time comes to rekindle the fire of your dream,
you must choose again, more wisely."

"They're coming," Captain America said. All eyes
turned in the direction of the advancing X-Men. They
knew they could not win—but they dared not fail.

"Aliya," Magneto said suddenly. "Follow your
heart."

The warrior from the future looked toward him, reluctant hope on her face. Unconsciously, she ran her fingers over the Time Displacement Recall Device slung at her hip. The mechanism could take her to the past, the future—or to the parallel universe that was home to the man called Cable.

"Xavier!" A howl from the distance. "I'm comin' fer ya, Chuckie—ain't gonna be nothing but mincemeat left when I'm through," Wolverine shouted. Of all the X-Men, he was the most brutal—government sponsorship was little more than a license to kill for the Canadian-born mutant.

"Yer mudder wears army boots," Ben Grimm growled under his breath.

"I want to follow Cable," Aliya said, forcing the words out with an effort. Her cheeks flushed with the confession.

"Then go," Magneto said urgently. "With gods to fight beside us, your presence can make little difference in the outcome of this battle."

Charles Xavier glanced at him in surprise, but said nothing. Behind them, there was a rush of flame as the Human Torch lofted once more into the sky. It had begun to rain, but the droplets sizzled into steam long before they reached his body, and he moved in a glowing cloud.

"Then I'll go," Aliya decided. "I won't forget you, Eric."

Magneto raised his hand in farewell and Aliya turned away, retreating to a distance where the geo-chronal displacement of the TDR would not affect Magneto's forces.

"It will only be a moment more," Xavier said, pointing. The X-Men raced across the broken ground that separated them from the former prisoners. Wolverine—despite the fact that his adamantium skeleton made him one of the most vulnerable to Magneto's power—sprinted out in front, impatient for the kill. His claws flashed dully through the rain.

"It won't matter," Magneto answered. "Look." He pointed toward the sky.

The thunderclouds that Storm had raised in her elemental battle loomed black against the sky, but out of the west came a force blacker still—a monumental wave of dark energy rolling across the sky, crushing everything in its path.

"It troubles the very gravimetric lines of force that hold our Earth in its orbit," Magneto said. "I sensed it coming several minutes ago but did not know what I sensed. Charles?"

"I don't know," the once-leader of the X-Men answered, studying the phenomenon. "It's like nothing I've ever seen. We can only wait to see what happens."

"X-Men—take them!" Scott Summers shouted, stopping to fire an optic blast that knocked Captain America's tricolor shield from its spinning trajectory.

There was an orange-white pillar of radiance as Jean Grey rose into the air to meet the Human Torch, her telekinetic shields wrapped around her like veils of flame. She drew back her hand to strike. . . .

But the darkness reached them first. It spread its velvet wings over the battlefield, wrapping god and mortal alike in its dark embrace.

And in moments their battle—and their world—had ceased to be.

CHAPTER ONE

LIMBO, THE ETERNAL NOW

This is not a place for the sane.

Those who have heard of it call it Limbo, and speak of it in whispers. It is a dimension not of time, but of space, where now is all there is, and now is a darkling plain where ignorant armies clash forever through Limbo's twilight mists.

In this place that is not a place, in a time that is not a time, there is a castle called Tenebrae, borne upon the rolling sea of mists in the realm which exists in the gap between time and physical reality. It towers above Limbo's shadowy plains, and its ornate, non-Euclidian geometries—where walls are floors, and shadow-haunted staircases rise to nowhere and doors open on the void—could raise nightmares in the souls of the bravest. This is the land where all the stories end. There is no tomorrow in Limbo.

In a chamber within the castle lies the heart of what may be. Perhaps this hall tailors itself to expectations—Schrödinger's cat is raising a family here—and so in this unmoment of not-time it is a war room belonging to some far-flung future. Viewscreens cover every wall, and each one shows a thread of might have been and yet may be.

His name is lost in history. Whole universes know him as Kang the Conqueror. Descendant of a mysterious time traveller, Kang came of age in a century of peace and brought it war.

Once he reigned as the Pharaoh Rama-Tut in ancient Egypt. Once he fought beside the twentieth century's greatest tyrant, Von Doom of Latveria. In a galaxy two millennia removed from our own, he conquered all of known space, save for one tiny kingdom on the planet of his birth, home to the woman he loved.

The king had been old; the Princess Ravonna was his

only daughter. Ravonna had defied Kang from the moment of their first meeting, on behalf of her people and her realm.

He remembered the first time he had seen her.

It was early in his career. His legions had swept across all the countries of his homeworld. He held the satellites that orbited above; his battle fleet wove a steel cloak about the planet.

Only one kingdom still resisted him. It was a tiny place, a toy kingdom, holding sway over lands that were only a fragment of the planet's surface. It was so irrelevant that for years he had ignored it, intent upon bigger game.

Until now. It was the last, after all. All the rest of the world acknowledged Kang as its ruler, and he was reaching for the stars.

His legions encircled the tiny kingdom, his resources so vast against its tiny defiance. He had come to parley beneath a flag of truce. The kingdom's inhabitants had asked for this; Kang had been sure they meant to surrender. He had been willing to indulge them in this, the way a cat indulges a crippled mouse by allowing it to believe it can escape.

It had been springtime, the rolling acres of the kingdom green and flowering, an Eden in the midst of the dark mechanical culture that Kang had forged elsewhere. She had come riding out to meet his battle tank upon a white horse, her dark hair flowing free about her shoulders. There were flowers in her hair, as though she had just come from the garden, and she wore a riding habit in all the colors of spring flowers. In her hand she carried the silver wand of truce, its shaft entwined with white roses.

She was the Princess Ravonna, the king's only child, a child only barely a woman.

"So you are the man who has enslaved all our people," Ravonna said. Her eyes were as dark as her hair, and she gazed at him fearlessly.

"You mock me, child," Kang said. "I have set them free."

"Free to slave all the hours of their life for a grand design they will not live to see," Ravonna said scornfully. "Very well, conqueror, give us your terms."

"I do not make war with children, nor do I accept the surrender of kingdoms from them," Kang said crossly. The soft spring wind blew across the surface of his armor, but he did not feel it. The air, the sunlight, everything that the day could offer to him had been reduced to a series of readouts on the interior display of his armor. He was insulated from it all.

"Surrender?" Ravonna said in haughty disbelief.

She stared at him for a moment, and Kang realized she was trying hard to keep from laughing. He was amazed as he had not been in many long years, and wondered if the intelligence his spies and advisors had prepared for him could be wrong. What secret did Ravonna's people possess that she mocked him with such an easy heart?

"Oh, do forgive me, Kang the Conqueror," she said, amused. "I did not come here to bring you our surrender. We will defy you to the last babe in arms rather than submit to your tyrannical yoke. We did owe you the courtesy of telling you in person—my father would have come himself, but he had pressing business with the architect of the royal gardens."

Ravonna smiled mockingly.

"With the architect," Kang said, as if assuring himself that his ears did not deceive him.

"Indeed, Lord Conqueror. And so I have come in his place to assure you that you need not await our surrender before behaving like the brute that you are. Neither today nor any day will my people call Kang *master*, lord of murderers."

Kang very nearly did not hear her final insult; certainly he did not react to it. Gazing out from the turret of his massive tank at the laughing young woman on the spirited white horse, Kang felt an emotion growing within him unlike any he had ever known.

"You are aware that my army possesses enough power to not merely subdue your kingdom, but to obliterate it entirely?" Kang asked harshly.

"So you have said, and often, Lord Kang. And so here is my father's word to you—and mine. Leave us in peace, or be prepared to slay every one of us," Ravonna answered, her eyes flashing.

It was a strange feeling. Something delicate yet powerful; of gossamer lightness that yet stayed his hand with bonds of unshatterable alloy.

"Mock me at your peril, Princess Ravonna. If Kang stays his hand, it is from mercy, not weakness. I shall give you more time to consider—perhaps to consult with your nurse?"

That insult had hit home. Ravonna had reigned in her steed until it danced and reared. Without another word, she had turned her mount and ridden away. Kang had watched until she disappeared from sight, through the wall of the city's force field.

With one thing and another, it had been two years before he returned. He came as the conqueror of an empire that stretched a hundred light years in every direction from his home star, and when he came, it was with new terms for the tiny kingdom.

If Ravonna would marry him, he would leave her kingdom in peace.

It was a small concession. He was already master of time. He was already looking to the day when the son the two of them would have would rule the kingdom in her stead, and it would be but a tiny mote in his father's empire.

And once more she had defied him. Their clash of wills had been the clash of flint upon steel, and in the conqueror's heart there was ignited a passion to rival his love of conquest. From that moment Kang had loved the fiery princess. Years passed as he spared her father's kingdom out of love for her, hoping that one day Ravonna's heart would turn to him freely and he could crown her queen of all his far-flung empire.

But at last, frustrated beyond measure by her constant refusals, Kang broke his tacit vow and turned the might of all his armies against her father's tiny kingdom, and even the power of the twentieth-century super heroes known as the Avengers—snatched through time to be her defenders upon Kang's whim—could not lead Ravonna's armies to victory.

And so, at last, Kang was master everywhere upon the planet of his birth.

But when Kang would have taken by force what had so long been denied him—the hand of the princess—Baltag, commander of Kang's elite guard, had led the legions in revolt. He demanded Ravonna's death, as all had died who had dared to defy Kang by force of arms.

It was love (of a sort) that Baltag demonstrated in that hour. He had followed his master across a thousand battlefields, nurturing his own hopes of rulership at the heat of the forge of Kang's iron will to win. He had prized that inflexibility nearly as much as the spoils that his master's victories had brought him, and when he had seen it waver because of the horrified expression in a woman's dark eyes, he had not been able to bear it. He had led Kang's legions in revolt.

Perhaps he had always hoped he would not win. Perhaps he had only meant to punish Kang for turning away from the holy chore of conquest. Perhaps he meant to step back from the void of mutiny once he'd made his point.

But Kang was Kang, and he knew only one way to deal with any sort of obstacle whatever. In the face of hopeless odds, he had joined forces with the Avengers who had so recently been his pawns, in order to save Ravonna's life and her kingdom.

And all for nothing.

He had won. His rebellious field commanders had been defeated, Baltag himself in chains awaiting Kang's pleasure. The Avengers—who had been his tools, nothing more—had been dismissed to their own time again. And Ravonna looked upon him with eyes of love, seeing beneath the armor to the man beneath, the expression on her face that of one who discovers, with dawning joy in the discovery, that she has at last found the man she must love through all eternity.

But such moments are not made to endure. In the moment of Kang's supreme triumph, the treacherous Baltag had somehow gained one of the guards' weapons, and used it in a final bid for mastery. He had sought Kang's death.

But Ravonna had thrown herself into the path of the bolt to save the man she had only now discovered that she loved.

She had died almost instantly.

He had executed Baltag, of course, and every member of Baltag's family. For a time Kang had soothed his soul by crossing the timestream and executing every avatar of Baltag he had been able to find. A thousand bewildered men died in agony, never knowing the reason for their deaths.

It did not make the pain any less. Ravonna's death was something that the master of time lived with daily. Every hour he realized anew that Ravonna was dead, lost to him forever.

Ravonna's kingdom he had preserved intact, converting it to a necropolis. Her people became her priesthood, ministering to the thousand effigies of his Ravonna that Kang caused to be erected in the streets of the city that had once known her step.

But in the end, his love was still dead. And with her death, Kang had failed to achieve his objective, to make Ravonna his bride.

Kang had failed. The knowledge was nearly enough to drive him mad.

He tried to forget. Uncounted years passed, as Kang wandered the timestream, seeking to deaden the pain of this one defeat in battle, conquest, and war. Empires toppled. Queens cried out for mercy that was denied them. Heroes who had been the hope of their people fell before the man in the glittering armor who mocked them as they died.

Kang, who was his own myth, his own legend, the general who eternally returned from the mists of time to conquer again. At the sterile heart of the universe, where stars battered lifeless stone to powder with their unceasing hail of hard radiation, Kang's fortresses of glass challenged the brilliant night. Circling stars where light itself was blinded by the sheer weight of the gravimetric pull, Kang's towers of collapsed iridium mocked the stark tyranny of gravity. Through worlds made of water, his amphibian legions swam.

He was Kang, and he lived to conquer.

But always, through the branching tributaries of might have been, he had returned to that black moment of his failure, seeking escape. Seeking to be reunited with his lost love once more. Only that would heal the wound within Kang's soul.

And now, as master of his time-twin Immortus's stronghold—and of its one malleable defender, Immortus's servant Lireeb—he had come closer to achieving his goal than ever he had done in all his long and bloody career.

He would gain Ravonna once more.

And a thousand universes would die.

Kang's command center was filled with dead glass eyes, monitors that mimicked the cathode-ray tubes of a dead civilization. They were controlled by the mighty central brain of Tenebrae's computer, which had once served another master. Each screen showed another facet of what might be. They did not show all facets—for there were millions upon uncounted millions of variant time-lines, so many that no one could say which among them had come first—but they showed a random shifting sampling of those timelines which conformed to the parameters Kang had specified when he first came to Limbo and began his quest.

Now and again one of the screens would go dark for a moment before its watching eye moved on. Those flickers of darkness meant that an entire universe—from the tiniest dust mote to the most gigantic sun—had, in that instant, ceased to be.

"Another timeline vanished. And just when things were getting interesting there too," Lireeb said wistfully. "I do hate not knowing how things come out, don't you? Or are you the sort of person who reads the end of the mystery first to find out who killed the butler?" The tall, gaunt albino—a creature of Limbo itself—tucked his hands into the voluminous sleeves of his robe and turned away from the viewscreen he had been observing, a faint smile upon his bloodless lips. His eyes were the mad scarlet color of the fire at the heart of a blasphemous jewel and his skin was the grayish white of tainted snow.

"Your amusement is of no concern to me," Kang said absently, not really paying attention to Lireeb's babble. One day his servant would finally overstep the bounds of Kang's forgiveness, and Kang would extinguish him with no more thought than he gave to ordering the death of a star. The conqueror's eyes roved from screen to screen as if he would watch all of them at once, though he stood with the stillness of one who has watched empires shatter at his command. Even at rest, his darkly cloaked and battle-armored form radiated vitality, energy, and a lust for mastery that had brought him uncounted victories.

Except against the super-powered barbarians of the twentieth century. Except against Death herself.

"Naturally I only strove to congratulate you, O Conqueror, on yet another triumph," Lireeb said smoothly. "And to remind you that with each victory, the time grows shorter—"

Kang held up one dusky armored gauntlet for silence, but Lireeb spoke on.

"—and you must trigger the timequake that will eradicate the web of time and parallel realities that you hold in stasis. The temporal field is already—"

Kang's patience—never his strongest feature—snapped.

"Cretin! Do you think that I don't know how far the laws of time can be bent?" he demanded, still without removing his eyes from the flickering, ever-changing montage.

On the screens all around both of them, those universes remaining—thousands upon thousands, though Kang had already destroyed easily twice their number—flickered before his sight. Every possible variation on what might be, every deviation from what the deluded savages who called it home thought of as reality.

"—showing signs of collapse," Lireeb finished inexorably. "As of course the master of time is aware, since after all, he *is* the master of time. For that matter—"

At last Kang tore his eyes from the display before him and turned to his servant, fixing him with a baleful glare more unhealthy than the effect of any of the weapons concealed within the smooth violet-and-viridian shape of Kang's invincible battle armor.

"Speak, then, if you will not be silent," Kang grated, "but know this, albino: should you try the patience of Kang the Conqueror too far, eternal oblivion shall be your portion."

The albino regarded him with an expression that might—between equals—have been approval.

"And you'd certainly be an expert in oblivion," Lireeb murmured appreciatively. "But as I was saying, the barbarian Earth hero Spider-Man and the mutant outlaws who call themselves the X-Men happen to have repaired their crude and primitive Time Displacement Core and solved the riddle of your Time Arrows. In their childish passion, they will now no doubt seek to discover the location of Your Puissant Majesty through the Time Platforms themselves, and, should they succeed—"

"Are you trying to drive me from my wits by telling me what I already know, albino?" Kang demanded, turning away sharply. In moments, his attention was caught once more by the ever-shifting panorama of the viewscreens that covered the wall before him. In one of those worlds, Ravonna waited for him—a Ravonna who lived, who was ready to welcome Kang as her true love.

"How could any man possibly do that in the face of the mighty Kang's, ah, might?" Lireeb enquired of the empty air.

"Chaos take you—will you not leave me in peace?" Kang shouted. No matter how many realities he searched, there were always more, but only one of these countless universes held the woman he sought—alive and loving.

"As much as Spider-Man and the X-Men will," Lireeb answered. "Should they discover how to reach Limbo, not even the walls of Tenebrae itself can defend you from their concerted assault. And a pitched battle here—"

Kang gritted his teeth. The trouble with inferiors was that they *were* inferiors. Unfortunately, Lireeb's warnings had a certain conventional wisdom to them, so allowances must be made. It was true that if Kang triggered the timequake now as Lireeb urged, he would indeed obliterate all the irritating tangle of proliferating timelines containing super heroes that sprang from the late-twentieth-century nexus point, and end the threat of Spider-Man and the X-Men to his plans. The only trouble was, the timequake would destroy all the possible Ravonnas as well as the irritating super heroes. And time was running out, as the forces he held in check grew increasingly unstable.

Unstable or not, they must await his whim.

Once he had found his Ravonna, Kang could ready the mechanism of the timequake, then journey to wherever his princess was with the Force Shield Generator that would preserve her timeline while the timequake swept the rest of the selected timelines out of existence. Until he found her, he could not act.

And besides, Kang liked a challenge—even if, as was so often the case, he had to choreograph it himself. So let the X-Men continue to struggle on. The battle would divert him; a welcome counterpoint to the frustration of his search.

"Once my foes have determined which of them journeys to which platform," Kang said, enunciating as slowly and clearly as if he were speaking to one of his Time Troopers, "they can be obliterated with ease by enemies recruited from within the very eras themselves. Do these schemes not suggest themselves to you? Must all the burden of conquest fall to Kang? See to it, albino!"

Not that he needed Lireeb's help to defeat his foes and gain his victory. The albino was a mere convenience, nothing more. Just as the Avengers had been, on that long-ago tragic day.

"Yes, master," Lireeb responded. "All shall be precisely as you command."

Kang closed his ears tightly, certain that if he did not he would hear the albino snicker.

CHAPTER TWO

MAINLINE, THE PRESENT

The Hudson Valley was once prime wine country, and the shells of bankrupt vineyards still dot the rural Upper Hudson landscape like ghosts—though in some places, the ghosts are more tangible than in others.

For example, the long-defunct Rosendale Winery in Rosendale, New York.

The barn that once housed the main press and fermentation tanks now housed the fruit of far different labors. Here, in a sub-basement, in the secret laboratory of the mysterious being called Blaquesmith—willing pawn of the Askani Sisterhood, guardian and sometime mentor to the mysterious time warrior called Cable—was the Time Displacement Core that had carried Cable back to a time that was both his past and his future: twentieth-century Earth.

He had been born scant miles from here, a very long time ago. Nathan Christopher Summers, the son of Scott Summers and Madelyne Pryor, a woman genetically identical to Jean Grey. To save his infant son's life, Scott had relinquished him into the care of the mysterious Askani, to be raised in a distant future world.

But it hadn't lasted—either the care or the future.

The machines that filled the old barn were created out of knowledge that would only be mastered centuries from now; knowledge that only the Askani (who had little interest in it) retained. In this laboratory the threads of past and future cross, and what may be—all the what may be's—could be viewed as easily as *Nick at Night* reruns.

But no one here is interested in watching television just now.

Half an hour ago.

Lights flashed, as power demands were answered by

draining storage batteries, by shunting the charge from a catch-basin designed to keep Central Hudson from wondering just what there was up in Rosendale that needed all this power. The poisonous tang of ozone was harsh in the air; the scent of Frankenstein's laboratory on a thousand fabled midnights.

The time platform flashed, and two figures stumbled from it, clutching at each other for support. Around them for a brief moment swirled the volcanic ash they'd brought with them: Gambit and Wolverine limped away from the platform, knowing—hoping—that there were others behind.

Gambit looked as if he'd been rolling in mud. His glowing red eyes seemed less out-of-place against skin that was streaked white and black with ash. The long leather duster he wore was stained black with water all the way to his hips, and the leather across the shoulders was charred with the pinpoint burns of falling sparks. The ash smeared into his face only served to emphasize the haggard exhaustion of its lines.

Bad off as he was, his companion was worse. Wolverine's costume was nearly gone, much of his yellow and black mask scorched away along with the hair beneath. His shoulders—he was bare to the waist—were spotted with white blisters the size of golf balls, that broke and oozed as his accelerated healing factor attempted to cope with the massive insult of an attack by the super-villain Electro. His normally hirsute form was as pink and hairless as a boiled pig.

"You okay, Cajun?" he asked.

"I been better. An' you?"

Wolverine's only response was a mirthless smile.

Storm and Iceman appeared next, both spattered with mud. Storm wove unsteadily on her feet, her long silver hair draggled and choked with mud and weeds. Iceman watched her anxiously, obviously wanting to steady her, but in his ice-sheathed form he'd do her more harm than good. Storm shook her head as if to clear it, forcing a smile to reassure her teammate, but there were dark circles beneath her slanted blue eyes.

The next to appear were Cable and the Beast, and when their condition became clear, the other three—Iceman not included—rushed forward to strip them of arctic survival gear that had become deadly, its insulating layers soaked with icy water. Wolverine ruffled his fingers through the Beast's blue fur, forcing it to shed its cargo of half-frozen water. Hank smiled in absent gratitude, flexing his cold, stiff fingers.

Cyclops and Phoenix arrived last of all, and with a flick of her telekinesis, Jean Grey was able to remove all the water from the Beast's fur, though there was little she could do for the others.

That was when they'd found out that they'd lost. That in attempting to destroy Kang's time bomb, they'd armed it instead.

And two of their comrades were still missing. Bishop and Spider-Man—lost somewhere in a parallel universe in which the malfunctioning Time Platform had marooned them—were still missing, and every minute they were gone increased the possibility they could not be returned. The Time Displacement Core would not have been running at all if it had not been jacked directly into Professor Charles Xavier's magnificent mutant brain: even now the X-Men's mentor sat crouched over the control console of the platform, gossamer-thin wires snaking from the needle-thin limbic jacks implanted within his brain to the machine before him. He looked drained beyond measure, but his struggle was far from over. It would not end until Spider-Man and Bishop were brought safely home.

If they could be.

•　•　•

The two-minute recall had been sent, giving Spider-Man and Bishop a moment's warning before the recall was triggered.

"Sixty seconds," Blaquesmith said. "Retrieve signal encoding."

Professor Xavier and his X-Men watched tensely as Blaquesmith made his final calculations.

"Thirty seconds," Blaquesmith said. "Dimensional interface up and running."

There would be only this one chance to retrieve their friends, and so far they'd lost every battle with Kang except for one. Even while they defeated Kang's agents, those successes had only loaded the gun that Kang the Conqueror had trained upon the beating heart of everything they knew. Even the gentlest of them was out for blood now, and they stood strained and tense as Blaquesmith threw the final switch.

Silence.

"It didn't work?" Gambit asked, staring at the empty TDR platform.

As if in answer, there was a lightless flash—reality turning itself inside out—and suddenly the empty space was filled once more with the forms of a small crouching man and a much larger one standing upright.

"So, what took you so long?" said the latter, dressed in blue and gold.

"We're baa-ack!" The crouching blue-and-crimson figure sprang from the platform to hit the wall of the barn with a distinct thump. "We're back—we're here—New York—hot dogs—rush-hour traffic—subway strikes—happy, happy, joy, joy—we're back!" Spider-Man caroled as he bounced from wall to wall far above the heads of the others.

Professor Xavier sighed, a deep sound of relief and weariness, and began unlinking himself from the Time

Displacement Core. His hands shook with overwhelming fatigue, but there was no time to rest.

Bishop merely shook his head. His guns were still in his hands—Bishop had spent his whole lifetime fighting, so that even now he relied more upon his futuristic weapons than his mutant powers. The burly black mutant had been born with the power to absorb energy from anything he touched and redirect it as explosive blasts, but Bishop's future, a time centuries beyond the X-Men's "present," was one in which the persecution of mutant-kind had reached nearly its ultimate unfolding. The grim scar—*M* for "mutant"—that Bishop bore over his right eye was mute witness to the terrors of that future.

On the opposite wall, Spider-Man froze, clinging effortlessly some twenty feet above the others' heads.

Bishop gazed over the assembled heroes dourly, his mouth quirking in a humorless smile as he surveyed their battered condition.

"We've failed," he announced. "Kang is still free, still destroying universes even as we stand here. We still have to stop him."

"Tell us something we don't know," Iceman muttered.

"Granted," Cyclops agreed, shooting Iceman a minatory look. "Unfortunately, he's now more powerful than ever." He glanced toward Professor Xavier, his face beneath the gleaming battle visor worried as he assessed his mentor's weakness.

"So. Kang's still the target for tonight. Learn anythin' else on yer package tour, Curly?" Wolverine growled toward Bishop.

Bishop sighed, holstering his hand cannons and stepping off the teleport platform. Spider-Man leapt from the wall to land lightly behind Iceman atop one of Blaquesmith's computers—at least he thought it was a computer.

Bishop drew himself up to his full imposing height,

casting off the weariness of a battle that he had only left moments ago. His dark eyes glittered like hostile lasers, directed at an enemy who was not present.

But it was Cable who spoke.

"We know that Kang has been attacking our time-stream from four different alternate universes, at points ranging from scant decades in our own future to a time over a millennium distant. What we must do is split our forces into four teams: Iceman, Wolverine, and Bishop will go to—"

"Just a minute, here—" Bobby Drake protested, absently brushing the last of the frozen mud from his icy exterior.

"An' just who elect' you leader of de X-Men, *hahn*?" Gambit angrily wanted to know.

"Gambit—" Phoenix began.

"Stop it—all of you!" Blaquesmith said urgently.

"What is it?" Cable asked, turning away from them and stepping to Blaquesmith's side.

"Someone is trying to cross between timelines, using a technology whose energy signature is identical to my own," Blaquesmith said in his reedy, dispassionate voice. "They should materialize within the Core momentarily."

Bishop swung back to face the platform, his hand cannon leaping from its holster to his hand as though it were a living thing. The same thought was on the mind of every one of the X-Men: that Kang had at last come to face them here.

"Guess it ain't over 'till it's over, eh, Bish?" Spider-Man said, tensing himself to spring.

Bishop appeared to ignore him.

Iceman spared a moment to glance up at the crouching figure above his head. "Um, you know, he *hates* being called 'Bish,' right?" he said in a low voice.

The impassive scarlet mask with its tracery of black

webbing tilted as Spider-Man cocked his head to stare back at Iceman.

"Yeah?" he said, equally softly. "And your point is?"

Iceman grinned and returned his attention to the teleport platform. In the flicker of an eye, a slender figure in a blue-and-gold battlesuit appeared there. The X-Men stared at her blankly: friend or foe?

"Aliya!" Spider-Man said.

Bishop lowered his weapon, but it was Cable who moved fastest and farthest.

"You're alive—oh, Cable—praise the Askani that it is so!" With a gasp of relief, Aliya flung herself into his arms.

In many ways the young time warrior that Spider-Man and Bishop had come to know in the alternate universe was Cable's mirror image. Almost before the others had registered the fact of their emotional reunion, Cable and Aliya had broken apart and were regarding each other with identical expressions of closed wariness upon their faces.

"Something is wrong," Cable said, glancing toward Blaquesmith.

"Magneto sent me away," Aliya said, stumbling over the words as the strangeness of the leader of the Power Liberation Front's actions became fully apparent to her.

"In order to save you, perhaps," Blaquesmith said dispassionately. "Had you remained, you would have been destroyed—just as your home and everything you have ever known and held dear has been."

The ancient technowizard's voice was as remote as if he were announcing his opinion of tomorrow's weather, so that it took a moment for the assembled heroes to understand what he was telling them. Another universe was destroyed.

Aliya's home was destroyed.

"Jeez, what a party kind of a guy," Spider-Man muttered. Iceman shrugged. He'd had more time than Spider-Man had to get used to Blaquesmith, Cable's self-appointed guardian and mentor. In technical terms, Blaquesmith was *weird*.

"Gone," Bishop said in shock. Terrible as the world they had just left had been, with its Project: Pegasus to entomb supernormals in eternal stasis-generated hibernation, it was still a world in which Sentinels did not exist—where there was still hope for mutantkind's future. And now that world itself had no future. It was gone.

"Time to get it in gear," Wolverine grated.

"All right," Cyclops said briskly. "Blaquesmith, how long to program this buggy to send us to the four alternate timelines you've isolated?"

"It can be done quickly enough, Cyclops. You had best use the time to prepare yourselves to fight again," Blaquesmith said.

In an hour the deep violet burns on Wolverine's skin had faded to pale pink, and hair was beginning to sprout once more on his skin and scalp. The X-Men had taken the short breather while Blaquesmith worked on the Time Displacement Core to eat, change into fresh uniforms, and erase the effects of their injuries as best they could. But they'd been in a fight and they all looked it, and now they were going to fight again.

"Listen up, people," Cyclops said, as they gathered once more in front of the platform. "Kang's still destroying timelines and so far all we've done is help him. We don't have time to mourn, but we still have time to beat this thing once and for all. There are four of Kang's Time Platforms, and we know where they are. We know that they were used to deliver the Time Arrows, but Kang didn't destroy them, so they may contain the information we need to take the battle to him. On his home court we can beat him once and for all—he won't have the advantage of surfing through time to pick and choose his fights. We'll split into four teams and hope at least one of us brings home the brass ring—that team can return here to give the coordinates to Blaquesmith, who will use them to coordinate our efforts further.''

Swiftly, the X-Men's first field commander made his tactical dispositions: Storm, Gambit, and the Beast to the year 2099; Wolverine, Bishop, and Iceman to the year 3000.

''Cable, Aliya, Spider-Man, you'll take the nearest one, in 2020. That's only a few years away—Blaquesmith doesn't think it's diverged from our own present much, so things should be fairly familiar to you.''

Professor Xavier, in his golden hoverchair, a product of alien Shi'ar technology, descended slowly to the level of the Time Platform.

''Remember that Kang must have chosen these specific times and places for a reason, even if we don't know what it was—yet,'' he said. ''Fortunately, these Tempometric Meters will help you locate the platforms by the temporal radiation they give off. That should be some help. It is odd to think so, but speed is of the essence.'' The X-Men's mentor was exhausted, running on sheer indomitable will alone as he briefed the X-Men with what little information Blaquesmith and Cable had been able to put together in the past hour.

The Tempometric Meters resembled large golden ankhs—the Egyptian symbol of eternal life—with a tiny display sandwiched into the hole of the oval. They would be the teams' only guide to the location of the Time Platforms once they'd arrived in the various futures. The location mechanism was simple; a tiny blue dot functioned in much the same way that the needle of a compass would, its shape thickening or elongating in a crude measure of height or depth. It was the best the X-Men's techies could come up with on such short notice, and Cable had been hard-pressed to build four of them, even with Hank McCoy and Blaquesmith's help. As Professor Xavier spoke, Cable handed one each to the Beast, Cyclops, and Bishop, and kept the last one for himself.

"You'll be dropped as close to your goal as possible, folks, but there are no guarantees," Scott added. "Here. You'll need these too."

"These" were the other item Cable and the others had labored frantically over for the past sixty minutes—enough Temporal Recall Devices for each member of the team to wear one this time.

Each of them was a circle about eight inches across and three inches deep, attached to a chartreuse webbing harness that would allow each of the heroes to strap one to his or her chest. In the center of each silvery device a rounded hubcap shape could be lifted with a fingernail, exposing an almost humorously prosaic red button with the word RECALL carved into it.

By rights it ought to say DON'T PANIC, Spider-Man thought, staring at the button. He'd never felt less like taking a trip in his life. He didn't belong here. These guys were all so *organized*. And—except for Wolverine—so tall.

These were the Personal Recall Units that would return them to this time and place at will . . . providing, of course, that it was still there. Slowly each of them strapped on what would be his or her lifeline back to Rosendale.

Spider-Man started to shrug into the awkward harness, then got a brainstorm. He put the harness on backward, so that the heavy silver casing of the TDR rested between his shoulder blades. A squirt of webbing cemented it immovably to his costume (even with the lower-grade web fluid that was currently in his shooters, the bond should last longer than he would), and he'd notice it less there than if he were wearing it in front. And he was limber enough to press the button even if it was in the middle of his back—especially if coming home to MJ depended on it.

"That takes care of us, Scott, but what about you and Jeannie?" Hank McCoy said. His monstrous blue-furred form might have been the legacy of a genetic experiment gone wrong, but in his brown eyes was an entirely human worry for his friends and earliest teammates.

"We're going to 2035," Scott said, a faint reluctance to reveal the fact evident in his voice. "It seems to be a variation on the 2013 timeline Rachel Summers came from, which should give us a bit of an edge. Remember, folks—all of these are *possible* futures, not actual ones. Friend may be foe, and things may be distorted in the strangest ways—"

"Just as in any war, Cyclops," Cable said brusquely. "Let's go—even with the TDR, we may be running out of time."

"Yeah, Cyke—cut to the fight scene. I could use a good scrap after all this tail-chasing," Wolverine said. His claws glittered briefly in the dim light of the barn as he shot them to full extension and then retracted them again. Spider-Man winced. It looked painful.

"Come on," Cable said, staring right at him as if he knew Spider-Man's reluctance to plunge into the time-stream again. He and Aliya stepped onto the platform, and Spider-Man launched himself from his perch to join them.

"Why am I doing this?" he asked plaintively.

Before anyone had a chance to answer, there was an intense flicker of displacement and the three figures were gone.

•   •   •

''Heads up,'' Wolverine said, jumping onto the platform and crouching as though he expected to be attacked instantly.

''I just know this is going to be a really special experience,'' Iceman said crossly as he took his place beside Wolverine and looked back at Bishop. Bishop regarded him with impassive endurance as he mounted the platform, holding the Tempometric Meter as if it were merely another weapon as he mounted the platform.

''Second Team good to go,'' Wolverine said.

Then they too were gone.

In one sense, whatever the teams would do had already been accomplished, but in another, more real sense, all their battles were still to be fought.

Gambit and Storm took their places on the platform. Neither of them was at the top of their game, but Remy flashed a cocky grin at his fellow ex-thief as they took their positions. It wasn't Gambit's style to be seen worrying about the outcome of anything. Storm smiled back, unwilling to have him know how little she relished being flung crossways through time to an unknown and infinitely strange destination.

The Beast hesitated, still looking back.

''Your destination is a particular danger zone for the X-Men,'' he said to Scott. ''If that future is anything like Rachel's track, it will be full of Sentinels . . . who've won.''

''We'll be careful,'' Cyclops said soberly.

''Come back safe—all of you,'' Phoenix said, rising up on tiptoe to kiss Hank upon his furry cheek.

The blue-furred X-Man ducked his head, and then turned to close the space between himself and the platform with a single enormous bound as Spider-Man had. The moment his feet touched it, he and the other two were gone.

Scott looked at Jean, then at Professor Xavier.

"Godspeed, my X-Men," Charles Xavier said. "More depends on you than any of us can possibly imagine."

"Platform ready," Blaquesmith said. And in a moment, Scott and Jean, too, were gone.

Lireeb turned away from his console and regarded the man who styled himself conqueror of a thousand universes . . . because he *was* the conqueror of a thousand universes.

"The short-range probabilities are now fixed, Master," Lireeb said with satisfaction. "Storm, Gambit, and the Beast travel into the future to confront their own descendants, much as Cyclops and Phoenix, and even Spider-Man, do. In fact—"

"*Why* do you continue to torment me, witling?" Kang demanded, whirling from the wall of swirling monitors to confront Lireeb. "Is it not honor enough that I allow you to bear witness to my greatest conquest—that of the timestream itself?"

"It is a very great honor indeed, O Master," Lireeb said. "I only thought that you would wish to know that the woman Aliya has escaped her own timeline to rejoin—or meet—the simulacrum of her dead time-ravished lover, Cable. Not that it matters to me, of course. . . ."

There was a moment of electric silence as the echoes of Lireeb's voice trailed away.

"She's done *what*?" Kang screamed in a throttled whisper. "She's rejoined *Cable*?"

"I thought that would get your attention," Lireeb murmured, but Kang didn't hear.

"How *dare* she? How *dare* he? Those witless, insignificant *worms*—who are *they* to be reunited in defiance of Death when Kang himself cannot be?"

The diminutive figure in the green-and-purple armor nearly danced with all consuming rage, his entire body quivering with a fury even Kang had not expected to feel.

It was as if the posturing primates of the twentieth century knew his inner thoughts, his soul-pain, and mocked them both with a casual gesture. In that moment he was as mad as—if not madder than—Wolverine in the depths of the blackest battle frenzy.

"Their arrogance defies belief," Kang gasped in a rage-thickened voice. Crazed anger sang high and cold through his veins and hammered in his temples like the ticking of an enormous clock. "I shall fill their last pitiful hours of life with an agony undreamed of. I shall *show* them their deaths—"

"But, Master," Lireeb said in feigned innocence, "surely they are not worth your attention. Have you not already said that they will die in the future worlds they will journey to—and that even if they discover the remains of your Time Platforms, they will not be able to operate them, no matter how much Cable may—"

At the reiteration of that name, Kang emitted a shriek such as the very gates of hell must have made at the moment they were ripped asunder. The inanimate indigo faceplate of his armor—more impervious than any armor ever forged before it in all the space-time continuum, yet as flexible and responsive as a living human face—seemed to darken with a rage that transcended humanity itself.

"Do not speak to me of him! Do not speak at all! I promise you, albino, that should those mutant barbarians and the perfidious man-spider not each find an excruciatingly hideous death worthy of Kang himself—especially *him* whom I will not name—you will suffer in their place! Now leave me—go!"

Lireeb watched with interest as Kang turned away, his jerky furious breathing slowing as though Kang had recognized even his own rage as an enemy which might divert him from his quest. Kang dealt with his fury as he would with any enemy, and in seconds it was conquered;

both Kang's rage and his interest fading as though Lireeb had been only a transitory bad dream, a temporary interruption of his quest for Ravonna.

Lireeb shrugged. There were other places than Kang's volatile presence in which he could prepare suitable opposition for each of the four teams—who, in some sense of the word, had already been vanquished by whatever Lireeb would choose to send them.

Or not. In Limbo, the nature of both truth and reality was a very personal thing. . . .

CHAPTER THREE

T he first thing he realized after they'd made the jump was that the air was dead and desert-dry. Wolverine inhaled deeply and wished he hadn't. Dead air. Recycled air. Sterile and lifeless and containing no information at all.

It was a little like being struck suddenly blind, though he could still see perfectly well. The enhanced senses that he relied upon for much of his picture of the world were suddenly useless, as if they'd been ripped away, leaving him merely human.

Wolverine had wondered what it would be like to be human, sometimes. The puzzle had claimed his attention for, oh, five minutes at a stretch.

"Whoa!" That was Iceman checking in, to his left. Wolverine could taste, in the back of his throat, the cold radiating from Drake's body; it was an improvement over nothingness, and told him he wasn't victim to any sort of transformation. His senses worked the way they always did. There just wasn't anything for them to work on.

"What kind of a place *is* this?" Drake went on.

"Somewhere we don't want to be." That was Bishop. Wolverine glanced toward him. The burly mutant stared around himself impassively, foreboding radiating from him as cold did from Drake.

"Anyplace you recognize?" Wolverine asked.

"No."

Well, it had been worth a try.

The three of them stood in a corridor about ten feet in diameter. It curved away from them in both directions, as if they stood on the outer edge of a wheel. The corridor was tubular, flattened at top and bottom. The walls, floor, and ceiling were all made of a springy steel-colored material that had the texture of plastic. Handholds placed along the sides indicated that these passages were meant to be used both with gravity and without. Signs were lettered directly on the worn and battered walls, in an untranslatable script that bore a teasing resemblance to the alphabet of twentieth-century North America. Bland and probably cheap to produce; government issue looked the same wherever you went.

"We're out in space!" Drake said, gazing through the transparent slot of outer-curve bulkhead just ahead of them in the corridor. That was Drake all over, always announcing the obvious.

When he moved, Drake's body made the faint VLF sounds of shifting pack-ice, audible only to Wolverine. The recall device he wore gleamed against the ice on Drake's chest like some kind of cosmic bell-push, making him look even less threatening. Wolverine knew that Drake could handle himself in a fight—he wouldn't still be alive if he couldn't—but he lacked the killer instinct. Drake would always look for a way not to fight, even when his back was against the wall.

That was something that separated him from Wolverine—and a few other X-Men—even more surely than the x-factor they shared bound them together. Drake fought because he had to, not because he liked to.

Wolverine liked to.

But after the last several hours, even he was willing to talk first and slash second.

"I hate space. Every time the X-Men end up in space, something goes wrong," Drake griped.

"Don't be such an optimist, Frosty," Wolverine growled. His eyes were never still, searching everywhere for a threat or attack. "This time you could get lucky."

He secretly agreed with Drake, though he wouldn't give the twerp the satisfaction of saying so. Wolverine hated space travel, sealed environments, and running through mazes like a laboratory rat, and this little pleasure cruise seemed to involve all three. There were windows along the outer curve of the ring, and through them the unwinking stars of black space were clearly visible. At the edges of the windows there was a brown corrosion, as if something had bubbled through the joint between wall and glass. Sure they were out in space. What else could this be but a space station?

But if this was a space station, where were all the people?

Just in case anyone in ultimate authority (for the first time in his considerable experience) cared about Wolverine's opinion, he thought this deal was already blown and getting sourer by the minute.

But they were the X-Men. It was a way of life for them to walk straight into traps. *Like the flamin' six hundred back in the Crimea. Not that anyone listened to me then, either.* The fragment of memory dissipated like smoke when Bishop spoke.

"If we've been sent here, then this is where the Time Platform is."

"Where?" Wolverine snapped. He wasn't sure what it would look like, but he knew it wasn't here in the corridor with them.

Bishop pulled the Tempometric Meter from a holster on his belt and powered it on. Almost instantly the tracking device began to return a positive signal. "There. Kang's Time Platform is nearby." Bishop began to walk in the direction that the signal pointed.

As the three X-Men moved out of the area into which they'd been transferred by Cable's rebuilt Time Displacement Core, the air changed. Soon it was filled with a harsh chemical stench that blotted out both scent and taste for Wolverine. They must have been standing directly beneath one of the main air filters before, and as they moved away from it, the air had begun to thicken with the discordant alien scents of an artificial environment.

The thing Wolverine hated most about civilization was the way it smelled.

"We seem to be moving about the rim of a giant wheel," Bishop said. "We need to find a spoke to take us to the center. That seems to be the direction in which the meter is trying to point," he added, studying the crude display critically.

"Assumin' that thing's pointin' you to the center o' this thing, an' not to the other edge," Wolverine growled. He was less at ease by the second and he wasn't sure why. *This must be how Storm feels when she gets locked in somewhere small.* As if there was no room for anything else in the world except your deepest primal fear.

Only, Wolverine wasn't afraid of anything.

As they rounded the long curve of the corridor, there was a set of blue-tinted blast doors off to their left. At least that would get them off the rim of the wheel and heading in the direction that the Tempometric Meter was pointing them.

"This is too easy," Drake said.

"Shut up, Drake," Wolverine said, a thrill of atavistic dread coursing down his spine. Iceman snorted mockingly.

Bishop put his hand on the door. To the surprise of the warrior from a future that might never be, the pale-blue pseudometallic surface flaked away under his hand, and the doors rolled back easily.

"Drake's right," he said, slowly. "There's something wrong here."

"You mean other than another tin-pot tyrant tryin'a remake the world in his own image an' playin' snakes an' ladders with time to do it?" Wolverine drawled mockingly. "Hands up, everyone who doesn't think this is some kinda trap."

"Yeah," Iceman said. "But *what* kind of trap? That's the question." He stood on tiptoe, craning to see around Bishop's massive bulk. "God, this place is dry."

The corridor behind the blue door was dark, but in the light from the ring they could see that the insides of the doors were eaten with acid. Looking down the corridor, the three X-Men could see the marks of obvious acid damage extending far down its length.

"Oops," Iceman said, very softly.

The acid was the source of the stink that had overpowered Wolverine's enhanced senses. With the doors to the spoke corridor open, it roiled toward him with an intensity that nearly made him gag. It was strong enough that the other two noticed it as well; Bishop made a moue of distaste and Iceman wrinkled his nose.

"Euwww," Iceman said.

"There's been some sort of a battle," Bishop added unnecessarily.

Now that they were looking for it, all of them could see it; the marks on the bulkheads as if some sort of pitched battle had been fought with acid-cannons here. And as they looked behind them, they could see that there were traces of acid burns on the walls of the corridor they had passed through as well.

"Hey, guys," Iceman said edgily, "do you get the hairy feeling we're all in some sort of unauthorized remake here?"

Bishop turned to look at him, an expression of incredulous incomprehension on his face. But then, Bishop had never seen any of the *Alien* movies.

"Heads up, people!" Wolverine snapped. His claws slid out of their housings to gleam dully in the sourceless light of the station. There was a scrabbling behind the walls—at first only audible to him, then loud enough for the other two to hear.

And then everything happened at once.

Slugs—each longer than a human—burst through the weakened sections of the walls and deck. Only the three-flanged beaks and the tiny cluster of beady eyes differentiated one end of the featureless gray forms from the other.

"Kee-ripes!" Iceman yelped. He flung a hand up, gesturing in the direction of the nearest slug. The air shimmered as he gestured, the moisture in it coalescing into a bolt of ice.

But not enough ice; he could feel the aridity of the air as an ache along his muscles. It should have been quick work for him to wall up each of these slug-uglies in its own quick-frozen cocoon, but Iceman's real battle was not with them, but with the station's own runaway engineering, and it was a battle he could not win.

He concentrated grimly, not wanting either of the others to sense his distress. From the moment they'd arrived here, the space station's housekeeping systems had been sucking at him, trying to strip the moisture from his icy shell—just as if it were a frost-free refrigerator and he was a tray of ice cubes. In such a parched environment, there was little free moisture for Iceman's mutant power to draw on to work his cold magic.

The first slug launched itself into space and slid helplessly over Iceman's slick icy carapace, oozing acid slime all the while. Iceman slapped at it with an open hand, sucking all the moisture from its body and effectively freeze-drying it on the spot. He turned to look for fresh targets, trying not to dwell on the source of the moisture that had just been added to his arsenal.

The only other source he could draw upon for the moisture to create his ice shields was his own body, and there were limits to how far he could go before he was fatally dehydrated.

He was probably going to learn those limits before today was over.

The monsters were swarming through the walls, moving rapidly for all their clumsy leechlike shapes. Bishop brought his hand cannon to bear upon the slug arcing through the air toward him just as his mind registered the fact that he didn't dare fire on his enemy. Not inside a space station, where to rupture the skin of the station would mean a quick death by decompression for all three of them.

Out of the corner of his eye, he saw a flash of brightness as Iceman coated one of his opponents with frost. Bishop ducked back out of the way of his own foe and the slug fell heavily to the floor just beyond him, rearing up and snapping at him with its threefold beak. Its underside gleamed wetly, and beneath its body, the deck began to bubble as the slug's secretions ate into it. Bishop stared, momentarily transfixed by horror as the source of the acid burns on the walls became brutally apparent. If the secretions of these creatures could eat through metal, they could breach the hull of this space platform as easily as an energy blast—if more slowly—and the result would be the same: decompression and certain death.

In that moment of inattention, one of the slugs flowed over his foot and began coiling up his thigh. With a roar of disgust he kicked it away, using his weapon as a bludgeon on its unprotected belly. His battlesuit protected him for the moment, but Bishop could feel the chemical heat of the monster's alien metabolism even through the heavy unstable-molecule fabric.

How many are there? They seemed to be coming out of the walls. . . .

Wolverine growled deep in his throat as his claws sliced into the tough rubbery body of the slug. His hackles rose at the sound of its ultrasonic squalling, and he hastily shook its acid blood from his claws. The body had no memory for pain and with time even the mind forgot, but it had been only a few hours since he had faced Electro, and Wolverine could still remember the agony of being nearly crispy-fried. Being dissolved in acid did not make a good followup—fortunately, his adamantium claws were impervious to any form of corrosive he'd ever met. He attacked again, cautiously (for him), and was rewarded by a sudden cessation of the slug's ultrasonic death-agonies.

His claws were slimed—he didn't dare retract them into his body until he'd cleaned them. Wolverine looked around for fresh targets. They weren't hard to find. The corridor was crawling with the things. And while Wolverine's accelerated healing factor would help him regenerate, neither Drake nor Bishop could come to grips with the enemy except at the risk of severe burns. Drake was fighting at less than peak efficiency, and there wasn't any energy here for Bishop to siphon. This was not going to be a good day.

"Retreat!" Wolverine shouted above the sounds of the slugs' squeals and of blows hitting the armored bulkhead. "Back up the spoke toward the center!"

"Well, I think that went well. Don't you?" Iceman said with poisonous cheer as Bishop and Wolverine slammed the second set of blast doors shut behind them.

The only thing that had saved them was that they moved faster than the slugs did, but speed wouldn't save them for long. This was a space station. There was nowhere to run.

"We're toast," was Wolverine's succinct assessment. It was only a matter of time before the slugs found their way here into the main part of the station, although it seemed on the evidence that they hadn't made it yet.

"We have our mission here to complete," Bishop said in a matter-of-fact voice. His uniform was sheened with slug slime that none of them dared touch, and his face had the set, weary expression of a man who'd already fought too many battles without rest.

This is the part where the shouting starts. Iceman was not especially interested in refereeing a brawl between two of the hardest heads in the X-Men. He looked around instead. At least the lights were on, though they looked like they were burning at half strength. He could feel the dryness in the air sucking at him, and it occurred to him that the enormous aridity was another indication that something was wrong. Whatever life-support systems this place had, they were going off the rails.

They'd reached another, inner ring. Its contours mirrored the outer ring they'd just left, down to the boring beige construction material covered with alien supergraphics. The outer wall of the ring had a door every few feet as all the spokes converged; the inner ring was blank. As Iceman stared at the slowly moving marks on the inner wall of the ring, he realized that the center pylon must be counterrotating.

"It'd be nice to figure on getting out alive, Bishop," Wolverine snapped. "So far, all I've seen is the odds stackin' up higher against us. There're three other teams, an' we ain't any use dead."

"And if they all fail?" Bishop rumbled.

Iceman never got the chance to hear Wolverine's answer to that question. As the inner ring rotated past an open hatchway, its darkness began to . . . wriggle.

He didn't bother to think of a snappy comeback or an amusing way of alerting the others. Iceman simply hit the doorway with everything he had.

Wolverine didn't want a fight with Bishop, but—as much as he hated to retreat under any circumstances—he was sure he didn't intend to buy in on any more suicidal cavalry charges. He was trying to decide whether it would be simpler to coldcock Bishop or simply wrestle the Tempometric Meter away from him when the temperature in the access ring went from a chilly fifty to somewhere near thirty below in the space of three seconds.

Drake's body shimmered in a corona of frost crystals as he poured everything he had at the open doorway coming slowly into view. The slugs that had been writhing through the slowly widening aperture were already frozen. Their bodies looked like an obscene sculpture in frosted silver.

Bishop had reached the same conclusion Wolverine had in about the same time it had taken the battle-hardened Canucklehead to reach it: Bishop let loose with both blasters at the frozen slugmeat, and the zero-chilled aliens shattered like crystal, their acid venom refreezing in beautiful emerald-green arcs in the steadily dropping temperature.

They'd been wrong. The slugs had already infested the core. And the X-Men's bolt-hole had suddenly become Grand Central Station.

Wolverine launched himself between the streams of fire and ice, using his claws to slice his way past the frozen layer of slugs to the living ones beyond. If they couldn't hack their way through the barricade, in a few moments they'd be trapped in this inner ring between two walls of slugs.

And they'd be dead.

Wolverine wasn't an easy man to kill. Bullets, knives, radiation, poison . . . his accelerated healing factor dealt with all of them fast enough in a melee for him to easily gain the upper hand.

Fire—and its toxic cousin, acid—was another matter. The damage they did wasn't easily localized. Now he was facing slugs with acid for blood, and there was no way out of bathing in the stuff. His instincts had not misled him. This was not a good day.

Wolverine swore feelingly as he plunged his arm elbow-deep into an unfrozen slug-body. He felt the heat of the chemical reaction, and above his glove the acid burned furiously on bare skin. And the slim protection that his gloves offered wouldn't last forever.

"Drake! Get this off me!" Wolverine shouted, slashing recklessly through the slugs. Either Drake could backstop him or he couldn't, and either way these things needed to be killed.

But, Lord, it hurt.

As the slugs began to realize what was happening to them, how many of them were being killed by the man with the knives in his hands, they began to flee—or regroup. Wolverine could see a second sealed inner door behind them, amazingly intact despite their onslaught.

Drake responded gallantly to Wolverine's demand for help, though Wolverine could see that Drake was in trouble. The acid sludge covering Wolverine's body solidified into rime, and Wolverine brushed it away. The blistered and bleeding—and frozen—skin beneath began to recover almost immediately.

"Come on!" Wolverine shouted. In another few minutes this doorway with its promise of haven would have rotated past Drake and Bishop—it was now or never.

The other two X-Men crowded into what Wolverine now suspected to be some kind of airlock system. With his remaining strength, Iceman threw up an ice barricade between them and the outside corridor.

For a few blessed instants there were no slugs to be seen.

"I think I can open this," Bishop said, looking at the hatch.

•   •   •

A few minutes later the inner hatch had fallen to Bishop's handiness with far-future technology. Except for a few slime trails, the chamber was bare of slugs.

This had been some kind of a control room, once. The unfamiliar control panels and displays gave the room the oddly distancing look of the set for a television show. The equipment had been battered by the station inhabitants' last defense, but it still seemed to be running under power. The arrays of darkened displays served as a grim reminder that in this place, their lives depended on the space station's life-support systems. And none of them knew how badly damaged those were . . . or how long they would last.

Bishop stepped through first, his guns angled to cover the widest field of fire. Anytime he fired he would risk killing all three of them, but against the slugs he had no choice.

"Oh, wow," Iceman breathed, staring around himself at the banks of sensors and visual displays. One of the viewscreens had been twisted like a sheet of plastic, but three others still showed an arc of exotic starfield. "This looks like a really bad episode of *Blake's 7*," he said.

"Drake, can you possibly confine yourself to meaningful information exchanges?" Bishop said.

The mission was going bad. He could feel it in his bones, and suspected that Wolverine did too. But Bishop also knew what it was like to go into battle woefully outmatched by the enemy but having to fight on regardless. Wolverine was right: they were only one of four teams and the odds against them skyrocketed with every new fact they learned. But sensible or not, the three of them couldn't afford the luxury of taking Wolverine's advice. What if the other three had already failed and were counting on them to succeed? Bishop and his two companions would probably die here sometime in the next hour, but the slim possibility that they could get their hands on Kang's Time Platform and make it give up its secrets was more important than their mortality.

All three of them were mutants. And in Bishop's world, that fact alone was a ticket to oblivion. From the first moment he'd drawn breath, Bishop had been living on borrowed time.

"So where's this platform?" Iceman demanded, as if Bishop might now produce it from his back pocket. "And what do you think this place was?"

"That is hardly important to our mission," Bishop snapped.

Ignoring them both, Wolverine hunted around the wreckage until he found an energy rifle with a dead powerpack. Stripping the powerpack out of the frame, he jammed the barrel into the door frame and broke it off. There was no retreat in that direction, not with the outer ring and most of the spokes filled with acid-spitting slugs.

"Wolverine," Bishop said thoughtfully, "you said this was a 'no-win' situation and you were right. I think that you and Iceman should use your recall devices to return to Blaquesmith's lab and leave me to seek out the Time Platform with the Tempometric Meter. That way, we only risk one of us."

Iceman glanced at Bishop, the stubborn disbelief on his face plain even through the blurring sheath of ice. But it was Wolverine who put his thoughts into words.

"An' I think you should take that Tempometric Meter, Bishop, an'—"

"Somebody's coming," Iceman said quietly.

The other two turned, looking around for slugs, but Iceman was not referring to anything inside the station. He was looking in the direction of the monitors that ringed the room.

In one of the three remaining viewscreens, a spaceship was approaching the station.

•   •   •

"It's a wonderful thing, the freemasonry of High Space," Lireeb mused to himself from his vantage point outside time's shimmering lemniscate. "When doughty adventurers meet, who knows what may happen?"

The tall albino paused for a moment, to allow the echoes of his own voice to fade against Limbo's walls.

"*I* do, of course," he answered himself.

At the moment Lireeb was alone, in a small chamber designed for the examination of one timeline at a time. As painstakingly as a pathologist studying a biopsy, Lireeb had made his tiny insertions into the fabric of this one thread, shaping events until they proceeded along the track that he knew Kang would wish them to take.

It was an enormous amount of work to stage a confrontation that, in the greater cosmic scheme of things, was totally unnecessary, considering the point in the timeline at which the X-Men's team had inserted itself. However, after this long, Lireeb knew his master's whims. Kang wanted a show battle, so a show battle he would have. And if creatures who had as much claim to reality as Kang himself bled and fought and died for less than nothing, what was that to Kang? The nature of conquest was that only the victors would live.

A pity Kang had not absorbed and applied that lesson when he might still have profited from it. Still, it was not for Lireeb to question his master's wishes, only to carry them out.

To the letter.

"The local *gendarmerie* is going to be in no mood for long conversations after the highly artistic transmission I sent them. Isn't it wonderful what can be done with computer animation these days?" Lireeb asked the empty air.

She was a gracious lady, and her name was *Icarus*. Her body was made of steel and energy, glass and dreams. She swam through a sea of charged particles and plasma shoals, her hull battered by the solar winds and pelted by sheets of hard radiation. She was on her way to a rendezvous, and *Icarus* had promises to keep.

Icarus was one of the largest Starcruisers ever built, and she was home and transport—and weapon—to one of the most unique cadres of individuals ever assembled across all space and time. Each was the last survivor of his or her culture, each was blessed with powers beyond those of the ordinary run of humanity, and each was dedicated to justice above all.

Answerable to no temporal authority.

The Guardians of the Galaxy.

"Those murderin'—"

"Take it easy, Charlie," Major Victory said. "We can't afford emotionalism."

Charlie-27 looked more superficially human than any of the others on the bridge of the *Icarus*, as if he were a normal man distorted by some cruel funhouse mirror, but Charlie-27's vast strength and nearly impervious hide were sufficient testament to his Jovian ancestry.

"But they killed everyone on *Cherryh*—and broadcast what they'd done to the rest of the galaxy!" the woman beside Charlie-27 burst out. "I say we take them out—hard!"

Her skin was the dusky gray color of volcanic rock, her hair and brows an ever-shifting tapestry of flame—for Nikki's ancestors had been genetically engineered in a kinder, gentler time to survive life on the surface of Mercury. Now she—the last survivor of her race in a war that had taken no prisoners—stood alone, her membership in an elite starfaring cadre signified only by the red-white-and-blue star that she wore upon the shoulder of her emerald jumpsuit.

"And I say we take them alive if we can," Major Victory repeated, the hardness of command in his voice.

Against the bright glassteel surfaces of the *Icarus*'s flight deck, the eerie black sheath that had succeeded the copper foil suit that had kept Major Vance Astrovik, USAF, alive for nearly two millennia ate light like the event horizon of a black hole. When he'd played at *Star Trek* as a boy dreaming of starflight, who knew to what bittersweet realization of his ambitions his dreams would lead him?

"We need to find out what they know—and why they did it—before we turn them in."

It was the right thing to say, the reasonable thing. It didn't go over well with any of Astro's four companions, and he knew it. But that was what being the leader was all about: making hard choices and making them stick.

The transmission had triggered all of *Icarus*'s alarms a scant four hours ago. Signal coding indicated that the patrolling Guardians had intercepted a broad-beam distress signal transmission from the deep space station *Cherryh*, a crossroads station in a galactic backwater that did not contain any suitable planets on which to erect a navigational beacon and refueling stop. Roughly a thousand men, women, and children had lived on *Cherryh*.

Until now.

They'd only received a scrap of the transmission, the signal torn to bits by the distance over which it had travelled. They did not know how the marauders had reached the station, or what had triggered their spree. All the Guardians knew was that the three men had moved through *Cherryh*'s defenseless inhabitants like a plasma beam through a stick of warm butter, executing them slowly and horribly.

The message was at least four hours old, and possibly more. There was very little chance that any of the inhabitants of *Cherryh* were still alive, or even that the attackers were still there. But the five who had heard the message were the Guardians of the Galaxy, and they could not afford to ignore the chance that someone remained alive on *Cherryh* to rescue.

Or to punish.

"I've been to Stockade, remember?" Charlie-27 said, referring to the local prison planet. "It's a hellpit, but it isn't bad enough for animals like those." Like Nikki's, Charlie's race had been genengineered to withstand the daily stresses of life on an alien planet—Jupiter, whose vast resources called out for a race of miners and engineers to exploit them on behalf of a hungry Sol System. "No matter how far we've got to chase them, they aren't getting away with it. That's how I see it, anyways."

Nikki the Mercurian smiled grimly. "You got that right, Chunkie."

Charlie-27 had been a man of small contentments, once. When the war came, he had laid down his ore cutter for a commission in the Jupiter militia, as the people of Jupiter rallied gallantly against their inevitable defeat. Now he, too, wore the tricolored G-star, fighting a battle that was always different but always the same—the battle for right against the uncaring greed of absolute power.

"What are you planning to do, Major?" Martinex asked coolly. Like the other Guardians, he was the only survivor of his kind. Though sprung from human stock, Martinex's people had been given a crystalline structure to enable them to withstand the unearthly cold of Pluto as part of a bid to colonize that dark and distant world in the days when humanity's ambitions had been restricted to its own solar system.

"We'll give them a chance to surrender," Astro answered slowly, darting a glance aside to the fifth member of the *Icarus*'s small force.

Yondu's people, unlike the others', had not sprung from earthly stock. The Centauran's primitive mystical race had been encountered in the earliest days of Vance Astro's recovery from his ten-century sleep, and Yondu recruited to join Astro's band. The enigmatic blue-skinned archer was often the voice of reason and balance in their deliberations.

"As we must, so that the greater Balance is served," Yondu agreed. The red crest that added a full half meter to his slender height waved slightly as he sadly shook his head. "But it will be difficult to find any understanding of their actions."

"I still say it's a put-up job," Nikki grumbled. "You saw the tapes, Yondu—one of them made up to look like Geeze, here, and one of them looking like a cut-rate Pluvian—sorry, Marty!—and that short guy with the claws . . ."

Wolverine. Iceman. Bishop. *Harsh names for ruthless killers*, Astro thought to himself. Everyone—even pacifist Yondu and emotionless Martinex—would want to be in at the kill.

"Meant to impersonate one of the Inhumans?" mused Martinex. "That close-knit race keeps to its hidden lunar city—save for exceptions like our own Talon," he said, speaking of the absent Inhuman member of the Guardians' band. "But it will hardly matter who they wish us to believe they are once we've docked with *Cherryh*."

Major Victory took a deep breath. Led to this purpose by their own turbulent lives, the Guardians of the Galaxy were difficult to command at the best of times, and angered by the atrocities they'd witnessed in the beam-cast only scant hours before. . . .

Now he had to try to convince them not to all go charging into the battle. Like the pragmatic and cautious Martinex, he suspected that this might be a trap. And so he wanted to split the Guardians up, leaving two to remain aboard the *Icarus* and bringing two with him into the station to investigate—in case the brutal deaths of all of *Cherryh*'s men and women were nothing more than a feint designed to gain the killers the first starcraft that responded to their transmission.

"We're coming up on *Cherryh*," Nikki said tensely from her position at the helm's console. "*Icarus* says most of her automatic systems are still online and under power. She's extending a docking cradle for us."

"Good," Vance Astro said. "Now, listen up, people, because here's how I want to play this."

At that moment, *Icarus*'s communications console woke into life.

"Attention, unidentified spacecraft! You are approaching—" A transmission was coming from the station. "—a derelict station. Do not attempt to dock! Repeat: do not attempt to dock! Attention, unidentified spacecraft!"

"It isn't going to work," Iceman said under his breath.

Bishop glared at the comm system in murderous disgust. That he'd been able to figure out how it worked at all was something of a minor miracle, but the X-Man from the future was in no mood to go easy on himself.

"I don't even know if they're receiving our transmission," he growled, before losing his grip on his frayed temper utterly and smashing his fist into the screen. Pieces of not-quite-glass flew everywhere, and the bank of lights darkened with a despondent groan.

"Great," Iceman muttered. "That's really useful, Bishop."

"Do you have any *constructive* suggestions, Drake?" the burly mutant growled. Bishop's mutant power was to siphon and channel energy used against him; useless against Iceman, who relied on his body's power to radiate subarctic cold. But there were always his fists. Bishop had learned early that force was the final arbiter of any discussion, and while he would never turn on his own teammates, he'd reached the point where he'd feel a lot better if there were something he could hit.

Wolverine—who nearly always felt that way—had reached that point several hours ago, but at the moment his body was immobile as he looked back toward the hatch through which they'd entered. The harsh stink of acid filled his senses. All four edges of the seam around the door were filled with green slime that bubbled corrosively against the glassteel hull. In a few minutes—at most—the slugs would have eaten their way through the door and into the control room.

"C'mon. Let's move," he said to the others. "We've got to find a way out of here. Don't waste your time on that ship. If they dock here, they're dead men."

"You want a way out, guys? Allow me."

For years Iceman had dismissed himself as the weakest of the X-Men, until age and experience had taught him that guile was more effective than any show of brute force. Now that the X-Men needed a route out of the killing jar, Iceman was the one who was going to find it for them.

"Space stations need ventilation systems. Ventilation systems need vents."

Ever since the three of them had arrived in this might-be-the-real-one future, Bobby Drake had been locked in an unceasing struggle with the space station's life support systems. They wanted to defrost him. He wanted to keep his icy form. The struggle wove a connection between him and the central air processing plant of the space station that was as perceptible to him as weather currents were to Storm.

"Big ones, actually." He turned toward the source. He didn't see anything, but that didn't matter with the high-powered help he could field. "The system's broken. It's doing its best to freeze-dry this place. That makes it easy to spot. This way, guys," Iceman said, pointing toward what seemed to be a blank wall.

The air for the control room was coming through a grilled vent placed high on the wall opposite the door. Bishop tore out the air scrubbers, exposing a long, dark

shaftway that might lead anywhere. It would be a tight
fit for Wolverine, and a *very* tight fit for Bishop.

"These shafts will lead directly to the Power Core,"
Bishop said, "if they also lead to the Housekeeping Systems. Those two usually go together. But it means that
the deeper we go, the more security systems we'll have
to fight."

"We ain't gonna find anything better," Wolverine admitted dourly, gazing into the dark. "I'll go first. The
slug that meets me, dies." He hauled himself up into the
vent and vanished. The other two could hear the faint
sounds of his boots scuffling along inside the vent.

"Clear," he called back after a few moments.

Bishop looked dubiously from the vent to the hatch
that sealed off the only other possible escape from the
chamber. Acid was running freely from the seams now,
pooling on the floor. Opening that door would be the
same thing as suicide, but the vent would provide a tight
fit at best.

"You're next, Bishop," Iceman said. "I'll go last to
seal us in."

"If you're wrong about the direction the air's coming
from, we're going to suffocate in there, you know,"
Bishop said. "We won't be able to reach our TDRs to
implement recall."

"What's the matter?" Iceman said, shrugging. "You
want to live forever?"

Bishop didn't answer; Iceman hadn't expected him to.
Holstering his weapons, Bishop began squeezing himself
into the vent.

Iceman stared at the door and wished Bishop would
hurry.

It had been a brisk fight, but Astro had won it. Martinex
would stay behind to guard *Icarus* from harm,
and Charlie-27 and Nikki would accompany him into

Cherryh to apprehend the killers of the station's civilian population. Yondu would split his efforts, staying with the ship at first but catching up to the others once they'd located the terrorists. Yondu's mystic arrows were the perfect weapon in an environment where no one—friend or foe—dared to pierce the station's glassteel skin and rupture its structural integrity.

Astro exited the docking bay, Nikki and Charlie right behind him. Perhaps it was his imagination, but the station already seemed haunted, as if it were a living thing capable of mourning its lost occupants. There was no sign of life, and in his sinking heart Major Victory began to believe they'd come too late to do anything but punish the guilty and memorialize the dead. Even the normally ebullient Nikki was silent, and Charlie-27 stalked at Astro's shoulder like some brooding monolith of doom.

Where are the bodies? No one appeared to impede the three Guardians as Astro led the other two up the lower spike from *Icarus*'s docking cradle and into the station itself. There had been almost a thousand souls on *Cherryh*, according to the statistics that Main Frame held. Where were they now? Herded into the main storage compartments to die? Were any of them still alive?

That's what we'll have to find out. Astro stopped and spoke into the tricolored star-shape that was both communicator and emblem. "*Icarus*, this is Astro. Any sign of the terrorists from your end?"

"Negative, Major," Martinex answered. "The peculiar interference we noted while docking still seems to be in effect. It's blocking the biosensors from being much use. But we're pretty sure they're still there. Near-space sweeps report that the last ion-wake through this area was over a month ago."

And the time stamp on the signal they'd intercepted was less than a week old. The enemy was here.

"Keep trying," Astro said. "I want to know *where*

they are, not just that they're here. And I want to know if there are any survivors—any life readings at all.''

"Wilco, Major," Martinex said.

"Meanwhile, we'll search *Cherryh* inch by inch—if that's what it takes to find them. Stand by. Astro out."

This stuff didn't smell like steel. It wasn't cold like steel—or any other metal—and it was oddly resilient. Every time he inhaled, Wolverine was reminded that he was in the future, as far from home as he'd ever been, on a mission as hopeless as any he'd ever run.

But he was an expert in hopeless missions, sour-milk runs, and cakewalks that were anything but. They'd follow Bishop's bouncing ball down to the end of the line and see what was there. They'd do what they came to do.

And then they'd leave, if they still could.

Down to business. Wolverine had no intention of staying in the vent any longer than was necessary to bypass their dead end and find another clear route to the Time Platform. The vents were clear, and in the back of his mind the trained warrior part of him chewed over that anomaly. He would have expected the slugs to take over the vents first thing, but either the station's defenders had managed to seal them against the bogeys, or the things preferred more open spaces. At this precise moment he didn't care which explanation was true, and the three of them weren't going to be here long enough to find out.

The stench of the slugs faded as he wormed forward on his hands and knees, his shoulders brushing against the sides of the vent. Its well-scrubbed air referred no information at all to Wolverine's enhanced senses, and this was *not* a time when no news was good news. They had to get out of here, to someplace where that gadget Bishop was carrying could do them some good in whatever time they had left. Time travel was supposed to mean that you had all the time in the world to do what you had to do, but that didn't look like it was going to be the case this time out. For one thing, they were about to have company here at ground zero.

Wolverine thought about the ship that they'd seen on the screen back in the traffic control room. It had probably docked with the station by now, and unless its crew were the official space-slug cleanup crew, something he doubted, it was a good bet that whoever was on her had no idea what they were walking into here. And unless they had something unusual up their sleeves in the way of reflexes, armor, and firepower, they wouldn't be alive to wonder long.

Until he'd joined the X-Men, Wolverine had always been the expendable one—the point man, the rear guard, the one that no one would weep for if he never came back. He'd walked into death without a single backward glance; sent men and women—ally and enemy both—to dance with the Reaper without a second thought. A faceless group of unknowns from a maybe-future walking into a trap was nothing that was going to disturb his rest.

He didn't think he'd mention that to the others, though. Bishop probably had a few ideals left in that battered soldier's carcass of his, and Wolverine had seen Drake mist up over roadkill.

Still, if there was a free chance to warn the bogeys, he'd take it.

Probably.

His muscles were starting to cramp from the confined space when he reached a vent opening. This one gave into what looked to Wolverine like a maintenance corridor. He didn't see any slugs, or much sign of acid damage. Good enough.

"First floor, everybody out," Wolverine said, bracing himself against the vent and ripping away the grille.

• • •

"Did you hear that?" Nikki said edgily. The boom and screech of tortured metal echoed eerily through the deserted station, audible even over the ragged sound of the life-support system.

"Sounds like we've found them," Charlie-27 said with satisfaction. "What are we waiting for?"

With reflexes honed under Jovian gravity, the massive heavyworlder began to run toward the sound, his mercurial companion close behind. Astro did not even try to stop them. Part of successful leadership was knowing what orders wouldn't be followed and not giving them. Instead, he summoned the reinforcements they were almost certainly going to need.

"Yondu!" Major Victory said into his star communicator. "Time to join the party!" The G-star had barely begun to broadcast the Centauran's reply when Astro started after his fellows.

"So what's the story?" Wolverine said to Bishop.

The time travellers stood at an intersection of two corridors. After so much time spent in the station's circulatory system, they were beginning to build a map of their environment—enough, as Drake had insisted on saying, to enable them to get there from here.

His acute hearing and scent tracking were both useless; something Wolverine didn't bother to mention. And Drake wasn't looking so hot either, Wolverine thought to himself. His icy surface had gone opaque and furry with patches of sloppily formed crystals. Cold radiated from him in waves, and normally Drake had better fire-discipline than that. Only Bishop looked as if it was business as usual, and Bishop had already been in the field for days, fighting an alternate universe's battles.

It almost seemed as if something had arranged things to drop him and Iceman in particular into someplace where they had two strikes against them going in. But no one save Cyclops had known where the three of them were going, and all Cyclops had known when he picked the teams was the year, not the place.

"I believe the Time Platform lies somewhere directly above us, in a location that may well be the Central Power Core for the entire station," Bishop said.

"Which would be the place hardest to get into," Wolverine agreed. He'd seen enough top-secret military installations to know that, and it looked like they didn't build them any different in the future.

The mutant time warrior looked up from the Tempometric Meter in his hand. "Correct," he said.

"Then let's get going," Wolverine said. He wondered what kind of problems Cable and the others were having wherever they were, and how many of them he'd ever see again.

At that moment his stifled senses belatedly registered the sound and smell of intruders. The people from the ship—he'd lay money on it. *And of all the flamin' corridors of all the flamin' space stations in this flamin' universe, they had to come down this one*. He turned in that direction, claws popping, and ducked even before he consciously realized the X-Men had been fired on.

"Surrender! This is the only chance you'll get!" Astro shouted at the terrorists. This close, the three looked even less like the Pluvian, Jovian, and Inhuman they were supposedly impersonating—but they looked even more like trouble.

The pseudo-Pluvian's body seemed to be made of ice—as befitted its name—not crystal, though it moved like a man. Astro could feel the cold radiating from its body even from where he stood, and—to his quiet amazement—patches of frost seemed to be forming on the walls around it as well.

Beside it, the dark-skinned giant—Bishop—looked almost baseline human, though when he turned to face the Guardians Astro could see some distorting glyph cut into his scarred and bearded face. The man's rippling muscles spoke of time spent under multi-G acceleration, such as was often used as punishment on the prison planets, and he was carrying enough weaponry strapped to his body to more than make up for any lack in the armament of his companions.

The might-be Inhuman—Wolverine—in the black mask and blue-and-yellow battlesuit had seen them first. Wolverine looked almost dwarfish in comparison to the dark-skinned giant, but the glittering spikes extruded from his gloved hands left no doubt he meant business. On the beamcast, Astro had seen those claws used with barbaric efficiency on the station's inhabitants. If it came to a fight, Wolverine was the one they needed to take down first.

But they were the Galactic Guardians. They did not kill. Marshalling the power from Within Yet Beyond, Major Victory sent a bolt of pure mutant psychokinetic energy fountaining toward the three terrorists.

Wolverine didn't know what the bolt that sprayed off the bulkhead above him was, but he knew it wasn't a peace flag. And the crew facing off against his team was something out of a forty-inch-pizza nightmare.

"Bishop, go on! Follow the tracker! We'll hold them here," he shouted. He saw Bishop's face settle into heavy lines of acceptance, and turned away. For just an instant Wolverine locked eyes with Iceman, and saw him shrug. When it came to the crunch, Drake was do-or-die with the best.

But he was under no illusions either. He was the one who'd have to carry this fight, and the faster the better. Wolverine charged, flinging himself at the biggest of the attackers, claws glittering lethally. Once he'd left Project

X he'd sworn that his days of jumping through hoops on missions he didn't understand were over—and he'd been doing nothing else since this caper went down. It was a good day to beat the living daylights out of the first available target, and the big bruiser in the lead looked like their designated winner.

"That was your first and last chance, butcher!" the big guy shouted, clenching his fists.

"Hey. And he doesn't even know you," Wolverine heard Drake mutter.

He smiled. A little blood never hurt anyone, in Wolverine's opinion.

His claws didn't punch through anything except the uniform jacket the man was wearing. They slid over the surface of the big guy's skin as if he were made of steel. Wolverine barely had time to register the fact that his strategy hadn't worked when the man mountain flung him into the bulkhead.

"Hey!" Iceman said, when Wolverine went flying. *Couldn't we talk this over?*

Part of his mind wondered why they had to fight at all, even as he filled the air around the blacksuit and his two companions with a hail of ice bullets.

"Nikki! Get the one called Bishop!" the man in black shouted. *They know who we are.* Iceman thought with a sinking feeling. *What's going on?*

"Looks like you and me are gonna have a hot time, Icey," the gray-skinned redhead—Nikki—said. His ice bullets melted as they reached her.

"Hey, do you know your hair's on fire?" Iceman quipped, sliding out of her way on an ice carpet. *Why do I say these things?*

"And your butt is toast," the girl called Nikki snapped back, flinging a firebolt at him. He felt it singe his icy hide, and the unforgiving environment quickly sucked the moisture away.

Drake, you are going to be out of luck quick if you don't think of something fast. Because it'd be a cold day in hell before he let little torch-top get to Bishop and sabotage their mission.

A cold day in hell.

Literally.

Bishop had left men to die before. It was always in a good cause.

He'd never gotten to like it.

He focused his whole being on the Tempometric Meter he held in his hand, trying to match the blue blip on its surface to the map of the station he was building inside his head. When he reached a maintenance go-down Bishop stopped to look back, but he'd rounded the curve of the station and could see nothing of the fight he'd left behind.

He could hear it, though. When Drake made ice it hissed like falling sand; he could hear it in the silence between the taunts that Wolverine roared. He could hear other things, too, battle sounds for which he had no referent. The enemy was still engaged, then, and if the X-Men hadn't already taken them down, it meant that the intruders had enough power to give Iceman and Wolverine a real fight, and both of them were still recovering from their last battles.

The two of them might not win. And, even more horrible to contemplate, their recall devices might be destroyed in the battle, marooning them here. It had already happened once on this mission.

Voluntary exile to an alien timeframe was one thing. Temporal shipwreck on a decaying space station filled with alien slugs was another.

Get the platform and we can all go home. That's what

the generals always say, isn't it? And somehow, every time, everyone doesn't get to go home.

Bishop stuck the Tempometric Meter back into its holster loop and began to descend, his eyes fixed on the tiny blue star.

If Bishop had been in open country to begin with, it would have been quick and easy: see the blip. Follow the blip. Attain objective. But the very architecture of the station conspired against him, forcing him to turn left when the Tempometric Meter said that platform lay on his right. The sounds of battle faded behind him, and he tried to shut his mind to the probable fate of his teammates.

But as he descended, he realized that Wolverine's guess had paid out. The Time Platform was in the heart of the station, at the Power Core.

By the time he reached the level the Power Core was on, Bishop was sweating. The lights had dimmed until the only illuminations were the deep amber failsafes and the bright constellation of red warning lights on the control panels he passed. The temperature in the dying station had risen steadily the closer he got to the Core, and it was at least a hundred and twenty degrees in the passageway. Iceman had been right—the climate control for the station was out of kilter, running wild and decaying along with everything else around it.

Not that Bishop was devoting much of his attention to Iceman's guesses at the moment. He had other things on his mind.

The corridor ahead was filled with slugs.

They were piled in the corners like drifts of old socks, stuck to every surface like the decorative magnets that covered the refrigerator in the kitchen back in Westchester in a time far, far away.

Bishop backed quietly out of the corridor and around

the corner, weapons at the ready. Then he thought about it for a moment and looked again.

None of the slugs were moving. They'd registered no sign of his presence. In fact, he couldn't tell one end of the things from the other, and they were only about half the size of the ones the three of them had fought earlier. Neither beaks nor eyes were showing.

What if they weren't slugs—or at least, weren't *adult* slugs?

Even in the crippling heat, Bishop's blood ran cold. Larvae. Eggs. The promise of a whole colony of the monsters, ready to reproduce and spread across the galaxy.

But if they were eggs—or even just sleeping—they wouldn't attack him. And the Tempometric Meter assured him that the Time Platform lay at the end of the corridor, inside the Power Core itself.

As stealthily as he'd ever moved in his life, Bishop catwalked through the tangle of slug bodies to the security hatch leading to the Power Core.

It was open. All three of the interlocking doors that shielded the Core from the rest of the station were open. Even in the baking warmth of the corridor, Bishop could feel the heat gushing from the Power Core as if he stood before the open door of a furnace, and within he could see the gleam of bright metal, something that looked out of place set in the middle of the rest of the station's construction. He didn't need to consult the Tempometric Meter to tell what he was seeing.

Kang's work. The Time Platform was inside this chamber.

Bishop didn't need any machines to know why Kang had chosen this location, just as he needed no machines to tell him that the air was filled with energy; a soup of radiation so lethal that even Wolverine would have survived exposure to it by only minutes. Someone standing where Bishop was now would die within hours: crossing the threshold of that room would shorten that time to minutes.

Fortunately, Bishop, of all people, had no need to fear radiation poisoning. His mutant gift treated it as if it were any other energy assault. He felt the half-painful rush as his body converted heat energy to kinetic energy inside his mutant body. It trickled through his skin, washing away some of the grinding weariness of the last few days, lending him its energy to complete his mission.

But his boot soles smoked as he stepped forward, and he knew that he could not spend more than a few minutes inside that sweltering place without dangerous consequences. He walked slowly forward, utterly aware of the fact that his retreat line was compromised by scores of alien slugs.

He'd been right.

It was a nursery.

The Power Core was a scene of unremitting horror. It had been transformed—first by the arrival of Kang's staging platform, and then by this hellish infestation. The air was filled with a mist of dissolving metal and vaporizing plastic, and poisonous orange smoke hung in the air like the mist on an alien moor. Pools of the bright green acid he had seen the slugs spew lay cupped in every depression, bubbling slightly as the vitriol ate through the metal beneath and released noxious fumes of decomposition into the air. Hardened accretions of acidic slime and half-dissolved bulkhead covered every surface. Beneath their glabrous coverings, the whole Power Core had the look of something that was melting, oozing slowly away into the primordial ylem from which life first sprang. The slugs were everywhere, twitching faintly like a carpet of grayish maggots swarming over a long-dead body.

And at the center of this inferno, Bishop could see the Time Platform itself. It was covered with slugs and their secretions, its clean curves pitted, smoking . . . and utterly useless to him, even if he could reach it.

As Bishop watched, he saw one of the slugs begin to fission, dividing as if the heat and radiation here gave it the power to do so. Perhaps it did, but that fact was of little interest to Bishop. The slugs' feverish breeding was as useless as the Platform, for in the glow of the red telltales and critical lights that illuminated the chamber, Bishop could see that whatever the slugs had done here in their makeshift nest, their depredations had nearly eaten through to the heart of the Core's reaction chambers. There was a Cherenkov glow where the containment baffles of the Power Core were thinnest. Soon they'd go entirely, and the reaction would build until the Core reached critical mass.

The station was going to blow. And from the sharply rising temperature, it was going to be soon.

Kang had won. The Time Platform was unrecoverable. Even now, Wolverine and Iceman might have paid the ultimate price in a mission that had been doomed before it began. He had to get back to them. The three of them had to hit their recalls while there was still time.

Bishop's jaw clenched. Kang had just been playing with them. All that they'd suffered and risked here had been for nothing. They might as well have stayed home.

The slugs nearest to him began to twitch. A ripple went through the living carpet of voracious flesh that surrounded and covered the Time Platform.

They'd scented prey.

CHAPTER FOUR

MAINLINE +3, THE YEAR 2035

T he translation nimbus of Cable's Time Displacement Core faded, and the two X-Men were able to look around at this world's version of 2035.

Like comedy, it wasn't pretty.

Once upon a time this might have been any major city, and there was still a distinctly American look to the rubble. Phoenix took a step away from the empty space in which she and Cyclops had appeared only seconds ago. Her foot struck something that skidded away across a surface of tilted concrete and shattered masonry. She reached down and picked up a battered rectangle of tin.

"'Attention: You are leaving a Controlled Zone,'" she read aloud. "Controlled by what, I wonder—or do I?" she asked, turning to her partner, lover, husband, and friend. "Scott, where are we?" Phoenix dropped the sign back into the rubble and scuffed it aside with her boot.

All the color seemed to have been leeched from the world, leaving behind only dun gray, weathered browns, and dispirited beige. In these bleak surroundings, Phoenix's red hair stood out like a bright battle flag, and the clear colors of the two X-Men's blue-and-yellow combat suits were dazzlingly conspicuous against the gray overcast of the day. A cold wind blew steadily, unbroken now by any intervening skyscrapers, and though their suits were insulated, both shivered.

"Still on the East Coast, I think," Cyclops said, looking around the devastation for clues as to their location. "Welcome to downtown . . . well, someplace."

"Right. See any Time Platforms yet?" his wife quipped.

As she spoke, Phoenix continued to look for something—anything—that would tell her where they were. It hardly mattered to their mission, but she wanted to know. As far as the eye could see, there was only dev-

astation and ruin, and no familiar urban skyline anywhere. How could this have happened in less than forty
years?

In tacit response to her question, Cyclops activated the
Tempometric Meter and began turning slowly in a circle,
searching for the blip that would tell him that Cable's
device had picked up emanations from the one of the four
Time Platforms that was based in this time.

"Nothing," he said after a moment. "The screen's
dark."

"What? Cable said he was dropping us right on top
of them," Phoenix protested automatically.

"He may have missed; the meter may have malfunc-
tioned. Keep in mind, Charles and Blaquesmith repaired
the TDC with the equivalent of spit and bailing wire.
We'll need to run a search pattern on foot; see if it shows
up." Cyclops's voice was neutral, though his own disappointment must be as great as her own.

"Right." Phoenix sighed. "Let me see what's out
here, first." As she spoke, Phoenix reached out with her
psionic powers to mentally scan their surroundings for
any signs of sentient life. If she could make contact with
another mind, it would give them more information about
the world of 2035 than any amount of scouting possibly
could.

"Scott," she said after a moment, "there's something—
someone?—at the very edge of my range, but—"

Suddenly the air was filled with the scream of shattered
air, as if of incoming artillery. At the moment both of
the X-Men began to react there was a *crump* as the giant
android figure landed, its tons of mass crushing the rubble beneath its armored boots to powder.

"This unit is Group Leader Sentinel Prime—you are
under arrest, X-Men!"

Sentinels, Jean Grey thought with a pang of soul-deep

revulsion. She'd known that 2035 was on a timeline that Sentinels all but ruled, but still she'd managed to hope they wouldn't meet any.

No such luck.

The Sentinel Prime was sixty feet tall, able to look through a fifth-story window while standing on the ground, providing there'd still been fifth-story windows. The purple-and-pink enamel of its bodywork—a legacy from its original designer, Bolivar Trask—gave the monstrosity a ludicrously clownish appearance, though Sentinels had long ago stopped being a joke to the X-Men or to any other mutant. Sentinels were every mutant's nightmare, originally created by Trask and his son Larry to put an humane end to the unilaterally perceived "mutant menace," but having long since evolved through generations of redesign and self-creation into self-willed hellhounds that had come to generate fear and revulsion through their very presence.

Neither Cyclops nor Phoenix needed to say a word to reach their decision—with the speed of thought itself the X-Men's team leader lashed out at the towering figure with a full-power optic blast that struck it directly in the chest. The shattering sound of the blast's impact masked the faint sizzling of ionized plasma as Phoenix lofted telekinetically into the sky and took a quick look around.

Scott—it isn't alone!

Five more Sentinels—these only twelve feet tall and looking strangely tiny beside their enormous Group Leader—were advancing quickly on foot across the shattered urban wasteland.

At the same instant that Phoenix sent a telepathic warning to the man who was both husband and battle comrade to her, she launched an assault upon the nearest of the smaller Sentinels. Hovering above it, Phoenix wreathed the mechanoid in a cocoon of telekinetic energy and squeezed with all her power.

And "pop" goes the weasel. I hope. . . .

• • •

Cyclops had entertained a fleeting hope that his first blast would take down the Sentinel leader, but fortunately he hadn't counted on it. The force of his strike had flung the enormous machine backward—pulverizing more ruins—but even before the cloud of powdered cement had finished rising, the Sentinel Prime was climbing awkwardly to its feet once more. Behind it, he could see the forms of other, smaller, Sentinels advancing.

"Resistance is futile!" the Sentinel Prime announced. "We were alerted to your arrival hours ago!"

But we only arrived minutes ago, Cyclops thought, before shelving that part of the puzzle for later. If his first shot hadn't taken the Sentinel down, he needed to open up some breathing room—preferably before even more reinforcements arrived. Cyclops fired again, directly into the Sentinel's optical sensors.

As he did, a loud explosion from above rocked the area.

They aren't making them like they used to, Phoenix thought fleetingly, as the Sentinel in her telekinetic grasp crumpled like a discarded candy wrapper. As far as she could see from her position—and even at this moderate elevation she was already far above the tallest structure that remained intact—the entire city had been reduced to rubble, far worse than it had been in Rachel Summers's 2013. Phoenix had been an X-Man almost half her life. She would not admit to fear or despair. But a tiny unquenchable part of her mind flinched away from discovering how bad things could get in a future that she might yet live to see.

She pulled her shields tightly around her as the Sentinel exploded, using the shockwave to thrust her higher into the sky. On the ground below, she could see the crimson flicker of Scott's optic blasts through the roiling dust cloud. Cyclops hadn't taken down the Sentinel Prime yet and thought he might not be able to alone, but he wasn't worried.

In fact, through her psi-link with her husband, Phoenix could tell that he was actually more puzzled than anything else. These future Sentinels didn't seem nearly as formidable as those ancestors of theirs that the X-Men had faced on numerous occasions—why?

But even while she wondered, Phoenix searched the ground, looking for other enemy targets. One Sentinel down. Three of the small ones on the ground, plus their enormous leader.

But that meant that she could only account for five of them now, and a moment before there had been six. . . .

In that instant, a flash of intuition made her look up. The sixth Sentinel was above her, flying silently through the gray sky.

At the same instant she saw it, the hunter-killer flung its arms wide, and a shimmering net fell through the air toward her, hissing as it fell. Once the Sentinels had wanted to take their prey alive, but Phoenix could see that this net sizzled with energy. It was meant to kill anything it touched.

Reaching out quickly with her telekinetic powers, Phoenix grasped the edges of the charged net with hands of pure mental force, and before the hovering Sentinel could register the fact that its trap was no longer falling freely, Phoenix had taken the deadly webbing and had wrapped it around the Sentinel's body. When the net touched the Sentinel's metal skin a bright blue corona of energy flared, and the air was suddenly rank with the scent of ozone. The Sentinel, all its internal circuitry destroyed, fell from the sky like a stone.

Two down. Three to go. She looked around.

Scott? Where are you?

* * *

This was getting boring, Cyclops decided. It wasn't that evading the attacks of the Sentinel Prime was actually easy, but it wasn't as difficult as it ought to have been. He'd already destroyed what he suspected was the entirety of the Prime's missile reserves, and it didn't have much left to use on him besides its fingertip lasers. He had a hunch that the Prime's neural-net programming hadn't gone up against something that could actually fight back in a long time.

A very long time.

The thought made him shudder.

Retreating quickly over the broken ground—there was no way that Cyclops alone could make even a second-string Sentinel back down, no matter how depleted its resources—Cyclops ducked under the laser array that the Prime deployed, firing back in a brief aimed pulse. Out-gunned or not, the battering he was dishing out was beginning to show. The Sentinel's head—which was where most of its main sensors were housed, if not its brain— was battered from repeated force-blasts, one gleaming red eye already shattered and dark.

Of course, it could still fracture every bone in his body if it connected with even one backhanded swat. And Cyclops didn't have Wolverine's augmented healing ability, or even a first-aid kit.

Three of the Prime's smaller acolytes had been moving forward in a pincer movement, attempting to encircle Cyclops. Their actions might have been more of a cause for alarm if he hadn't known what they were doing from the moment they began . . . and planned for it.

Cyclops had drawn them away from the open area where he and Phoenix had first arrived. While no less ruined, the part of the city he was in now had more standing rubble, and in some places the truncated shells of building stretched fully two stories into the leaden sky.

Though Cyclops was no telepath, a sixth sense honed

through years of battle warned him when one of the Sentinels was behind him.

Right where he wanted it.

He waited until the last possible second—then, diverting his attention from the Prime for a precious instant, Cyclops whirled, hitting the wall of the building to his left with every ounce of force his mutant optic beams could deliver.

The wall disintegrated, turning to a hail of rubble that travelled away from him with the speed of a shotgun's charge. The Sentinel scout in its path was annihilated. Its head was struck from its shoulders as cleanly as an executioner's ax would have severed it, and a moment later several hundred pounds of building materials punched through the positronic brain in its chest, putting a period to its brief existence.

That's three.

A bright arc across the sky told him that Phoenix had rejoined him.

"Jean—catch!" Cyclops shouted. He jerked his head sideways, the scarlet fire of his force beams shearing loose a section of wall. As it began to fall, Phoenix seized it with her telekinesis, catching it up and using it to hammer the Prime with piledriver force. It flung up its massive hands to protect itself; laser beams sprayed everywhere in a spuriously festive display.

"See what you can do with Robbie the Robot," Cyclops shouted to her, although he knew that with their psi-link in place he did not even need to speak aloud. "I'm going to bat cleanup."

Gotcha, came the instant response in his mind.

With Phoenix keeping the Prime Sentinel occupied, Cyclops was free to turn his attention to the remaining ancillary units. They moved in for the kill, just as he'd expected, and as they did, it came to him that their smaller size was much better adapted to moving easily through the tangled labyrinth of ruins than their leader's enormous bulk was. He wondered if that meant there was something left here for them to hunt.

Better adapted or not, it was clear that whatever central battle brain controlled the units, it had not faced powerful, highly trained opposition in Cyclops didn't like to think how long. While these Sentinels would make a formidable enemy for any human or untrained mutant, it took Cyclops less than a minute to get both of them firing at him and then catch them in their own crossfire. As he'd thought, their own weapons were more than adequate to pierce their armored hides, and his optic blasts were enough to finish the job. They fell in a tiny avalanche of rubble, still sparking faintly.

Five down and one to go. He only hoped they hadn't called for more reinforcements.

He turned to see how Phoenix was handling the Prime Sentinel, and for just an instant, his eyes behind the shield of their ruby-quartz battle visor widened in astonishment.

"The first thing you have to do is get the mule's attention," Jean quoted absently to herself. In contrast to the languid tone of her thoughts, the plasma bolt she hit the Sentinel Prime with was anything but.

And it'd worked. She'd gotten the mechanoid's attention.

She heard the sound of overheating servos whine as the monstrous head rotated on its universal joint to bring her within primary sensor range.

"Here I am, big boy!" Phoenix taunted it. "Take your best shot." Memories of all the times she'd faced the Sentinels in the past flickered through the back of her mind. She suppressed them. She would not fail here.

As if it were actually capable of hearing and understanding what its opponent said on a human level, the

Sentinel raised its massive arms. All three sets of beams—fingertips, palms, chest—fired at once, turning Phoenix's hovering figure into an earthbound star.

To no effect. And though the Sentinel was powerful, it was not as quick on the uptake as its previous incarnations. It kept firing, though the energy fountained harmlessly off the shields Phoenix had wrapped around her.

And slowly the hulk began to rise into the air.

Once Jean Grey had been unable to move more with her mutant power than her own muscles could physically lift, but that time was long past. The Sentinel's armored form weighed uncounted tons, yet Phoenix, hovering in the sky above it, plucked it from the ground as easily as another woman might lift a kitten.

She wondered how high she'd have to lift it before dropping it would destroy it, and instantly rejected the thought. Through their psi-link, she'd picked up Scott's guess that this ruined city might still be inhabited. Sending the giant Sentinel hurtling to the ground might kill hundreds of people.

Jean spared the ruins a quick glance. Well, dozens, anyway.

Finally, almost six seconds after she'd begun lifting it, the Sentinel began to react. She felt it struggle against her, attempting to fly under its own power.

She refused to let it go.

The Sentinel was now fighting back with all its not-inconsiderable armament, but the beams were all deflected before they reached their intended target. Phoenix was stretched nearly to her limits to hold the two of them—herself and the mechanoid—aloft, and to keep it helpless. It was, as Wolverine might have said, a Mexican standoff.

Mind if I join in? Cyclops asked through their psi-link.

I was waiting for you to offer, Phoenix responded. Before she had finished forming the thought, a scarlet lance of pure force shot up from the ground below, striking the Sentinel Prime in its armored side. The mechanoid's body recoiled with the impact.

Or it would have, if Phoenix were not still holding it locked in an unbreakable telekinetic grip, pushing its bulk down as hard as or harder than Cyclops's optic beam pushed it away. Like some armored insect caught between hammer and anvil, the Sentinel writhed, suspended between earth and heaven in the grip of both an irresistible force and an immovable object.

In the end, something had to give. Though it felt as if it took forever, only scant seconds passed before the Sentinel's chest armor buckled, and an instant later its remaining optic sensor was lifeless and dark. Carefully, Phoenix lowered the inert mass to the ground, and floated down after it.

"Some welcoming committee," Cyclops said. "I wonder when the second wave is going to show?" Even as he spoke, he'd pulled the Tempometric Meter from his belt and was scanning once more. Watching him, Jean felt a tiny flare of pride. Scott Summers was simply the best there was; an absolute professional in a field where one was either professional or dead.

"Probably about—Wait! Scott, I'm picking up someone's thoughts. I thought I was before, but I'm sure now."

Cyclops froze, his attention suddenly removed from the Tempometric Meter and riveted on Jean. She was equally still; only her eyes moved.

There. At the entrance to those ruins.

She'd seen the labyrinth from above while fighting against the Sentinel. Now, in a flicker of their psi-link, Cyclops saw it too. Without another word between them, the two X-Men pounced like two cats on a single mouse.

A particularly tatterdemalion mouse.

The gaunt man crouched in a narrow space that had once been an alleyway between two buildings. Both structures were gone, but pieces of their walls remained, as well as piles of bricks where someone, sometime in the past, had begun a hopeless attempt at cleanup.

His clothing was stained and threadbare, musty with neglect, his face drawn and prematurely aged. His left ear had been sliced away cleanly, as if with a laser. But the brown eyes that gazed up into the time travellers' faces were bright and unafraid.

"Mutants?" he said. "You guys're super heroes, aren't you? I haven't seen anything like you in *years*. It's nice to see somebody giving the Big Boys some of their own back." The man smiled in feral triumph, then sobered once more. "But there's always more where they came from," he added, glancing nervously up into the sky. "You have to get out of sight—and cover up those colors you're wearing. Come with me—to the Casbah."

Trust him? Cyclops asked silently.

He's being truthful, Phoenix responded.

And though it meant abandoning momentarily their quest for the Time Platform, it would give them a breathing space in which to plan a search pattern to lead them to it.

"We're with you, friend," Cyclops said.

"Keef," the stranger said, sticking out one hand in an aborted gesture before shoving both hands deeper into the pockets of his overcoat. "Hurry."

Keef scurried off the way he must have come, moving with surprising speed for one so gaunt and undernourished. Cyclops and Phoenix followed.

"How perfectly marvelous," Lireeb said, watching from his vantage point a thousand continua distant. All around him were the bizarre artifacts of Limbo; as he watched the screen he toyed with a withered monkey's paw. "The doomed innocents have taken the bait."

Lireeb set the paw down next to an ornate jeweled box covered with carved Greek lettering and settled back to watch the fun.

Keef led the two X-Men quickly into the city's still-intact underground. At the entrance to the underground warren, Keef removed a tiny lantern from a secret cache and used it to light their path, though he actually didn't seem to need the faint light to find his way through the darkness.

For a while there was still light, filtering down through broken ceilings, reflected into the depths by a series of cunningly placed mirrors. Jean, knowing that Scott's night vision was almost nil due to the red visor that protected the world from his uncontrollable optic blasts, did what she could through their mindlink to help him find his way; but even with Keef's torch it was hard going for both of them, and Jean was glad when they stopped for a breather—at least until she recognized where they were in the maze of utility tunnels, trunk-line accesses, sewer systems . . . and subway tunnels.

New York subway tunnels. Phoenix had her answer, not that it did her much good. They hadn't moved very far through space, and less than forty years into the future. But it was world enough and time for the destruction the two X-Men had seen around them.

"Well, there are certain sections of New York, Major, that I wouldn't advise you to try to invade," Rick Blaine had told Major Strasser in a fictional encounter in a long-ago war. But that was sixty—or, rather, a hundred—years ago. Times had changed. And New York had been invaded . . . by Sentinels.

The open space Keef had stopped in was lit with hand-made torches that danced and guttered wildly in the gusts coming through the tunnels. This, then, was what New

York would come to, less than forty years in their own future.

But it isn't our future, Jean Grey told herself stubbornly, trying to cling to the warning Scott had given all of them back in Rosendale even as her heart ignored it. *The future is not fixed. This is only what* may *be, not what is.*

But it was hard to remember that while staring at the cracked tiles of what had once been a working subway station in a world where the Sentinels ruled everything upon the surface.

"Not much farther," Keef said. He looked at them hopefully, as though he might be worried that they'd bolt.

"Let's get on with it," Cyclops said grimly.

The small party came out into the daylight blinking owlishly as their eyes adjusted to the relative brightness of the gloomy afternoon. Keef looked out across the stretch of open ground, plainly reluctant to cross it.

"Well, we're here. At least, we're kind of here. It's over there." He pointed, the gesture small and close to his body. Keef had survived by wits alone for so long that this supernatural caution was more than second nature to him. It was a small thing but, to Phoenix, more frightening than any trumpeted lists of atrocities could ever be.

"There?" Phoenix asked him.

Across the no-man's-land of rubble that stretched before them, one of the warehouses that clustered along the Hudson was still intact, its very normalcy more shocking than any amount of new devastation could have been.

Keef eyed her blue-and-gold costume dubiously; the bright colors obviously offended even as they fascinated him. "Yeah—but it's all open ground to get there . . . and there are worse things than Big Boys out here, youdambetcha. We'd better wait for dark."

Worse than Sentinels? Phoenix wondered. The memory had flitted across the surface of Keef's mind too quickly for her to catch it, and she was reluctant to invade his privacy any more than she had to.

But it was something worth worrying about.

"We don't have the time to wait," Cyclops said. Even as he spoke, Phoenix saw him glance down at the Tempometric Meter in his hand. Its surface was still dark; wherever the Time Platform was, it wasn't within range.

"Then allow me, gentlemen," Phoenix said.

Before either Keef or Cyclops could react, Phoenix seized them both in a telekinetic grasp and lifted them across the dead zone in the space of a heartbeat. A moment later she settled to the ground beside them.

Keef stared at Phoenix. On his face was an expression of mingled worship and bitterness that she found almost impossible to interpret. But despite the fact that the telekinetic joyride could not have been a new experience, he settled almost at once.

"C'mon, folks," Keef said. "Time to face the music." Lifting a concealed door in the ground almost beneath their feet, he slipped down inside. The X-Men followed.

The entry tunnel was short—built more to slow the Sentinels than for any other purpose, Cyclops guessed—and once he and Phoenix were through it, they were able to stop and look around themselves.

They were standing in some interior open space, illuminated by dim, though natural daylight. Standing in front of them was a crowd of people, all holding weapons—even if only primitive clubs or spears—and regarding them with suspicion. The crowd was dressed in dark, tattered clothing, some still with the embroidered letters— *H* for human, *M* for mutant, *A* for anomaly—that marked this (as Cyclops had expected) as a close relation to Rachel's future reality, a reality that had diverged from the world the X-Men knew almost two decades ago. A few—

no more than two or three—of the crowd showed visible signs of mutation, but most of them looked merely human.

"Keef, what have you done?" someone called from the back of the crowd.

"Yeah, yeah, yeah—it's always Keef's fault," their guide shot back good-naturedly. "Can't you see what they are? They're *super heroes*."

"They're nuts, going around dressed like that, is what they are." A short black woman, her graying hair elaborately braided and beaded with beads of hoarded tinfoil, pushed to the front of the group, a crowbar in her hand. She wore a purple T-shirt, scavenged from a gentler time, with a large, defiant *M* painted on it in Day-Glo paint. A mutant.

"They killed Sentinels," Keef said. "I saw them."

The statement ran through the crowd like wildfire, and suddenly it parted for Cyclops and Phoenix like the Red Sea, its members all talking among themselves. Keef slipped away, apparently glad to get out of the spotlight. The woman in the purple T-shirt frowned at the two X-Men, as if she still wasn't sure of them.

"Careful, Vette," a tall blond man said. He wore a T-shirt with an old logo and the motto BE YOUR OWN DOG across it. For one heart-clutching minute Scott thought it might be some future ghost of Sam Guthrie—the X-Man known as Cannonball—but the chance resemblance was only a trick of the light.

"You hush, 'Rover, I'll handle this; you go get Dream. Who *are* you guys?" the woman called Vette demanded suspiciously.

There seemed to be little point to concealing their identities, though Cyclops wondered if their names would mean anything to these people. "I'm Cyclops and this is Phoenix. We're the X-Men."

Understanding broke with something like shock across

the black woman's face. "Oh my God . . . I met you once, when I was just a baby." The crowbar dropped from her nerveless fingers to clatter on the cement floor. She took a step backward, as if they might be a threat. "But you were killed. I saw it on television." Tears gathered in her eyes.

"Not yet," Cyclops said, and in his voice was the grim promise: *not ever.*

"I don't know how, but you . . . They really are X-Men," Vette announced to the crowd.

"The X-Men are dead, *chica.*" A husky Latina woman, years younger than Vette, came up to stand beside her. "They died years ago, when there were still camps." She swept Cyclops and Phoenix with a scornful glance. "These people are just fools." She put an arm around Vette's shoulders, but her words and her eyes were directed toward the time travellers. "You want a cup of tea, fools?"

A few minutes later, Cyclops and Phoenix were sitting on battered chairs beside a small alcohol stove. The Latina woman—she'd introduced herself as Esperanza— was carefully pouring tea into two chipped mugs. Vette hung back, as if unwilling to approach them. She'd said she'd seen the X-Men when she was a child: Cyclops tried to remember her—or did that meeting exist only in this continuum's twisted history?

Around the two of them the small enclave of hunted New Yorkers went about its business—mending weapons and bodies, cooking, living. Cyclops could see more clearly now, and saw that the open space of the warehouse was subdivided into scores of smaller cubicles by cardboard sheets and blankets hung from ropes. The trappings gave the impression of a vast refugee city, but Phoenix had psi-scanned her surroundings and informed him that there were fewer than three dozen people here.

"Jyrel's going to see if he can find you fools some-

thing to wear—what got into you, flashing colors like
that?'' Esperanza said. ''What do you think it is, 1980
or something?''

''Just a whim,'' Phoenix said, taking the tea and
breathing in its warm fragrance gratefully. The contrast
between the woman's bellicose words and kindly manner
took some getting used to.

''Well, welcome to New York, now go home. You
don't got time to indulge yourself with your upmarket
'whims' here, Nixie—this is the big leagues,'' Esperanza
grumbled. ''You draw too much attention, you endanger
the whole Resistance.''

''The Resistance?'' Cyclops asked.

''That's us.'' Keef was back to cadge a cup of tea from
Esperanza. ''The few, the proud—the Anti-Sentinel Resistance League. Now playing at a theater near you.''

''Or what's left of it,'' Esperanza grumbled. ''Quit
talking your trash, Keef.'' Keef shrugged, obviously used
to being hushed.

Cyclops and Phoenix glanced at each other, trying to
correlate what they were hearing with what they remembered of Rachel's journey from 2013.

''The Anti-Sentinel Resistance? But . . . you're not all
mutants, are you?'' Phoenix asked doubtfully, though her
psi-scan had already told her that most of the people here
were human—or thought of themselves that way.

''What are you, some kind of bigot?'' Esperanza demanded in irritation. ''Human—mutant—it doesn't make
any difference anymore. The Sentinels want to kill *everybody*.''

It makes a certain horrible sense, Cyclops thought
grimly to himself. Eliminate the human race, and you
eliminated mutation—and mutants. It was the sort of
warped logic a Sentinel might embrace. Years ago, Cyclops himself had convinced a group of Sentinels to fly

into the sun in a doomed attempt to reverse human mutation by stopping it at the source.

What price human/mutant harmony? Phoenix said through their psychic link. *These people don't care about the difference between human and mutant anymore—all they care about is the difference between living and dead.*

"We need to talk to your leader," Cyclops said to Esperanza.

"I'm here."

For a moment Cyclops hoped it was Kitty—she'd be called Kate, now—Pryde, who would at least be a familiar face in this dismal land of What Might Be. As Shadowcat, she'd been an X-Man and a founding member of the X-Men's British counterparts, Excalibur. Once, Kate had managed, with Rachel's help, to timeswitch herself with her younger counterpart in an alternate timeline—Cyclops's own—to try to prevent an assassination.

But as the speaker stepped forward out of the shadows, Cyclops saw that she was nothing like the Kate Pryde who would have existed now.

For one thing, she was too young. She was the youngest person he had yet seen here; slender and frail, with flaming red hair badly cut into an unruly crop. She wore a mechanic's jumpsuit, crudely tailored to fit. The blond man Vette had called 'Rover stood behind her.

"My name is Dream," the redhead said. "Who are you?"

"Say they're the X-Men—huh! We *all* gonna be exmen—*and* women—s'what I think," Esperanza said.

"They killed a Sentinel pack," Keef said boldly. "I saw them, Dream. They're alpha mutants—really."

"All the alphas are dead," 'Rover said from behind Dream. He glared at Cyclops and Phoenix.

"Quiet, all of you," Dream said gently. "They can tell me themselves." She sat down on a stool and accepted tea in a dented tin cup with no handle. Keef and Esperanza retreated a few feet, taking the others with them and leaving the X-Men alone with the leader of the Resistance.

Scott sipped his tea—it was bitter and far too sugary at the same time—trying to frame a suitable response to this whole bizarre situation. It was true that these people seemed to be in desperate need of help—but he and Phoenix hadn't come here to help them. Was there any way to rescue these people from the Sentinels' genocide without endangering their own mission? He didn't think so. There was no time.

There was never any time for the things that really mattered.

"We *did* destroy six Sentinels," he said aloud, "and we *are* X-Men. We're from the past, but it's not the past you know, Dream. We've been sent here because we've discovered that your . . . world is being used as a staging ground for an assault upon the fabric of reality itself. We've come here to stop it."

There was a pause while the redheaded woman weighed his words. She was so young! Cyclops tried to guess her age, but privation and constant fear had aged her prematurely. Her hard green eyes were enormous in her young/old face.

"And if you stop the assault, will everything be all right? Will that change . . . this?" Dream could not disguise the ragged note of hope in her voice.

"I don't know," the X-Men's leader admitted reluctantly. "We'll do as much as we can outside of our mission to help you and your people. I promise that."

"You're telling the truth," Dream pronounced. "And you are who you say you are. I'm not an alpha mutant, but I *know* that—it's the only gift I have; the only thing that came down to me."

As she spoke, Dream searched both their faces with anxious eyes. Phoenix felt a faint flicker of recognition beneath the surface of her mind as she stared back into those burning green eyes. Who was this girl, to seem so familiar?

"Don't you recognize me?" Dream asked. "Don't either of you recognize who I am? I'm *Dream*—I'm Rachel's daughter. My father was Franklin Richards."

Jean stared. In a future not their own, Rachel Summers had been *their* daughter, hers and Scott's. And if Dream was Rachel's daughter, then in some time-twisted sense, Dream was their granddaughter.

"I was born in 2012," Dream began. "In the South Bronx Internment Center. My parents—Rachel Summers and Franklin Richards—died when I was about a year old, trying to stop the Last War. That was the war that changed the Sentinels' programming forever. They'd already repressed all scientific research because it could be a cause of mutation, and they'd also exterminated most of the mutant population of North America. But in those days, the rest of the world was still safe—it was a stalemate between the New America and the rest of the world, so long as they confined themselves to just the one continent . . . but they didn't. They broadened their mandate to include every mutant on Earth, and attacked Europe.

"It was the battle to end all battles: Dr. Doom and the Sub-Mariner fighting side-by-side with Inhumans and Genoshan proctors. It took the Sentinels over fifteen years to declare victory—to poison the oceans and level the mountains . . . and destroy everything alive that they could find. Because after the first few battles, the Sentinel Nexus changed their mandate again. It was no longer just mutants who had to die, but every living thing on this planet: human, mutant—*everyone*."

Cyclops and Phoenix sat silent, horrified. It seemed like the punchline of a bad joke, but it wasn't funny. The Sentinels—created by humans to serve humans—were literal-mindedly logical enough to feel that the best service they could render humanity was to destroy it.

"I grew up working in a Sentinel factory," Dream continued, "helping to build new units to answer the demands of the war. That's where I learned to sabotage the things too. You see, for a while we—the living—still thought we could win." Dream gazed down at the cup in her hand, her emerald eyes unreadable. "I don't know if we can, now. We've lost so many. Even the Rogues and the Wildpacks are gone. I don't know if anyone else is left alive on Earth but us. There aren't any more children—we think the Sentinels had something to do with that too. I'm the youngest person I know. They don't even have to hunt us to win. All the Sentinels have to do to win now is outwait us." Dream's shoulders slumped, burdened with all the weight of humanity's last stand.

"There's always a chance," Cyclops said brusquely. His voice was harsh with the effort of holding back his suddenly churning emotions. "You can't give up—ever. Do you hear me, Dream?"

Dream raised her head and gazed toward him, her green eyes brimming now with bright unshed tears.

"Do you think . . . ?" she asked, reaching out to him.

"I know you'll win," Cyclops said firmly, his gloved hand closing over her thin bare one. Dream clung to that grasp, as though trying to draw strength and confidence through it.

Jean wished she felt more of that confidence herself. Her emotions veered wildly between rage and shock. This was the future as if Rachel had never made her desperate attempt to change it, a world in which not only mutantkind, but humanity itself, stood upon the brink of extinction, its last defiance led by Dream.

Their granddaughter. Her granddaughter—child of a child she would never have.

"All right, then," Dream said, pushing the momentary

emotion away from her and getting to her feet. "You said you were here looking for something that didn't belong here? There's only one place it can be. Listen up, Rats—"

She raised her voice only slightly, but all the inhabitants of the warehouse quickly gathered around—Jyrel, Vette, Esperanza, 'Rover, Keef, and others whose names Phoenix did not know. All armed. All watchful. And all looking to their leader.

Dream.

"The Rats-In-The-Walls are the best Resistance Cell on the whole East Coast," she told them for the time travelers' benefit. "We see everything—and we haven't seen anything, right?"

Murmured—puzzled—assent from the gathered figures.

"And the Big Boys haven't seen anything, right?"

Scattered laughter and hoots of derision. *Big Boy* was obviously the local cant for "Sentinel."

"So if you're sure the thing you're looking for is here, X-Men, there's only one place it could be," Dream finished, turning back to Cyclops and Phoenix. "There's supposed to be a place in the center of the city—way downtown—where even Sentinels don't go. I've never been there, but I heard about it from the Tommyknockers—another Resistance group. They're all dead now. If your package is anywhere within a hundred miles, it's in the Dead Zone. I'll take you there—I'm good at avoiding the patrols, and maybe we'll meet somebody who's still alive."

As opposed to meeting someone who's dead? Jean looked at Scott. "But you can't! Dream, it's too dangerous—"

The young woman smiled crookedly at her. "What, do you think I want to live forever? Couldn't if I tried. Jyr's got your coverups. Put them on and let's go.''

We can't allow this, Jean sent telepathically to her husband. His bleak expression, she knew, matched her own.

We have no choice, Jean. We need Dream's help to find this taboo area. It's our only hope—the tracker can't even tell me where to look for Kang's Time Platform. And we can't afford to fail—for her sake.

But she's—Jean began, and abruptly sealed off the thought. Dream was their granddaughter, blood of their blood. Phoenix could not bear the thought of endangering her. But if they did not take this risk, not only Dream and her world, but untold others, would die.

Numbly, unseeing, Phoenix shrugged into the battered tan raincoat Jyrel handed her and pulled a dark beret down over her flaming hair. Beside her, Scott was also concealing his battlesuit, a hooded sweatshirt and gimme cap doing what they could to disguise the bulky gold-and-ruby visor. Pulling on the torn and stained sweatpants that went with the outfit, he looked like the New Mutant in the 'Hood.

Jean's mouth twitched in a faint smile. What did it say about her—about all the X-Men—that they were ready to make jokes at a time like this?

"You should think hard before you risk yourself, Dream," Cyclops said. "You're their leader."

The young redhead glared at him stubbornly, and in that moment Jean could see Scott in her.

"And that's why I have to—" Dream began.

"Sentinels!"

Keef skidded into the middle of the crowd. "Sentinels coming this way! *Lots of them*!"

"Go!" Dream shouted. "Rendezvous at Checkpoint Charlene!" Everyone scattered except for Dream and the two X-Men.

But fast as Keef had been, the warning came too late. The wall of the warehouse simply . . . disintegrated.

And silhouetted against the lowering sky were the forms of six Prime Sentinels.

CHAPTER FIVE

MAINLINE +4, THE YEAR 2020

T he first thing Spider-Man noticed about the year 2020 was the smell: wherever he was, it smelled as if it had *wanted* to be an open sewer but hadn't been able to get its hands on the right ingredients. The smell of rot was underlaid with a toxic chemical tang that made him recoil instinctively. He looked around.

It was night. It was raining. He, Cable, and Aliya were standing in a dump.

Terrific.

All he could see in every direction were undulating mounds of discarded *things*, looking oddly companionable and familiar. Pepsi now came in a cardboard carton. Jolt Cola had introduced a sugar-free version. He saw brand names like Toxic! and First Strike for products he didn't want to imagine. Most of the trash was paper and plastic; the glass and metal consumer waste of his own period seemed almost completely absent.

In the middle distance was a high-powered security light—apparently there for protection, as if trash could be mugged—and farther away there was the glow of city lights and a skyline that looked like New York on steroids.

The worst thing was, this place was less than a quarter of a century away. With more luck than you could really count on in the super hero trade, the three of them all might live to see this century, this decade. He tried to remember that Cyclops had said that all the places they'd be sent to were futures that might never be.

But it seemed too real to doubt. How could anyplace that smelled so bad be fictional?

Aliya shifted position, and Spider-Man heard plastic crackle under her boot. He glanced toward her. The gold metallic plates on her uniform reflected the night and the lights in weirdly distorted patterns.

"This place looks like a scene shot by Ridley Scott with a headache," Spider-Man said to her.

"This is the year 2020—*a* year 2020," Cable corrected himself, apparently thinking about the same thing Spider-Man had been.

"Welcome to the future, now go home," Spider-Man muttered to himself. There was no way this place could look enticing. "So where do we start?"

Silently Cable inspected the Tempometric Meter's display and then pointed with it. Aliya swung her rifle back over her shoulder and began picking her way carefully through the trash in the direction of Cable's gesture. Watching them, Spider-Man felt like the proverbial third wheel, as though he were eavesdropping on a conversation between lovers. What was it like to have loved someone and lost her, and mourned her, and then get a second chance in the middle of armageddon?

It would, Spider-Man thought soberly to himself, be pretty terrifying. But for all the surface emotion either Cable or Aliya showed, they might as well have been two strangers who'd just met in a fern bar. Spider-Man shrugged and followed them—on foot, little as he liked it. There wasn't anything here to hang a web-line from, so that meant walking.

The rain—dirtier than precip in the Big Apple, and that was going some—began to soak through his mask and the shoulders of his costume, adding to his discomfort and growing irritation. In the last subjective week he'd gone to an opening at the Museum of Natural History, visited the X-Men, spent most of a day in the Old West, fought androids from the future, been marooned in an alternate reality with only a slim chance of getting home, met a different set of X-Men, seen an alternate version of himself die, found out that everything he, Cable, and the X-Men had done so far had been achingly futile, and was now here in some kind of future on a wild Time Platform chase.

Ever since this had begun he'd been flung from frying pan to fire, with time itself turned into a meaningless jumble where effect preceded cause. It offended the meticulous sense of order he'd learned in darkroom and chemistry lab, long before he'd become Spider-Man and taken up a career practically defined by the phrase *near miss*.

And the worst of it was, he'd lost track of time so thoroughly that he wasn't sure anymore whether he was late for dinner. MJ was the patient sort—a necessity when married to a super hero—but nobody was that patient.

Thoughts like these went too well with his surroundings; to distract himself he studied Aliya and Cable, both walking ahead of him. Like reflections in an inverting mirror, they did not seem so much to be friends, lovers, companions—whatever they truly were, and Spider-Man sincerely hoped that nobody would tell him—as two sides of the same coin: the perfect soldier, represented here in male and female versions like some kind of well-armed full-contact Barbie doll. Dolls shouldn't have human emotions. Dolls were supposed to take anything you gave them and then go back in the box until next time, untouched and unscathed.

But even dolls could break. He just didn't want to be around when it happened.

Cable stopped. "Here is the entrance," he said, gesturing with the Tempometric Meter as though it were a royal scepter. His metal arm gleamed faintly; they were moving away from the one illuminated watch-light, and in the darkness it was hard to see much of anything at all.

"The entrance to what?" Spider-Man heard himself ask obligatorily. The rain became heavier, the moisture in the air releasing a host of new smells. His uniform was soaked, sticking to him in earnest now, something that gave it all the charm of being encased head-to-foot in soggy nylon. Which was what he was wearing, after all.

"Some sort of a—" Aliya paused to sniff deeply "—a sewer, I'd guess."

She was looking at a round grating about a yard across centered in a large block of concrete. A sewer, just as she'd said, and this was one of the ventilation shafts to keep explosive gases from building up in the tunnels below.

Meaning they came out here. Spider-Man tried to hold his breath, realized it was silly, gave up, and inhaled. *Lord, I hope this smell will wash out of my costume, or when I get back I'm going to be your* un*friendly neighborhood Spider-Man.*

A quick blurt of Cable's ion cannon destroyed the lock, and Aliya moved to pull the grate away. Spider-Man helped her, his spider-proportionate strength enabling him to pick up the grate and toss it like a giant mesh frisbee. It fell to the ground several hundred yards distant, the sound of its impact softened by the piles of garbage all around.

"There's something so universal about a sewer," Spider-Man said ruminatively, staring down the shaft. There were rungs set into the side—not that he needed them, but they were proof that *someone* used this access.

"Get out of the way," Aliya said, pushing past him. She swung over the side and began climbing down into the darkness. Cable threw her a flashlight and Aliya caught it, the unspoken communication between them quick and vivid. In moments she'd reached the bottom of the ventilation shaft, her footsteps sending up clouds of poisonous stink.

Hoo-boy—talk about eau de Newark, Spider-Man thought, wishing he could hold his nose through the mask. But he couldn't, and he knew you could desensitize yourself if you breathed enough of the stuff. Drawing a deep lungful of not-exactly-air, the wall-crawler followed Aliya into the sewer.

Where the ventilation shaft crossed the sewer main there was a ten-foot drop to the bottom—filled with thick, slowly oozing slurry—that Spider-Man didn't really feel like making. He edged along the ceiling instead, spider-walking along. It was comparatively clean, anyway, even if just as fragrant as the muck below.

Fan patterns of dried waste on the curving walls showed the various high-water marks of toxic sludge, or even out-of-season rainfall. Water was starting to collect at the bottom of the ventilation shaft and drip into the slow-moving river below. He wondered if waste water was vented through this system as well. If the rain continued, they might be looking at a high tide that could wash them away.

And Kang's Time Platform, too, come to that. Wherever it was.

Aliya waded through the sludge oozing down through the center of the pipe as unconcernedly as though she were crossing a city street and climbed up to the catwalk at the far side. Clumps of brownish-yellow guck the consistency of oatmeal slid from Aliya's battlesuit and dropped to the ground as she stood holding the torch to light Cable's arrival.

"Stay sharp," she said, looking up toward him on the ceiling, and swung her rifle in a short arc as if she would confront all comers. It was hard to remember that less than two hours ago, across a thousand timelines, the two of them had been fighting at Magneto's side, only to discover—after a single desperate gamble that would reunite her with a time double of the man she loved—that everything she'd known—her entire *world*—was gone and her battle had been for nothing.

It didn't seem to affect her much. *Or is that really fair?* Spider-Man asked himself, gazing speculatively down at the top of Aliya's head. Maybe it was just that she was hard—as hard as some of the hardest he knew, both good guys and bad. *If she weren't already in a relationship*, he quipped mentally, *I'd introduce her to the Punisher. They'd probably get along just fine*.

There was more splashing as Cable reached them. He hung from the last rung for a moment, regarding the effluvium with distaste, and then jumped.

At the moment Cable's boots splashed down, Spider-Man felt a tingle all over his body.

"We've got trouble, folks," he said, keeping his voice low.

But from where?

His name was Arno Stark, and his money had bought a legend . . . the name and the armor of Iron Man, the Golden Avenger.

There were times he thought the armor was laughing at him. Mocking him, because while its creator and original wearer had been a selfless—even masochistic—hero, Arno Stark was nothing but a mercenary.

Although, to be fair, he was a very wealthy one.

Stark couldn't really remember why he'd thought it such a good idea to buy the trademark. At first it was only the acquisitive need to make Stark-Fujikawa what it had been in the golden age, the Age of Heroes. He'd been younger then, and had still retained some belief that skill was rewarded, that ability led to power.

It didn't. He had power now, but he still wasn't sure where it had come from. He could enumerate the several separate betrayals that had led him to this place in his life, each time he'd cheated, each time he'd lied, each time he'd met reason and truth with cynicism and superior force. Every victory had taught him another piece of

the truth: the good guys didn't win. They never won—
they were too weak. Unwilling to use the only weapons
that would gain them victory. Each proof of that had been
a little death to him. Once upon a time.

The golden armor of Iron Man contained the weaponry
to level a city block and support systems that would let
him circle the globe and venture into the frontier of space
or the depths of the sea. The combination of power and
anonymity had seduced Arno Stark from the very first
moment. The sense of putting on not only the armor, but
another persona . . . one considerably more ruthless than
his own.

If that were possible.

Stark still vividly remembered the first time he'd worn
the golden armor; the sensuous feeling as its hypermag-
netic couplings closed over his own health-club-toned
limbs. In the second decade of the new century, robots
were the mainstay of the business world: Stark-Fujikawa
held all of the fundamental patents in the science of robotics that Baintronics did not. Robots were an invisible
workforce: powerful, subservient, endlessly patient.
Though society had long since stopped building robots
in hominid form, the suit of armor still looked like a
savage golden robot. When Arno Stark sealed himself
into the suit, he felt that savagery enter his blood, the
implacable, conscienceless patience of the robot: inhuman, without the concept of pity or mercy. Their brute
mechanical ruthlessness had never caused them pain.

From that moment forward, Arno Stark's star had been
on the rise. Soon he had no more reason to employ his
golden doppelgänger in defense of SF's market share,
and the thought of searching corporate America for in-
justices to right never occurred to him. But he'd developed a taste for blood.

And so Arno Stark placed Iron Man's services on the
market, for sale to the highest bidder. His price was high,

and he continually raised it, but it was always met. Because the jobs that Iron Man took stayed taken. The people he was sent after were delivered without fail into the hands of whoever met his price.

Along the way, he'd converted his site security into a mercenary cadre that few could equal. He named them Iron-Bots; a malicious joke that no one in Arno Stark's world would ever get.

But tonight he got to amuse himself with it once more, and this one was on the house. Because someone had brought him an anonymous tip that tonight there would be Wreckers in Queens . . . and it was always open season on Wreckers.

Iron Man glanced at his companion. It was her territory; he'd had to call her in on the operation or risk trouble. He regarded the shapely body revealed by the tight scarlet-and-blue combat suit; admired the spill of red hair down the woman's back.

"What are you looking at?" Spider-Girl snapped.

Spider-Girl was one of the last of the Independents; a lone vigilante protecting her territory from incursions of Wreckers, Illegals, rioting Vidiots, or worse. She was clinging to the curving wall of the sewer line, staying fastidiously far from the waste flow that Iron Man was forced to wade through. Her eyes were invisible behind the white shields of her mask, and Iron Man wondered what she looked like without that tight-fitting battlesuit.

"Nothing," Iron Man said.

He wondered if she was for sale. She'd make a fine addition to his Iron-Bots, with her strength, speed, agility . . . and lethal venom stinger.

There was a faint light ahead, just beyond the curve of the tunnel.

"There they are," Spider-Girl said, pointing. She'd located the Wreckers at the same time his armor's systems had. Iron Man was impressed. "Our target for tonight."

• • •

Cable and Aliya both turned in the direction Spider-Man
pointed. His spider-sense was screaming, warning of im-
minent attack, and an instant later, he knew why.

A searchlight flared, blinding all three of them.

"Well, if it isn't the same old Wreckers in fancy new
clothes," a harsh metallic voice snarled. "It's a good
thing I received an anonymous tip that you'd be here—
I wouldn't have thought of looking for you scavengers
this far north of your usual stomping grounds."

Spider-Man blinked hard, wincing as his eyes adjusted
to the brilliant light. The speaker was a glittering metal
man, and for a moment he thought it was another of
Kang's androids until he saw that it wore red-and-gold
armor similar to that of Iron Man.

But it was only a resemblance. The red-and-gold hel-
met looked eerily like a skull, with an articulated jaw and
jagged, Halloween-pumpkin mouth-slit. The armored
pauldrons where the metal-mesh sleeves met the crimson
gorget had been reinforced with what looked like heavy-
duty power conduits, and the shoulder pieces themselves
were now arching buzz-saw discs. Spider-Man had met
and worked with Iron Man on dozens of occasions, and
he knew that no matter how many design changes his
employer Tony Stark put the armor through, the billion-
aire industrialist would never have made it look this . . .
hostile.

"You can surrender," the inhuman amplified voice
came, "but I'd so much prefer it if you didn't."

Was there a man inside there or not? Spider-Man
wasn't sure. And it would make no difference in the way
Cable and Aliya played things. That was the worst part.

"Who are you?" Cable asked, playing for time. Aliya
moved away from him along the catwalk, trying to widen
the enemy's field of fire.

"The name is Iron Man, Wrecker—not that you're

likely to get the chance to remember it. The bounty on you scum is the same, alive or dead,'' the armored adversary said.

It wasn't actually too hard to figure out why this guy was here so opportunely. Spider-Man didn't know what a Wrecker was, but it was clear enough who'd been responsible for this Iron Man's anonymous tip.

"If Kang doesn't play nice," Spider-Man said under his breath, "nobody's going to invite him for any more sleepovers."

Cable had time for one baleful glance in Spider-Man's direction before Iron Man opened fire.

The red-and-blue figure on the ceiling behind Arno Stark froze there, almost a part of the masonry itself. She hadn't expected. . . . There'd been no time to prepare for the sight of the terrorist desecrating one of her most sacred memories.

I don't care what Iron Man does with the other two. This one's mine. Skittering along the ceiling as gracefully as her namesake, Spider-Girl headed toward the intruder whose costume was an echo of her own.

Whatever Iron Man was using for repulsor rays racketed off Cable's hasty telekinetic shield, spraying out in all directions. He and Aliya returned fire as if they were the two halves of one person, and the half-lit tunnel was made brilliant by the flashes of the explosions. Through the strobe effect, Spider-Man could see other shapes moving forward behind Iron Man—soldiers in blue-and-silver uniforms, with large guns and hostile expressions.

Maestro, a little travelling music, please, Spider-Man thought to himself just as he leapt.

He'd been a hero since he was in high school, but Spider-Man had never been the strongest kid on the block, or even the fastest (if you counted in people like

Quicksilver or the Speed Demon). But what that made him was someone with a whole career's worth of experience in taking on opposition that was bigger, stronger, and scarier—and winning. Because while the dudes he faced off against usually had the raw power to crush him like a fly, they could only do it if they could *catch* him.

Spider-Man touched down once—using the ersatz Iron Man's head to leapfrog off from—and smashed feetfirst into the first wave of foot soldiers right behind him. They went down as if by reflex, weapons flying to hit the walls and skid down into the sludge. Spider-Man sprang from the toppling bodies to the wall, the ceiling, the other wall, spider-sense taking the place of instinct and sight, keeping him out of the line of fire. He heard shouts, curses, and pain-filled screams that didn't care who heard them.

In midair he flung out a blanket of webbing shot from both web-shooters at once, to further tangle the enemy. It wasn't his best work, but it ought to slow them down. How many were there? Where had they come from? And what did they want, other than their three heads on a plate? *Of course,* he thought, *that may indeed be all they want. Too often, that's enough.*

A weight landed on his back and dragged Spider-Man from the wall.

''Impostor!'' a woman's voice screamed in his ear.

Spider-Man could not see who she was; she moved too fast for that and her strength and agility matched his own. She punched him in the face and then tried to rip his mask off.

Panic-edged reflexes thrust him away from an opponent he could barely see. There was an explosion beside his left ear—she'd shot at him with something—and then he found himself barely managing to avoid being engulfed in webbing much like his own.

''Lady, what *is* your problem?'' Spider-Man demanded as he flipped away from the webbing onto the sewer roof.

And stared.

Her costume was red and blue, just like his, with a black pattern of webbing against the red. Around each wrist she wore a gold bracelet of cylinders—possibly the source of the blasts she'd bracketed him with—and a half-mask above which her long red hair whipped around her face like Medusa's snakes.

"The name's Spider-Girl. *How dare you desecrate my father's memory?*" she demanded. And then she blasted him again.

It hurt. Pain and nausea crawled along his nerves, and there was a sickly metallic taste in his mouth. *Poison*, he thought muzzily, as his heart raced with the pain. *She's poisoned me*.

"Finish him! Finish him!" Iron Man roared.

His amplified voice boomed off the walls, its echoes jangling like shadows in Spider-Man's head as he tried to shake off the effects of Spider-Girl's venom blast. He was still standing; he flailed wildly and struck out with spider-strength against anything within reach. In that moment, Spider-Girl could have killed him, but she hung back as the Iron-Bots swarmed over him. For a moment their weight bore him down, down . . . and through all the noise and the pain he could still hear what she'd shouted at him when she'd attacked:

"How dare you desecrate my father's memory?"
Father . . . ?

There had been better days. There had been worse days. For Nathan Dayspring Summers, this was, in some sense, just another day. Another typical day for a man whose earliest memories were of his infant fingers being folded about the makeshift stock of a toy weapon.

The enemy had them outgunned, though that wouldn't

have mattered in the face of some of the tricks Cable knew. He knew he could win, but the important thing now was following the trail of Kang's Time Platform to whatever end it had.

No matter how many bodies he had to crawl over.

For a few seconds Cable traded shots with the red-and-gold armored figure in the tunnelway ahead. Spider-Man had disappeared, somewhere in the melee ahead. Aliya, above him on the catwalk, tried with some success for bank shots off the tunnel walls at the troops behind Iron Man.

Well, Cable had a job to do, and he wasn't going to get it done standing here.

He concentrated his firepower directly on the golden bull's eye in the center of Iron Man's chest and followed his firepower with his body. Cable was an imposing man—and here and now, an unknown quantity. It would take more than most people had to stand up to someone like that when he was coming right at them.

And as he'd expected, Iron Man flinched.

It wasn't by much, but it was enough. The golden mercenary hesitated, and Cable slammed into him with the fury of a runaway train. Iron Man hurtled backward, tangled among fallen members of his own forces for the crucial moment that let Cable and Aliya slip past him.

Beyond Iron Man, the enemy forces were softer. He cued the ion cannon he carried to ''full auto'' and sprayed a covering fire ahead of him.

''Spider-Man! Come on!'' he heard Aliya cry. He stopped. She ran past him as he whipped around and laced the air behind them with a rain of augmented laser-excited death. He hoped the web-slinger could keep up, because there wasn't any time to wait for him.

There was a flash of red and blue, and Cable relaxed; Spider-Man's bright costume made it easy to see him. The arachnoid mutate bounded away from some of the mercenaries, shot a web-line to the opposite wall, and followed it with his body.

Cable turned in the direction Aliya had gone and ran with all his might.

The sewer line twisted and turned, but the blue flicker of the Tempometric Meter kept the three time travellers on the right course. The enemy was only seconds behind them, though their greater numbers handicapped them in this confined space. Sensible people would be looking to find a suitable place to make a last stand, but Cable was still following the trail of temporal energy that would lead them to the Time Platform.

And when it led them into a shaftway that angled upward, he stopped, taking precious minutes to guide the other two into it.

"Aliya, you go first. I'll cover us," Cable said.

"They'll follow us right up the pipe," Spider-Man said quietly, his tone unwontedly sober. "It's too obvious to miss."

It must originally have been some kind of drain; water was already trickling down through it from the rain outside. Even if it was narrow enough to stop the twenty-first century Iron Man, it wouldn't stop Spider-Girl.

"Spider-Man's right," she objected. "They'll know where we've gone—and you're carrying the Meter. I'll go last."

Cable shook his head, gesturing again for Aliya to precede him.

"Look, *I'll* go last if it'll make the two of you stop arguing," Spider-Man said. "*Both* of you go." He turned away and began spraying the tunnel behind them, weaving a web-shield across it to slow their pursuers at least a little bit. Not for the first time, he wished he were carrying his usual blend—this stuff, concocted quickly on Aliya's alternate world, dissolved measurably faster—

but anything that would buy them a few precious seconds was worth trying.

Just think. If your experiment with permanent-bonding adhesives had worked out just a little better, today you might have been known as the man who invented the Post-It note.

He dismissed the random thought and concentrated on his weaving. Cable, who'd lost the argument, began climbing the pipe.

"That won't stop them long," Aliya said to Spider-Man as soon as he'd finished. "Go on. He needs you up there."

As what, comic relief? But all of them had a job to do, and they were going to do it as well as they could. Spider-Man followed Cable up the shaftway. He heard Aliya start her climb before he reached the top.

The shaftway flattened and narrowed to something that forced him to scuttle along on fingertips and toes. He could not imagine how Cable had made it through, but obviously he had. At last Spider-Man reached the top of the pipe. The opening had been closed off by a grille that Cable had already torn loose; the squarish opening was more than wide enough to admit one svelte web-slinger. He looked down.

He was eight feet above the floor of some white-tiled room. At least there was light here, and he could see Cable standing off to one side. Spider-Man dropped lightly through the aperture, bouncing to the floor in a crouch and looking around.

For a long moment Spider-Man thought that the chamber looked oddly familiar for someplace he'd never seen—until he realized that he *had* seen it before; on a daily basis, in fact. It was a subway stop—the first Queens-side stop for the R train. The line went elevated later on and farther out, but here it was underground.

How had they gotten here from the junkyard they'd

started out in? For a disorienting moment, Spider-Man lost all sense of where he was; as an antidote, he forced himself to concentrate on what was immediately before him.

The subway station didn't look as if the MTA had had much ridership lately. Its lights still burned, though the lenses were dimmed with dust. In fact, everything here was dusty, half dark, and deserted. Trash had been piled into monstrous mountains at each end of the platform, but it had been here for so long that rats and insects had already picked it clean. Beyond, the tracks still ran, rusted silver, between dark and dark.

"It's this way," Cable said, pointing down the track with the Tempometric Meter. "Hurry. We haven't much time."

Behind him, Aliya dropped down through the broken grille. Her rifle rattled faintly in its sling.

Terrific. I hope the third rail's turned off, or barbecued hero may just be the soup of the day. Although, if those nasties were still following them, a little high voltage might not be amiss.

"There was no one behind me," Aliya reported. "Maybe they've given up. Though that's not the way to bet," she added.

"Come on," Cable said, jumping down onto the tracks.

No! Spider-Man's spider-sense screamed, wakening into jangling life. He opened his mouth to shout a warning—

And just about then the roof fell in.

Or, actually, the back wall. It cascaded across the tracks, blocking the subway tunnel in the direction they wanted to go. But that wasn't all. There was a rumble as the heavy armored vehicles moving toward them up the tracks behind them shook the subway tunnel, and thin drizzles of dust began to filter down from above. Iron

Man stood in the headlights of the lead ATV, posing like General Custer on a John Ford ridge.

"I'd been hoping to surround you—I should have known you'd make for the high ground like the rats you are," Iron Man said.

They were trapped. The only direction left to run was back to the sewer, and Spider-Man could see the red-and-blue form of Spider-Girl as she slithered through it. Who was she? He knew of two different people who'd called themselves Spider-*Woman*, but one was a brunette, the other blonde. Was she someone he had yet to meet? Someone he would never meet, because this timeline diverged too far from his own?

She mentioned her father. . . .

They might have been able to make it over the rock-slide and down the tracks, but Iron Man and his goons could clear the roadblock and travel faster than the three of them could run.

There was no way out except through Golden Boy, there, and Spider-Man didn't think he was the type to let them go with a slap on the wrist. He flicked a glance at his companions. Neither Cable nor Aliya was the type to bargain, to try to point out that this was all a mistake, that they weren't Wreckers, but tourists.

"For the first and last time, get out of my way, Tin Man," Aliya said. "Or I'll see you in hell." Her voice was steady, but loud enough to be heard above the sound of the rumbling machinery.

"I'm sure you will, curve—someday. Throw down your weapons," Iron Man said. Behind him there was a ratcheting sound of a dozen weapons brought to the ready. Spider-Man looked for the woman in the red-and-blue costume so like his own, and did not see her through the glare.

"Do it," Cable said quietly.

Aliya glanced toward him, surprise and reluctance

plain on her face. But she dropped her rifle, and Cable followed suit. Their ion cannons clattered as they fell to the tracks.

Spider-Man sighed inwardly. Now came the really boring part where they got taken into custody and tried to figure out how to escape. Maybe they'd get lucky. Maybe there was somebody farther up the food chain who'd be willing to listen to reason. He wondered who among his acquaintances was still around over two decades later, and if he could convince any of them of who he was.

"All of them," Iron Man said.

Carefully Cable set the Tempometric Meter on the ground. It wasn't a weapon, but it could be easily mistaken for one, and now was not the time to argue.

"Good," Iron Man said, and raised his hands. But not to point at the three of them—to point at the ceiling, where it was already beginning to crack under the strain and neglect of decades. It creaked and groaned, ready to fall.

Ready to come down on all of them, with a little help.

How many times had Spider-Man played out this scene, fighting somewhere that was coming down all around both of them, where the hero lined the villain up for the money shot and then pulled it at the last moment because he couldn't make it without killing his adversary? Even some of the bad guys in that position wouldn't take that easy out.

Time seemed to stretch and slow. *He's going to do it!* Spider-Man thought in stark disbelief.

Iron Man was obviously no hero . . . nor yet an honorable villain. *He isn't going to take us anywhere—he really means to kill us.*

"No!"

He saw the woman in the red-and-blue run toward them from her sideline position, realizing what Iron Man intended to do; heard her shout a protest in the same moment that Iron Man unleashed a force blast at the roof.

This is it, Spider-Man thought.

There was no way to survive the blast, but at the last moment they pretended. Spider-Man saw Cable throw himself over Aliya's body as she made a desperate lunge to protect the Tempometric Meter. His eye flared bright gold in the dusty air, but whatever mutant powers Cable could field didn't seem to be enough this time.

Spider-Man cried out as a chunk of rock hit him numbingly in the shoulder.

And then the darkness began, and went on forever.

CHAPTER SIX

For a dazzling, terrifying instant as the light faded, Remy LeBeau thought he'd come home.

The air was sweet and thick and green and wet with the scent of flowering growing things and the undertang of rot. It was the smell of the Louisiana bayou, where a young adopted thief of the Clan LeBeau had run until the streets of the Big Easy became too hot for him. That heat and humidity had become a part of Gambit's life—everywhere he went, things always seemed to be too hot for a poor Cajun boy.

Of course (so Gambit told himself encouragingly) it was only to be expected that notoriety should attend the life of the greatest thief who'd yet been born.

The moment of disorientation faded. Gambit opened his eyes.

The three of them stood in the only clear spot in a jungle that looked as if it had never even heard of a machete. The yellow-green light filtered down in bars, thick as honey, sparkling with slowly drifting pollen motes. The leaves of the upper canopy rustled as small creatures scampered through it, dislodging showers of dew on the three X-Men below.

"How . . . beautiful," Storm said wonderingly. The lines of exhaustion and strain in her face eased as she surveyed the paradise surrounding them.

"Not as beautiful as you, Stormy, an' dat's de trut'," Gambit answered automatically, his Cajun accent as thick and heavy as the tropical sunlight. Despite his easy patter, this place made him nervous. In the bayou, something was always out to eat your lunch . . . or make you lunch. He doubted this place was any different.

"But where are we?" Storm asked, frowning slightly.

"It's 2099, do you know where your children are?" the third member of their team wisecracked automatically. Hank McCoy straightened up from his crouch and brushed ineffectually at the pollen gilding his blue fur. The Tempometric Meter in his hand gleamed brightly, like sunlight on water. "The trouble is, this doesn't look much like 2099 to me."

"But if we ain't where dat fancy machine o' Cable's sent us—" Gambit began.

Suddenly the ground began to shake. Dew and flower petals rained down from above, and the sound of the leaves rattling against each other was like the sound of pounding ocean surf. Then, cresting over the ocean sound, came the rhythmic pounding of running feet. For a moment it was impossible to tell from which direction the sound was coming.

"Stampede!" Hank McCoy shouted, springing with bestial agility for the nearest branch. "Talk about déjà vu . . ." he grumbled, staring down at the ground beneath his feet.

In a moment the flood tide of animals had reached the clearing. They looked like geckos gone horribly wrong. Bipedal, about five feet tall, their green-and-yellow hides blended into the jungle backdrop as if they were poisonous ambulatory flowers. Their jaws gaped horror-movie wide, showing forests of yellowing needle teeth surrounding pale yellow tongues. They ran as if something larger pursued them—but not as if it pursued them so closely that there wasn't time for a snack.

Storm simply used her elemental powers to loft her into the lower branches, safely above the herd. Gambit wasn't so lucky.

The Cajun-born X-Man stood frozen for an instant, directly in the path of the rampaging lizards. Then, with a sleight-of-hand flicker, his bo staff appeared in his hands. He used the gleaming length of metal to launch himself into the air, landing on the tree branch beside the Beast.

"Amazing," the blue-furred mutant biogeneticist said, gazing down at the lizards galloping past beneath his feet. "I seem to attract these things; I wonder if I should change my cologne? At least we haven't gone too far wrong; superficially those beasts resemble genus *velociraptor*, but certain differences would seem to indicate—"

"I got no interest in bein' on a first-name basis wit' dem, me," Gambit said feelingly.

Moments later, the swarm was gone, leaving behind them only a trampled swath through the jungle. There was no sign of whatever had frightened them. Storm drifted to the ground as gently as a falling flower. Gambit and the Beast joined her less gracefully.

"Dinosaurs!" Gambit spat. "Dat ain't no part of any future Gambit knows."

"Henry?" Storm said. The gold of her recall device glinted against her costume, making the wind-rider glitter like a Fabergé icon in the sunlight pouring through the canopy. "Gambit's right—this world doesn't seem like the future to me. It's so alive—so vibrant—"

"So full o' lizards lookin' for dinner," Gambit muttered.

The Beast gazed quizzically at the Tempometric Meter in his hands, his shaggy brows beetling. Crouched on the forest floor like some creature out of time's dark past, Henry P. McCoy looked as though he belonged to this far-flung reality far more than did his companions.

"Let's start with the good news. Wherever we are, this little doohickey is definitely registering the presence of Kang's Time Platform somewhere off thataway," the Beast said. "Which would imply that we've reached the destination our tour guide booked us through to: 2099, a hundred years from our own time, though not necessarily in our own future."

Gambit shrugged eloquently, brushing his unruly hair

back out of his eyes. His skin was already damp with sweat in this hothouse environment, and his leather duster weighed heavily on his shoulders.

"As for where we are in a more cosmic sense—other than about five miles away from where we need to be— since this probably is 2099, either Cable's Tin Lizzie has sent us 'way, 'way, away from our own baseline to some-place where dinosaurs still rule the earth—not impossi-ble, if what paleontologists call the Great Die-Off didn't occur way back in the Cretaceous Age—or we're some-where a little closer to home that still has dinos."

"Great choices," Gambit muttered, reaching for a cig-arette.

"The Savage Land?" Storm said. "That is the only place on Earth that still retains its primeval wildlife. But this does not resemble any part of the Savage Land I remember. And I have explored much of it recently." Gambit recalled that Storm had led a team of X-Men— including the Beast, but not including Remy—to the Sav-age Land only weeks earlier to face the threat of Sauron.

"Maybe we jus' in Jurassic Park instead," muttered Gambit, striking a match. He blew it out, then rubbed the burnt head between his fingers and slipped it into his pocket. There was something about this primeval beauty that discouraged littering.

"Wherever we are," the Beast said thoughtfully, "we'd better stick together until we see what other kinds of wildlife this place can field. If you take to the air, Storm, you're likely to become lunch."

"Or reveal our location to our enemies, if enemies we have here," the mutant elemental agreed. "And we can-not be certain that we do not. Very well, Beast. Lead on, and I shall follow."

Even if she had been willing to risk flying, Storm could not have carried the other two with her; one, but not both. Like it or not, the party was restricted to the pace of its slowest member.

Gambit trudged along between the Beast and Storm, trying to keep his mind blank. It could almost have been a picnic outing from happier times, save for the urgency of their task. At the other end of this road lay Kang's Time Platform and another fight for the X-Men. And this time they were fighting for reality itself.

The danger was almost too big for Gambit to believe in. He'd faced Ragnarok before, gone toe-to-toe with the Four Horsemen of the Apocalypse, but this time he wasn't being offered a ringside seat at the end of the world, or even the end of the universe. This time the X-Men and Spider-Man were playing for all the marbles: everything there was, everything that could conceivably be, faced destruction at the hands of a madman.

It wasn't fair, but Gambit was used to life not being fair. What it really didn't seem was *reasonable* that one man could cause this much trouble.

For a moment, like a tongue probing a bad tooth, his mind flicked back to that moment on the battlements of Notre Dame when Sabretooth had let go of the rope, and Genevieve had fallen to her death on the pavement below. He remembered the shock and disbelief he'd felt— and the guilt, because he'd only played at love with her.

Gambit would gladly kill Sabretooth for what he'd done that day, but he couldn't believe that killing Victor Creed would bring Genevieve back.

But what if he did believe it?

Don't go there, LeBeau. You won't like it, Gambit told himself bleakly.

But what if he did?

It was a fascinating field trip, but Dr. Henry P. McCoy kept yanking his mind away from the taxonomy of flora and fauna and back to the unwinking blue light on the

Tempometric Meter in his hand. At least that was just as it was supposed to be. The indicator would lead them to the Time Platform, which held—if a whole range of possibilities and fervent wishes came true—the only possible way left for them to beat Kang: by forcing him to fight them on his home ground, in realtime.

Wherever—whenever—that was.

It was an awful lot of hopes to be resting on the shoulders of a dozen X-Men and one drafted wall-crawler scattered across four timelines and most of a millennium.

Not that I'm nervous or anything, Hank reminded himself. He'd been in on the countdown to the end of the universe more than once in his time; played billiards with the Cosmic Cube, seen living gods debate the wisdom of unmaking their creation. Worse, he'd seen people who took on the mantle of gods toy with that power.

Just like now.

When you came right down to it, it didn't matter how many galaxies Kang had conquered. He was no god. Some perverse accident had given him godlike power, which he wielded in an entirely human manner.

So much the worse for humanity.

After a brisk hour's walk, the forest began to thin, the great trees growing scarcer, actual grasses replacing the thick fertile detritus of the forest floor. They could actually see a horizon now.

"Ocean," Gambit said, sniffing experimentally. He frowned; the scent wasn't quite right. The water was more brackish than salty.

A few moments later they reached the water. The far shore, if any, was hidden in mist, but about a mile out Gambit could see the looming bulk of an island, a darker gray-green smudge against the mist.

And was it his imagination, or did he see a glint of metal within that verdant overgrowth?

"Behold our destination, somewhere within the next three kilometers due west," the Beast said. "Though one must admit, that island does look like the place." He shielded his brow with one massive blue-furred hand, squinting toward the island.

"An' Gambit wit'out his boat. Gonna be a long swim, I t'ink, me," Remy said, lighting another cigarette.

"Storm?" the Beast said.

The wind-rider looked up at the sky. It seemed empty enough. "I can ferry you each over one at a time, but I'd rather scout ahead on my own first. I'll be back shortly."

She lofted gracefully into the air. Remy watched her out of sight.

"I got de bad feelin' about dis, *Bête*. How come dere's nobody tryin' to kill us, hahn?"

"This's got to be another false trail in a long history of false trails," the aircar's driver complained.

He was tall and slender, his Eurasian features sculpted into the classical beauty that belonged only to the rich or the privileged these days. And in his time, Henri Huang had been both: the golden child of a corporation in a world where only corporations had power. He still dressed as if he were one of the privileged, in a bright red, gold, and indigo bodysuit. But he'd left that life behind . . . for a dream.

Only the triangular flash on his left shoulder indicated that Henri Huang might not be working for himself these days. But he'd gladly left the Alchemax Corporation lifestyle behind long ago. When it came to authority, Henri Huang had always had a . . . mean streak.

"Cheer up," his companion said. "It's probably a trap." Timothy Michael Fitzgerald—sometimes known as Skullfire—grinned, his white teeth flashing against a mask of dead-white syntheflesh. He had the fresh pretty-boy handsomeness of a James Dean loner, and was dressed ominously in black leather; heavy gold bracelets ringed each wrist like fetters . . . or battery packs.

"I still say it's some kind of red herring. Sure, the Savage Land is filled with exploitable resources. Sure, the corporations are bulldozing the clans into submission and ignoring every treaty ever signed. But why would Doom pick *now* to go after them?" Meanstreak asked again.

"Why not now? No time like the present, as the man says," Skullfire answered amiably.

"Oh, will you two boys cut it out?" the aircar's third occupant demanded. "Once Halo City intercepted the squeal between Doom and his flunkies, the X-Men couldn't afford to ignore it. If Doom gets it together for another grab at power, there isn't going to be *anything* left."

Her skin was the impossible white of paint—or milk, if any of them had ever seen milk that didn't glow in the dark. She was six feet tall, and hair as white as her skin stood up above her skull like an egret's crest before cascading down her back. Her eyes were glowing red slits, and her mouth was a glittering red-painted wound. Her only name was La Lunatica—the Madwoman—and she had once served the soul cancer known as the Theatre of Pain.

Before Timothy Fitzgerald. Before Doom's brief Presidency. Before so many things.

"You know, Lunatica, for a wannabe you talk almost like a real X-Man," Meanstreak drawled mockingly.

"Hey!" Timothy Fitzgerald moved to defend his lady.

"Thanks, lover," Luna said to him, "but I can take care of myself. You know, *Henri*, you've got no room to talk. You want to talk X-Men? Your idea of supporting the X-Men is to run off with an old school chum to take down Las Vegas while Xian—the X-Men's *former* leader—reverts to his days as a biker boy. I'd say I've done as much for the X-Men as you have, Meanstreak— and if I were you, speedy, I'd be nicer to a woman who can mess with your head the way Luna can,'' she purred.

La Lunatica was a psychic succubus who fed on the pain of her victims. She put the palm of her hand against the side of Meanstreak's neck. Meanstreak jerked away in revulsion, and his accelerated reflexes caused the aircar to sideslip dangerously.

''Watch it!'' Skullfire grabbed the steering yoke and tried to drag the aircar back on course, but only succeeded in making it sideslip it further. Meanstreak slapped his teammate's hands away and retook control, and a few moments later the aircar was again on course.

For a moment.

There was a *thump*, and the entire vehicle wobbled as its A-grav tried to compensate for the addition of a sudden weight to the back end.

''What are you people *doing*?'' Bloodhawk demanded. ''When I agreed to leave the high desert and join you in a return to the Savage Land to forestall Doom's grab for power, I thought that you at least took his threat seriously.''

Bloodhawk glared at them all impartially, and La Lunatica snickered.

The winged X-Man was a metamorph, and though he could change his form to pass for human, he much preferred his present winged shape. His armored skin was the deep vermilion of the rock of his desert home, and enormous veined wings combined with lateral airfoils to give him the power of unaided flight. Now he clung to the aircar's back deck with taloned hands and feet and glared at the other three X-Men as crossly as his avian namesake.

''We do,'' Timothy and Meanstreak both said, looking at each other.

"We do," Timothy repeated. "Uh—"

"The aircar's sinking," Meanstreak said under his breath. "Get out and walk, would you, Hawk?" he said aloud. "We're lucky this buggy I borrowed from McAllister will carry us, let alone you."

La Lunatica just smirked.

"Look!" Timothy cried, pointing out over the aircar's windscreen. "People!"

"Must be Doom's flunkies," Meanstreak said.

"You think everything has to be Doom's flunkies?" Skullfire demanded.

"You think everyone isn't?" Meanstreak shot back. "Especially *here*?"

"One of them is taking to the air," Bloodhawk announced. "I shall give chase." The aircar lurched as the mutant metamorph took to the sky once more.

"I wish Shakti was here," Timothy said. "Cerebra could tell us whether these were mutants or not."

La Lunatica peered through the windscreen. "One of them's glowing and the other's covered in blue fur. They're mutants. Doom's henchmen get kinkier every day."

"You should talk," Meanstreak muttered. La Lunatica ignored him.

"So let's waste 'em," Skullfire said cheerfully. A faint emerald nimbus was collecting around his fists; he'd been sure to suck up a full charge from the Halo City generators before they'd left, and he was itching to expend it on someone.

"No, Tim—wait," Meanstreak said, sounding uncharacteristically hesitant. "These mutants—look at the closeup in the view-scanner. Aren't they the Beast, Storm, and Gambit from the old twentieth-century X-Men?"

There was a frozen moment of hope mixed with fear. The conflicting emotions played across Timothy's face as the X-Men's newest leader leaned forward to stare at the images captured in the scope. Ever since Xian had brought them together, all of the newest generation of heroes to bear the proud name X-Men had hoped for and dreaded the day they might meet some of their mutant predecessors. They'd come close on a number of occasions, but . . .

"You flatscan," Timothy said with mingled anger and relief. "Those aren't the X-Men—the Beast had a tail and only three fingers on each hand and used to teleport—Gambit was taller than that and wore a visor over half his face—and Storm had a mohawk. Everyone knows that. . . ."

"You're right," Meanstreak said with relief. "They're just hired muscle."

"So what are we waiting for?" La Lunatica demanded enthusiastically. "Let's smoke 'em!"

"*Hélas, Bête!*" Gambit shouted. "We got company!"

There was a moment, perhaps, when things did not have to end in fighting. The flying car spiralled gracefully to the ground; small and silvery and elegant, closer to one of the cigarette boats that used to ply fast times and contraband out of Miami than to some grim and over-engineered example of future technology.

Gambit knew he ought to be impressed. When was the last time a poor Acadian lad—even one who was a member of the Big Easy's notorious Thieves Guild—had seen the future, right here and close enough to touch?

But he didn't like the looks of the three climbing out of it, and the red-winged nightmare was flying in the direction Storm had taken. Toward the island.

Keep your mind on your own problems, LeBeau.

He narrowed his attention to the car's occupants. Two men and a woman. The woman was the tallest, and her dead-white skin sweated like snow in the tropical heat of the jungle. Her eyes glittered with red fire and her mouth—the red of a wounded tropic flower—bore a crazy smile Gambit could see in the mirror any day of the week. Reckless.

Her companions were much less interesting; a preppie spear-carrier in red, blue and gold and a young frightener in black leather with a white-painted face. The frightener glowed faintly, like a fluorescent toy left out in the sun, but whatever power he had, Gambit was sure he could match it. And he was better looking, besides.

"*Chère*, call off your bad dogs, an' we talk," he called toward the woman. "Nobody wants trouble, no."

"Then why's your buddy in the fur coat playing least-in-sight?" the boy on her left with the white-painted face said.

Gambit could have prepared a number of good explanations—including the truth, which was that McCoy had just happened to be under cover when the aircar landed and had stayed where he was to avoid frightening the newcomers with his exotic appearance—but the leather-boy was pointing at Gambit with both fists clenched now, and Gambit felt that it was mainly a good time to be getting out of the way.

The glow got brighter, and in its sun-bright blaze the boy's body became transparent, until all that could be seen was the negative image of his form, black against intolerable brightness.

The shot blazed past Gambit's head and struck the trees only a few feet from where Hank McCoy had been stand-ing—purely an accident, as the young hothead had been aiming at Gambit and hadn't bothered to see what else was in his fire line—and the Beast, too, bounded out of the way. Gambit wasn't in any danger—their opponent's reflexes were too slow for that—but the Beast, too, had seen the red-winged flyer light out after Storm. Behind him a stand of trees exploded into toothpicks with the force of the blast; something electrical in nature, McCoy was sure.

Something, also, meant to kill—which automatically seated their potential playfellows on the "villain" side of the arena. McCoy scrabbled up the nearest tree.

"Oh, shock. Where is he?" Skullfire looked around for the man he'd just blasted. "I didn't disintegrate him, did I?"

Behind him the forest smoked with the aftereffect of the blast, and Skullfire realized that he was a long way from someplace he could pick up his next charge.

"Great going, Skullfire," Meanstreak muttered. "You didn't even leave something to ID." Skullfire turned on his teammate, a blistering reply rising to his lips, but Meanstreak ignored him.

"Where's the other one—the furry one?" Luna asked.

The other one, Hank McCoy thought to himself, *is right—*

"Here!" the Beast shouted, springing from his treetop cover in an enormous bound. They had to wrap up these homicidal maniacs—probably more of Kang's hired help, they'd arrived too quickly to be anything else—fast and sweet in order to be there if Storm needed assistance.

He aimed to land on the one in the bright uniform, but fast as he was, his target wasn't there when he arrived.

"Miss me, monster?" his foe said. He was a blur in the air as he moved, stopping only to hurl a taunt at the Beast. "Don't worry—Meanstreak is right here to turn out your lights." Then he moved into hyper-acceleration again.

And tripped.

Having fought the mutant known as Quicksilver in a number of battles over the years, perhaps the Beast had an unfair advantage. While there was no way he could beat the super-speedster's reflexes, he knew that Mean-streak's attack could be only as good as his footing. Swooping up one of the branches festooned about, all the Beast had to do was sweep it around himself until Mean-streak tripped.

But he had no time to follow up his advantage. Suddenly there was a weight on his back and a cat-squalling voice in his ear:

"I don't like Meanstreak—but if you mess with him, you mess with La Lunatica!" the woman snarled.

"Don't do me any favors, Luna," Meanstreak snapped.

No one who'd spent ten years with the Theatre of Pain could by any stretch of the imagination be a sissy, and La Lunatica had gone toe-to-toe with some of the best muscle the World of Tomorrow could offer. But strong as she was, the blue-furred monstrosity's form was stronger. He reached back, and Luna felt the crushing power of a hand bigger than her head laid against the nape of her neck.

She dug into the fur with her nails, preparing to use her powers to turn this guy's brain inside out. She was looking forward to the rush she'd get from turning his id into scrambled eggs—that was what most of these sanctimonious crèche-raised X-babies couldn't understand. Your power was there to be used—and if using it made you a predator, so be it. That was all there was room for in this world: predator and prey.

And pain.

Luna struck with all her power, deep for the heart of his pain.

And nothing happened.

The Beast felt a warning tingle over the psychic shields that Professor Xavier had painstakingly implanted in each of his X-Men's minds many years ago. So in addition to being a formidable physical threat, the albino woman was some sort of psionic.

The fact that he was safe this time didn't mean she couldn't get to him, though. It simply meant that her first try wouldn't work.

It would probably be better all around if there weren't a second attempt.

"Luna!" someone shouted.

In the instant that it took the woman to realize that her best shot simply wasn't going to work, the Beast grabbed La Lunatica by the scruff of the neck and pulled. She went flying, tufts of blue fur between her fingers.

That hurt, the Beast thought. But there wasn't time to dwell on it. Meanstreak was back on his feet.

"Heads up, *cher*," Gambit advised genially. His eyes were twin red glows, and a cigarette dangled negligently from the corner of his mouth. His bo stick was a blur of motion in his hands, its ends glowing with infused kinetic potential.

Skullfire whirled toward him, a faint green glow manifesting around his gloves. But Gambit was betting— from instinct as much as from watching him hold back and leave the Beast to Meanstreak and the crazy lady— that the boy's first shot had left him precious little in the way of reserves.

It was time for Gambit to earn his keep.

And besides, he had a plan.

"Surrender now and we won't have to hurt you much," Skullfire said with a snarl. "I'll even keep my girlfriend away from you if you're real good."

The tone was half bluster. Gambit barely listened.

"An' deprive such a lovely lady of de chance to meet Remy LeBeau? *Vachon*, I t'ink you are trying to insult me."

''We do our best,'' Skullfire said, grabbing for the stick.

Gambit, ever helpful, let him have it.

Mistake.

It looked like Thor had been listening to his prayers, Skullfire told himself happily. When this LeBeau person's hands had started to glow, he'd banked on there being some kind of ambient energy there he could use.

Because wherever there was energy, Skullfire could siphon it.

The bo stick hit hard, but he almost didn't care. Energy came roaring into his body—power that LeBeau had just conjured out of the air as if he were a magician doing card tricks. Skullfire took it, sucked it down like Coca-Cola, and lashed out with it.

And missed again.

Gambit couldn't figure out why all his instincts were telling him these kids were amateurs fresh out of the box when at the same time they seemed to be as lethal a collection of powerhouses as the X-Men had ever tangled with. It was something about the way they moved—as if they'd never had to go up against anything other than third-raters.

Maybe there weren't any super-villains anymore?

It was a pity, Gambit thought, that there wouldn't be time to ask them.

The moment Skullfire had grabbed his bo stick Gambit had abandoned it, springing backward in a flip that let him bound forward again an instant later, feetfirst. The blow connected solidly but didn't put Skullfire down— he was glowing bright again with the energy he'd stolen from Gambit, and for a fleeting moment Gambit wished Bishop were here. Someone with the ability to absorb any form of energy should have a field day with a walking battery.

Skullfire came up swinging with those lethally glowing fists. Gambit cut the ground out from beneath his feet with a charged card, regaining his stick in the process. Skullfire's energy-siphoning power and his own kinetic powers were too evenly matched; almost like mirror images of each other. If Gambit were to win, he would have to move the fight to a different venue.

But Gambit had spent too much time thinking about tactics, and while he had, Skullfire abandoned mutant pyrotechnics for good old-fashioned streetfighting. His punch took Gambit neatly along the side of his jaw and dimmed his lights.

The island was in sight below her, its greenery offering a taunting illusion of sanctuary, but Ororo already knew that she wasn't alone in the air. Behind her, a great winged creature soared between her and the sun, his powerful webbed wings savagely slicing the air.

With a flick of her fingers, Storm generated a headwind to slow him and made a quick low sweep across the surface of the island. In this sylvan Eden, any sign of technology would probably be a sign of what they were seeking.

There!

She spread her arms and floated to earth. The hot white sun of the future burned down on alien metal violet as a bruise. Storm approached it cautiously, wary of traps.

The Time Platform towered before her, canted over to one side. Cautiously, Storm ran her fingers over the side, then lofted herself aboard. Here was the cradle where the Time Arrow had been set. The cradle was empty now, but otherwise, the machine appeared to be intact. Did that mean that Henry would be able to operate it—and use it to track Kang the Conqueror to his lair?

And if he couldn't—if he failed—if all of them failed—would there be time enough to know that they'd failed? Or would there just be darkness forever, with no one to see or to care?

This world was only one might-be future, and it and scores of others like it were balanced in the trembling grasp of a madman. It was up to the X-Men to save it—to save them all—if they could.

Storm shuddered, wishing she weren't possessed of such a vivid imagination. She, Remy, and Henry were all on edge—far more so than the mission gave them cause for. All of them were visualizing the specter of total annihilation, and none of them liked it much.

In the sky above her, a shadow passed between Storm and the sun. Her mysterious assailant. He would be here in moments. She must lead him far from the Time Platform, lest he destroy it.

But as Storm prepared to launch herself into the air once more, there was a sudden roiling in the earth that knocked her from the top of the Time Platform to land sprawling in the grass.

Earthquake. Storm's more-than-human senses could detect a natural change in the weather hours coming before it happened, just as she could now feel the coiling of gravimetric and tectonic energies beneath her body. As she staggered to her feet, the ground rocked again.

Whether it had been unbalanced by the forces released when the Time Arrow had been fired, or whether this quake was merely a part of nature, which destroyed in order to create, these tremors were only the outriders of a temblor of such severity that it might well destroy the island—and would certainly smash the Time Platform beyond all hope of Hank McCoy's reconstruction.

The earth shuddered again, mildly, like the quiver that passes through the fur of a sleeping cat. Storm cast one more agonized glance toward the Time Platform before summoning the winds that would bear her aloft to defend it.

There was so little time left.

CHAPTER SEVEN

MAINLINE +2, THE YEAR 3000

In the Power Core of a deep space station, an army of slugs rippled toward Bishop like a living carpet through the heat shimmer of hell's own oven. Behind them, the corroded remains of Kang's Time Platform melted slowly into radioactive metallic sludge. There was nothing here left to salvage. Their mission had failed.

If Bishop were a praying man, he'd be praying now. He needed to get back to the others and tell them it was time to go.

Assuming, of course, that either of them was still alive.

There was no reason now for Bishop to hold back. The slugs were destroying the station faster than anything he carried could. He was safe so long as he didn't score a direct hit off the Power Core's ravaged shields.

He tossed the Tempometric Meter into the midst of the writhing bodies and reached for his weapons.

They were the best of their kind, from the shop of an armorer who was both long dead and not yet born. The tiny missiles they fired gave up their energy in a neutron pulse that, so Bishop was told, could knock a hole through a '57 Chevy lengthwise. Bishop had only recently learned what a '57 Chevy was, but he had always known the lethal firepower he carried.

He unleashed it now.

The muzzle flash from the paired hand cannon was like a string of pearls. The booming report echoed off the walls, blending into itself as his shell/missiles found their targets. Their ultrasonic keening sent burning lances stabbing through his head, but Bishop didn't let up. He backed out of the Power Core as he fired. Mounds of slugs disintegrated in fountains of acid, and Bishop ducked to avoid the lethal spray.

He'd bought himself a few minutes—at least the time to reload.

He turned to run.

Ahead of him, the corridor was filled with slugs.

Wolverine had been hit harder—after all, he'd taken on the Hulk for fun once or twice upon a time—and he was back in the fight even as he rebounded from the wall. He faced the three intruders from the docking spaceship. They'd fired on the X-Men without warning, and that meant that they were fair game.

"Let's see how well you bleed, chubbo," Wolverine growled at the big man who put him up against the wall. He flourished his claws threateningly.

"We already know how well you can cut, Wolverine—why don't you take on somebody who can fight back?" the blacksuit with the power blasts called from behind the human tank.

"Over here!" Iceman shouted.

I just hope this is going to work, Iceman thought. Bishop had said that the power core for the station was probably sheathed by housekeeping and operations modules, and people needed water to stay alive. Even if the housekeeping systems were sucking all the water out of the air that they could, it had to be going somewhere, and that meant there had to be water somewhere behind these bulkheads.

That, or slugs.

Wolverine lunged in Iceman's direction as though he were going to run, taking his cue. Big Ugly swatted the feral X-Man out of the air like a volleyball, but Blacksuit had already fired another of those black-light power-blasts. Unimpeded, it sheared through the wall behind Iceman.

Steam and water—blessed moisture—vented around him. Now he knew how cacti felt when it was time for a drink.

"Par-*ty*!" Iceman bellowed, and hammered Blacksuit with toaster-sized chunks of ice for all he was worth.

Unlike his companions, Bishop was a warrior first and a mutant second. It took him a split instant to switch from guns to the redirected blasts of kinetic energy that were his birthright. The corridor's bulkheads bowed outward with the force of his initial blast, and the wall of slugs confronting Bishop simply . . . vanished.

Bishop was a professional. He didn't stop to congratulate himself on his success before moving to claim the territory he'd just taken. Seconds mattered now—he had to reach Iceman and Wolverine, and the three of them had to trigger their Temporal Recall Devices to get them out of here before this place became a temporary star. With every step Bishop took away from the Power Core, the temperature dropped. He ran through the corridor, his boots slipping in the acid mire of pureed slug. The air was thick with the ultrasonic trill of their communication, so intense that even Bishop could hear it. He'd gained a temporary lead, nothing more.

He sighed with relief when he reached the cross corridor unscathed. The cross-corridor seemed almost cold to him now, though he remembered it as being hot when he'd first come through it. Another few yards, and he'd have reached the edge of their main territory.

The slug dropped from above just as he reached the first ladder. It caught Bishop across the shoulders, burning a thin line of agony along the back of his neck. Its tri-flanged beak snapped terrifyingly near his face as it twisted around.

With a roar of disgust he flung it off, but the acid had scored bright welts everywhere it had touched his exposed skin. He felt chilled, light-headed.

And where there was one slug, there were more.

• • •

"Take that, you ambulatory ice-mine!" Nikki shouted shrilly. She had this guy's number now. He didn't like the heat, and she was just the hot ticket to make him cash in his chips. Using the abilities genegineered into her Mercurian cells, she raised the temperature around him, melting his ice bolts before they even reached her.

Yondu had joined them by now, and one of the Centauran warrior-priest's whistle-controlled arrows had buried itself in her icy sparring partner's chest. He staggered at the blow, but oddly no blood erupted. *Is this guy made of ice?* Nikki wondered.

Normally both Guardians would have stopped and offered their foes another chance to surrender, but not after the atrocities they'd seen. There would be no quarter given.

There was only one thing on Wolverine's mind at the moment, and that was finding some way to get his claws through the hides of his two opponents. He'd stood toe-to-toe with the one they called Charlie and had put him down a couple of times, but his best efforts had been unable to pierce either Charlie's skin or whatever kind of battlesuit the man in black was wearing, and after the first exchange of blows, Blacksuit had hung back and kept on pounding Wolverine with some kind of blacklight blasts.

The blasts didn't hurt. But each time they hit him, it was as if reality blipped *out* for a moment, and each time it came back Wolverine was just a little bit slower. He'd started using the big bruiser as a shield against the blasts, but it was only a matter of time before Charlie and Blacksuit figured things out and found another way to put him down.

On the other hand, maybe he could put Charlie down first. While Wolverine hadn't been able to pierce the skin of the big palooka yet (which made him a sparring partner worthy of respect), the big lug's vest and shirt were already in tattered rags and there were several long slices through his trousers. It was only, Wolverine felt, a matter of time before he got through. He backhanded the man in front of him with his claws at full extension.

Charlie the Two-Ton fell to his knees, but it had been a set-up. Wolverine locked gazes with the man in the black suit over the bruiser's head, and then a fountain of black light hammered him in the chest like a shell from the biggest gun in the universe.

The corridor was one Bishop didn't remember having seen before, and for a paralyzing moment he thought he was lost. He was no longer following the Tempometric Meter's beacon though the magic labyrinth to Kang's Time Platform, and without its electronic thread to follow, he realized, he might neither be able to find his comrades nor avoid the swarming slugs that followed him with the slow implacability of rabid molasses.

But when he stopped to gain his bearings, Bishop realized that there was a beacon for him to follow. In the distance, the sounds of battle were faint but clear, like the sound of a foghorn on misty nights. It was a good sound. It told him that his comrades were still alive, and it was something that he could home in on.

But the slugs were hard on Bishop's heels now, as if they'd finally become aware of intruders in their midst. His mutant resources were depleted, and his ammo was running low as well.

All the ice in the world wasn't going to help him against Lady Bic, the blue guy with the arrow wasn't Mrs. Drake's little boy's idea of a fun sparring partner, and Wolverine was down. That worried Iceman—about half as much as the fact that if Wolverine was just stunned, he'd probably come up slashing without any thought of appropriate force. And if he wasn't . . . while the Canadian mutant was notoriously hard to kill, there was a first time for everything.

The cut wasn't too deep, really; just a scratch. Still, he had to stay iced up. Once he reverted to his flesh-and-blood form, that piercing could translate into a nasty wound.

"You guys gotta listen," Iceman said desperately to his attackers. In another moment it looked like he was going to join Wolverine on the floor, and if they took his recall device away from him he'd be marooned in the third millennium for about as long as it would take for Kang to turn off the lights in every universe there was.

"Not to you, master of evil," the blue guy with the red fin on his head said. He sounded like he meant it too.

"Aw, geez, where do you guys get this stuff? Does somebody write it for you?" Iceman snapped. "Like talking's going to kill you?" *If I could only take a breather, just a minute. That's all. . . .*

But the two of them were moving in on him, and he had to do something. Iceman shot an ice pylon toward the guy in the black suit and was rewarded with a solid contact that sent the blacksuit sprawling. The effort left him dizzy and, unfortunately, it also got him the big guy's attention. The Hulk clone ripped Iceman's ice caber loose from the bulkhead and swung it at Iceman's head.

A bolt from nowhere shattered it into a thousand spinning ice cubes.

Bishop was back, and he didn't look happy.

"I suggest that we unite against a common enemy," Xavier's Security Enforcer shouted.

Disregarding his antagonists, Iceman took a quick look around.

Bishop had stopped a few yards down the corridor, his reluctance to come any closer easily explained. All around the combatants—oozing slowly from impossibly small openings in the bulkheads and vents—dozens— hundreds—of slugs slithered toward them.

"Harkov's bones—vacuum worms!" Blacksuit shouted.

"Logan—get up," Iceman said urgently to Wolverine, not quite daring to touch him.

Slowly Wolverine pulled himself to his feet. "I ain't— been hit—that hard—in a while," he said, pulling off the remains of his black-and-yellow mask. The cover of his TDR fell off as he stood, exposing the little red button that said RECALL and making him look a little like a kill- crazed doorbell.

I must be worse off than I thought, Iceman said to himself, listening to his own giddy thoughts.

Seeing that Wolverine had stood, Iceman looked around, then fixed his eyes on Bishop. The burly black mutant looked more battered than he had the last time Iceman had seen him, his dark skin sweaty and creased with burns. The big man looked battered, pushed past his limits.

In short, in Iceman's oh-so-humble opinion, Bishop didn't look like a happy camper.

"And?" he prompted.

"The Time Platform's been destroyed and the slugs are about to eat through the containment wall of the Power Core," Bishop said.

"Guardians, I think we've been set up," Blacksuit said. His companions—Blueskin, the Tank, and Lady Bic (Iceman knew that they had real names, but he didn't know what they were)—looked toward him, their ex- pressions fading from rage to puzzlement.

"Set up?" the Lady Bic said. "But, Vance, the trans- mission—"

"There isn't time to discuss it here, if what Bishop

says is true. We have to get back to *Icarus* and consider the rest of this later,'' Blacksuit said.

Iceman reached out and grabbed Lady Bic's wrist. "Where's your ride?" the young X-Man demanded.

"Vance!" the flame-topped hellcat said.

"Come on—you three too," Vance said. "I don't know how you got here, but I won't leave anyone to die by vacuum worms." He held out his hand.

Vacuum worms? What kind of name is that? Iceman wondered as he took the proffered hand.

Funny, Wolverine reflected, *how a bunch of guys can be whaling on you one minute and the next be ready to buddy up*. It was a phenomenon he'd encountered time and again in his long career, and he'd never completely understood it. Sure, loyalties changed and a lot of brawls were nothing personal.

But if you finished things right the first time, you never had to worry about when your new buddies were going to turn on you again. He looked at the rest of his team. Drake was stumbling and Bishop was burnt. Even assuming one of the other teams had struck paydirt, they were in rotten shape to take on a megalomaniac time traveller with an overdeveloped sense of gamesmanship.

"Time to go," Wolverine said.

And stopped, looking at the four Guardians. They were grouping together and retreating slowly in the only slug-free direction left. They had a space ship here, Wolverine remembered. He'd seen it dock. He wondered if they could still reach it, or if the slugs had cut them off from their only line of retreat.

"Where's your ship? We'll get you there," Wolverine said.

I just hope this isn't one o' my worse ideas.

• • • •

Cherryh was dying—it didn't take someone familiar with the thirty-first century to see that. The decay had been increasing exponentially since the X-Men had arrived. Now the vacuum-worms' work could be seen in the way the glassteel sheets of the bulkhead bowed inward, gaping to reveal the structural framing beneath.

The lethal space parasites known as vacuum worms drifted through space until they reached a radiation source—a ship or a space station—sliding inside hull and plating to eat what metals they could find, and spawning in the hard radiation of the power core. Vance Astro realized that the whole thing had to be a setup when he saw the size of the worms. In order to have reached this size, *Cherryh* must have become infested months ago.

There was no shortage of water in the air now. The air-purifying plant, running at overload for the last several weeks, had finally shut down, and with the steadily rising temperature baking the moisture from the bodies of fallen slugs, the air through which they moved had become a dank swamplike miasma. The frigid zone surrounding Iceman's ice-sheathed body caused the air to condense on surfaces and fall like rain, until it seemed as if *Cherryh* wept for what it had become.

Together the seven adventurers represented a concentration of power this galaxy had not seen since the final climactic battles of the War of the Worlds centuries before.

Vance Astro, with the mutant fire of Simon Williams's blood coursing through his thousand-year-old veins. Charlie-27, possessed of the sheer brawn of a Jovian militiaman. The raw savagery of Wolverine. Bishop's unyielding will. The mystic force of the Centauran priest-warrior called Yondu. And the fire and ice of mutant and Mercurian.

It was very nearly not enough.

Their retreat toward the *Icarus* had been a series of

skirmishes with an enemy of infinite numbers. No matter how many they killed—with ice or plasma or the power from Within Yet Beyond—there were always more. Never a definitive battle; the seven adventurers fought only to clear their line of retreat toward the docks, turning and running as soon as the enemy paused in its merciless, inexorable assault.

"These things are like cockroaches!" Iceman exclaimed indignantly, blasting another several slugs with a lance that was mostly pure cold. Ice crystals shimmered in the frigid path he made, melting quickly in the rising temperature and turning into droplets of water. The slugs blackened and died. If you could bring enough to bear on them, they went down easily—his ice-blasts, Vance Astro's weird black blasts, even Nikki's flames—all brought the slugs down easily.

But no matter how many slugs the seven of them killed, there were always more. Bishop was out of ammo, and Nikki and Astro were tiring—and all the rest of the refugees had to close with a bad guy to do any good.

And closing with these slugs could be fatal. The big bruiser—Charlie-27, the others called him—was covered with oozing red welts from near misses by the implacable acid-blooded slugs, and Wolverine, even with his enhanced ability to heal, didn't look much better. He'd been broiled by Electro not three hours before, and healing took energy too.

Thinking about healing reminded Iceman that he, too, was hurt. It hurt like a fiery bruise, but he'd fought with worse. However, it was distracting and exhausting, leeching his resources and reminding him that he had no way of knowing when rest was coming in this battle where enemies and venues changed while the threat just kept getting worse.

The hell of it was, he, Bishop, and Wolverine could

be out of this mess with the push of a button. Miracu-
lously, all three of their TDRs had survived more-or-less
intact. Wolverine's was battered, but even if it didn't
work, the field his and Bishop's generated would carry
their teammate along. They could be home in the twin-
kling of an eye.

But these Guardians couldn't. Without their ship they
were stuck here on the station. They'd been suckered into
this mess through a false distress call, presumably sent
by Kang, and that meant that the X-Men owed it to them
to get them out of it.

If they could manage it before they met more slugs
than they could scare. Or before the station blew.

*But we can, right? Because we're the good guys, and
the good guys always win, right?*

Right?

"Aargh!" Charlie-27 let out a bellow of pure frustration
as the decking gave way beneath his feet. Sweat beaded
on his forehead as he felt the plating sag further. The
acid-burns on his arms and chest throbbed like the lashes
of a slave master's whip—acid that could eat through
glassteel decking had not been slowed at all by Jovian
hide.

"Chunkie!" Nikki cried. She started toward him but
Vance grabbed for her and held her back. This whole
section of flooring was rotten. That was why Charlie had
brought up the rear; he was the heaviest. But any of them
might have been the one to fall.

Everyone froze where they stood, spread out in a ragged column almost ten meters long.

"Go on," the Jovian militiaman said, making the soldier's decision. "Leave me. I'll catch up to you when I
can."

He saw Vance hesitate. "Nikki, go on and tell Marty
to get *Icarus* ready for a quick flit," Astro said to her.

Charlie could see his best girl's eyes flash from here; this wasn't an order Nikki wanted to follow.

"I don't mean to hurry you or anything," the one called Bishop said irritatedly.

"No," Wolverine said. "We don't leave our own behind. Not for things like that."

"Wait," Iceman said. "I've got an idea. Get going, you guys. I think I can work something out."

"No!" Nikki said, advancing on Iceman furiously. The step she took made the floor beneath her wobble like a sheet of thin tin.

"Look," Iceman snapped, rounding on her. "If I can reinforce the floor enough—starting with the part that's still good—he can *climb* out—but ice is about the heaviest thing there is. The whole floor might collapse instead."

"If you kill him, you frostbitten—" Nikki began furiously.

"Good," Vance Astro said, cutting across her diatribe. "Do it, Iceman. We'll pull back and wait for you."

"If we can," Bishop said, looking across the imprisoned Guardian to the corridor behind. The slugs could be anywhere, and they knew for sure they were following them.

"Yeah, well, if you guys would give me some elbow room, we could see if this works," Iceman said.

Despite his flashy presentation and rapid-fire wiseass patter, Iceman wasn't really comfortable with being the one that everything depended on. In a team fight, who knew who did what, so long as the good guys won? But if this didn't work, everybody would know that *he* was the one who hadn't been good enough. Guys like Wolverine and Bishop never worried about things like that, but *he* did.

And despite the impression he'd tried to give the others, this was going to be a delicate operation. He didn't know how much of the floor was rotten, and how far he'd have to extend the ice. It would have to be a slab more than eighteen inches thick to hold Charlie's weight, and in itself would weigh a great deal.

No point in thinking about it. He began to pull water from the air.

White frost lace skated away from Iceman's feet, racing through the moisture that had condensed on the slightly colder bulkheads and portholes, until the entire section of corridor where he and Charlie-27 stood was filled with fog and frost crystals. Lace on silver, lace on the black of the hull ports, a faerie frost that dropped the temperature in that section of hull a hundred degrees in seconds.

And then Iceman began to build. Frost thickened, and then its own weight turned it to ice. Thicker . . . thicker . . .

The floor began to creak and buckle. Quickly Iceman braced it with ice pylons, until the slab of ice hung from the ceiling and not the floor, its weight supported by a structure of crossing ice girders.

But no matter how strong the structure Iceman crafted, the tropical environment inside the station made his work begin to melt almost the moment it was formed.

"Come on!" Iceman said, holding out his hand to Charlie. Even as he spoke, he was increasing the size of the ice slab, extending it in every direction he could so that no square foot of the station would have to take the enormous load alone.

Slowly, painfully, the big bruiser scrabbled out of the hole. The ice beneath his hands crazed and misted with a thousand fracture points from the stresses he placed on it, and all that Iceman could do to help him was make the sheet of ice thicker, longer, make it advance with the inevitability of a glacier through all the twisting maze of the station. With all his might, he concentrated on *cold*;

snowfields and blizzards and the stark unforgiving absolute zero of deep space.

"There," Iceman said with relief when Charlie-27 finally pulled free.

It should have been a moment for celebration, but there was no time. Charlie-27 pushed past him, heading for the docking cradles. Iceman followed, and without his attention the ice behind him began to rot and sag.

Never any time.

A hundred yards away, around the curve of the station, the others waited. The air was still now, rapidly losing its oxygen as the CO_2 in the atmosphere built to lethal levels.

Wolverine was in the forefront of the retreat toward *Icarus*. He wasn't even trying to kill the slugs now, just to keep them back long enough to get the others through. There wasn't time for anything else. Through the soles of his boots, the station told her story of grim defeat through the groans of overstressed metal, the pinging of welds giving way.

The docking cradle that held the Guardians' starship was up ahead, its branching corridor marked by the flashing light that would have told the absent dead station personnel that the docking cradle at the end was in use. *Get to the corner, a few more yards . . .* they were almost home.

Almost home was the place that most people died.

Frost crackled beneath Wolverine's feet like a message from absent comrades, constantly melting and reforming. Wolverine hoped Drake would have the sense to trigger his recall if he got buried. They should be moving, getting those of them who could reach it to a safe haven, going home themselves to do whatever patch-up job they'd be let to do before the next round.

If home was even there. If Kang won—or had won

already, in the twisted syntax of time travel—would there be anyplace to go home *to*? Or would that place already have turned into darkness and the everlasting night?

"We're here!" Iceman shouted, coasting up from behind along a wave of ice. Charlie-27 scrambled after him, his heavy footfalls shaking the sheet of ice on which he ran. He reached the end and slid; exuberantly, Iceman built a curved slide that sent him rocketing down the access corridor to the *Icarus's* docking cradle like a one-man luge team. The others ran after, in motion the moment they knew their comrades were safe. Iceman filled the space behind them with ice to discourage pursuit, and threw up a wall just beyond the cross corridor as well. The weight he placed on the station's decks didn't matter now; their remaining time here was going to be measured in minutes.

And suddenly all the lights went out.

"Hey!" Wolverine shouted. He'd jumped forward, but the gravity had ended with the lights and he found himself twisting helplessly, disorientingly, in total darkness. Only the faint glow from Nikki's fiery body gave them any light at all, but if she increased it, the temperature of their surroundings would rapidly become unbearable.

Wolverine twisted in midair like a cat, but the walls were too far away to reach. "Drake!" he bellowed.

It didn't take long for Iceman to get the idea. Within moments the corridor was crisscrossed with a network of ice pylons that all of them could use to pull themselves along by.

In the distance, the open hatch of *Icarus* sent an inviting glow out into the darkness. Charlie stood framed in the light from the open hatch, waving them on. Wolverine plucked Nikki out of the air and flung her down the corridor, bracing himself between an ice pylon and the station's bulkhead. Charlie grabbed her and flung her past him, reaching out for the next man.

There was a vibrating in the air, a sound so loud that all of them could hear it.

"We're out of time," Bishop said. Only seconds remained before the station became a cosmic fireball.

"Come with us," Astro urged, stopping short of safety to save others. "Whoever you are, there's a place for you among the Guardians of the Galaxy."

"Don't worry about us, Major. We've made other plans," Bishop said. The other Guardians were calling for their leader, fear in their voices. Bishop waved him off. Astro turned away, racing for the safety of the *Icarus*'s hatch.

"Move it," Wolverine growled.

Hanging in the corridor, Iceman reached for the covering of his recall device. Bishop had his open. Wolverine's had lost its cover a fight or two ago. "Let's blow this joint and go home," Iceman said.

On a wave of superheated plasma, *Icarus* fled the site of what had once been *Cherryh* Station for the blackness of interstellar space.

"So the whole thing was a setup?" Nikki asked Vance, trying to figure out what had just happened. At least the five of them were safe, and *Icarus*'s medical equipment would take care of any incidental burns.

She hoped the three strangers could say as much, wherever they'd gone.

At least, she was pretty sure she did.

"There's no way they could have done what we saw on the tape if *Cherryh* had already been infested by vacuum worms," Astro explained. "No, Nikki, the whole thing was a trap from beginning to end."

"I wonder if we will ever know its architect—or its purpose," Yondu mused.

"Or whether or not it worked," Charlie-27 added, looking back at the glowing veils of light that were all that remained of *Cherryh*.

One measures a circle beginning anywhere, and from that standpoint, this room in a castle called Tenebrae in a realm called Limbo might serve as well as any other place as the center of everything that was.

Were there a dispassionate observer available, he might wonder—in this place that so much more than any other conformed to its inhabitants' expectations—why this refuge was filled with the quaint exuberant technology of yesterday's tomorrows. Why should Kang the Conqueror, that lucid and experienced vandal of civilization's treasures, reimage this command center as an image of humanity's invention halfway between that of the grovelling cannibal apes and the dispassionate reach of the uncaring stars themselves?

Such enigmas had their place, in the study of gods and the damned, but in this place the questions did not matter. However, Kang had chosen to craft his scrying glass to suit his personal whimsy and at last it had brought him what he wanted.

Ravonna.

"I have you." He spoke in a tone barely above a whisper, in which true love and genuine grief were very nearly overshadowed by the guttural sound of triumph. In that instant it was less important that Ravonna had been found than that it was he, Kang the Conqueror, Kang the Undefeated, who had found her.

"I have won!" He filled his lungs with air for the exultant shout that rang from the walls of Kang's stolen battle center. The sound echoed from the cool eyes of the viewscreens that surrounded him, from the surface of his royal carapace, until the living component was gone from the sound and the echoes that remained were footsteps through the graveyard of empires.

Here was the timeline he'd sought—here was his Ravonna: alive and innocent, ready to be wooed and won by her Conqueror once more. Their love would rise like a bright phoenix from the ashes of all the might have beens around them; glories and empires that Kang was prepared to condemn to dust with the careless gesture of one armored gauntlet.

"You rang, Master?" Lireeb asked, gliding into the Control Room with his cat-footed walk.

"I have found her." Kang's joy in victory was such that he did not even resent the fact that he had not, as a matter of fact, rung for Lireeb. "I have found my Ravonna, and the single timeline which I have chosen to become the single—the only—the ultimate history of the universe. It alone shall I preserve when all others shall die."

Lireeb regarded him with a dispassionate feline interest, almost as though Kang had just become a very interesting mouse.

"I suppose, Master, that despite your discovery you do *not* mean I am to trigger the timequake that will obliterate all the other timelines now?" Lireeb asked.

Kang regarded the albino with narrow savagery, his cold eyes narrow behind the flexible mask he wore. Almost he began to suspect that the albino mocked him—but no. The creature was too subservient, too passive, to choose to contest with Kang the Conqueror in a battle where it would be so obviously outmatched. Kang was master, here as everywhere. He regarded his slave with a cool benignant smile.

"Not yet, lackey. There is yet one more task to be completed before Kang may enjoy the full flower of his victory. . . ."

CHAPTER EIGHT

A moment ago, things had been as peaceful as they ever got in the dystopian fourth decade of a twenty-first century that saw humanity wavering on the brink of extinction. The young woman known as Dream—the leader of the Anti-Sentinel Resistance League—was working out how get two time travelers to a place she'd never seen: the mysterious Dead Zone in lower Manhattan, a place that was off-limits even to the fearsome Sentinels that had proven so efficient in reshaping the twenty-first century in their own barren image.

In the course of half a dozen heartbeats, all of that had changed.

The Sentinels struck without warning, and in force. Though the embattled Rats in the Walls had placed sentries with their usual fanatic care (because in 2035 you were either fanatical or dead), they'd always known that even the wariest sentries could be overwhelmed by speed and brute force.

Just as they had been today.

An instant ago the western wall of the abandoned warehouse that had become the Rats' de facto headquarters had been turned into a cresting wave of brick dust and gravel by a blast from an Alpha Sentinel's chest beam. The inhabitants of the warehouse had scattered.

At least, most of them had.

"Sentinel Alpha Six: Termination program running—secure and execute!"

The overamplified words came from the unmoving mouth of the lead Sentinel. It stood framed by the powdered rubble of what once had been the back wall of a deserted warehouse just north of Manhattan . . . a place that now seemed about to be humanity's last stand.

"Die, sucker!" the Rat named Jyrel shouted, dashing

forward, a bomb in his hand. Cyclops had known him only for minutes—learned his name by accident, really. Even as the makeshift Molotov cocktail left Jyrel's hands, another Prime reached down and took him between thumb and forefinger. And then . . . Jyrel wasn't there anymore.

"Execute this, butcher!" Cyclops shouted. He stood his ground and opened fire. The harsh ruby light blazing from his eyes lit the dust-filled air, making it look as if he stood in the center of a shimmering veil of light. The force blast struck the Sentinel, making its neck joints squeal as its head was forced back.

Beside Cyclops, Phoenix capitalized on the force of his initial attack, adding her telekinetic punch to his optic beam a split instant later. Scott steadied her as she staggered back under the force of her own assault, but her target was in much worse shape than Jean Grey was. The outlines of the Sentinel in her psionic grasp seemed to blur as the giant machine vibrated madly in its efforts to shake off Phoenix's savage attack.

Smaller Sentinels—tunnel fighters—swarmed in around the six leaders, wading into the maelstrom of bombs, bullets, and energy weapons as if the desperate human opposition simply weren't there. The Rats gained some victories, but not quickly, and never enough. The smell of blood quickly became stronger than the smell of dust, river, and coming rain.

Between them, Cyclops and Phoenix had accounted for the lead Prime Sentinel, but as it terminated, it fell across the roof of the warehouse, and now the whole building shook and groaned with the strain of supporting an additional six hundred tons of metal.

As Cyclops looked for another target—he had to be careful to avoid hitting his own side; his optic beams could be as much of a threat to the Rats as the Sentinels were—Dream appeared out of the swirling smoke.

Her face was harsh and drawn with pain; her right cheek held a purple burn where the back-blast from her energy rifle had come too close. She was grimy and soot stained, and there was a spreading patch of blood—her own or a comrade's—on the chest of her tattered gray jumpsuit. Her people were badly outnumbered and were being slaughtered wholesale by murderous robots. But the defiant light in Dream's green eyes still blazed.

"Come on!" Dream shouted, dragging at the sleeve of the sweatshirt Cyclops had donned to conceal his uniform.

He turned toward her.

"We've got to get you out of here!" she yelled.

We can't leave the others! a small voice within Cyclops cried. But the two X-Men had little choice. They could not afford to jeopardize their own mission: to find Kang's Time Platform and turn it against him.

Jean! Cyclops shouted through their psi-link *Disengage, now!*

Just a minute, Phoenix snapped back. Her mental voice was thick with strain.

Cyclops looked for her, and found her at last, hovering up near the sagging rooftree. A glowing nimbus surrounded her, and as he watched, the burnt-out Sentinel began to move, jerking like a spastic puppet as it twitched and slid free of the roof.

Shambling like some out-of-time Frankenstein's monster, the Sentinel turned on its nearest counterpart, flailing at it with lethal effect. Swiftly the two titans retreated—still locked in combat—to the river, where the Sentinel under Phoenix's telekinetic control pulled its enemy beneath the water.

"Come on!" Dream repeated, and Cyclops relayed the words directly into Phoenix's mind. He felt her flash of assent as he turned and followed the young resistance leader.

The door Dream had used to enter the warehouse a few minutes before hung open now. As Phoenix caught up to the two of them, Dream passed through the door and into a small cement cubicle filled with scavenged electronic equipment. But the computers—or the room itself—were not her destination.

"Open it," she said to Cyclops, pointing at the manhole cover on the floor. He stooped to lift it, just as Phoenix closed the door behind her.

"They're dying out there," Phoenix said in a ragged voice. Through their psi-link, Cyclops could feel how the deaths of most of Dream's resistance cell still echoed against Phoenix's psychic shields, making it hard for the telepathic X-Man to think.

"No," Dream corrected her. "They're already dead."

There was a grating sound as Cyclops pulled back the cover to expose the opening in the floor. The opening led to some kind of utility access.

"Down there," Dream said, still leaning against the wall.

"You'll have to go first," Cyclops said.

Dream shrugged, pulling away from the wall. As she did, Phoenix saw the fresh smudge of red blood against the concrete, and realized what the dark stains soaking through Dream's coverall must be. As Dream grasped the first handhold, she left it wet with fresh blood.

Shrapnel. Phoenix could pluck the information from the surface of Dream's mind as easily as she could sense her pain. Dream was hurt. And though Phoenix had seen her teammates hurt this badly many times before, they either had a mutant healing factor to make things better or the services of the infirmary at the Xavier Institute.

Dream had neither of those things. The rest of Phoenix's almost-granddaughter's life could be measured in a series of bloody handprints descending into the dark.

Silently, stunned by the impact of the knowledge, Phoenix followed. Scott came last, pulling the iron lid back into place above them.

"Some of these cables are still live," Dream said, panting with pain and stress. "It confuses their scanning. If we can get out of range quickly enough, we'll lose them. But we have to keep moving. The Big Boys don't give up easily."

"But what about you?" Phoenix demanded. "You're hurt; you need help." *And all the rest of your people are dead—doesn't that mean anything to you?*

"We have no time for our sorrows," Dream snapped, as if she'd heard Phoenix's thoughts. "All that matters is the future. That's the only thing that's real. Come on."

After about ten minutes they came up out of the underground onto the surface again. The sounds that the Sentinels made reducing the warehouse to rubble could be heard in the distance, but for all the reaction Dream had to them, the evening might have been silent as the grave. Like the ghost of Virgil conducting some new tour group through hell, Dream's whole being was focused solely upon reaching her goal.

That nightmare journey through the rubble of the necropolis was something that would come back in dreams to haunt Jean Grey for the rest of her life. Though she'd seen things far more sinister and eerie, the quiet certainty that the murdered city seemed to project terrified her on some primal level. It was as if some heavenly judge on his celestial throne had looked down and said, *This is the end. It all ends here, for everyone.*

Dream did not let either of the X-Men slow their pace. She pushed southward ruthlessly; sometimes across the surface, sometimes through carefully tended catacombs, as the afternoon darkened into twilight. At one stop, she'd picked up a light. In its wavering beam Cyclops and Phoenix could see defiant graffiti painted on the walls; the only history of this war that would ever be written.

Spidey Rules. Mutants Live. Alpha Prime sucks AC/ DC. Sentinels 0, Daredevils 3. Humans Rule! Wonderbaker 478. Haqrs R Us. Rel, if you see this meet me at— the rest was gone, hidden under the soot from a blast that had scoured the wall.

As they went southward, Dream moved slower and slower, and finally agreed to stop and rest for a few minutes. She shivered in the cold; Phoenix made Dream take the coat she'd been given to camouflage her bright battlesuit, and Cyclops took off the hooded sweatshirt that had been serving the same function for him and made it into a makeshift bandage for the worst of Dream's wounds. The chest wound was still bleeding, something that worried both X-Men.

"It's just a scratch," Dream insisted, though her pain told Phoenix otherwise.

Jean glanced at Scott. The set of his mouth was grim, but their own harsh necessity made him willing to let Dream spend herself this way. The screams of the dying back at the resistance headquarters still haunted both X-Men, though Dream only looked determined, a mad sort of serenity shining from her glittering eyes.

All that matters is the future, she had told them, with the grim fixity of one who is living in hell.

Phoenix hesitated, and in the end said nothing. *This is my daughter's daughter. Somehow, in some way, blood of my blood.*

After a short rest, they went on.

"This is it," Dream said breathlessly, clinging to the ladder that led upward. "The closest access to the Forbidden Zone. It's all open ground from here."

The last rays of daylight leaked down through the improvised shelter of boards that concealed the access to the surface. Only brute determination had brought her this far. Dream's bloodless face was a pale smear in the darkness, and her skin was beaded with sweat.

"I've got it," Cyclops said, looking down at the Tempometric Meter he held. "The Time Platform's within range." The presence of Kang's Time Platform was a faint vivid spark on the sweeping display. Dream had been right in her guess: their goal was within the Forbidden Zone.

"Come on, then," Dream gasped. "What are you waiting for?"

Scott and Jean exchanged looks. They could never have traversed this route without Dream to guide them, but it was clear to both X-Men that she'd given far more than her all to bring them here.

Dream was dying.

"Ladies first," Cyclops said. What should have been a flip reply came in tones of grating violence.

Dream gathered herself for one last effort, then slumped back, dazed, at last unable to force her body to obey her through will alone.

Cyclops caught her before she fell, lifting her frail weight in his arms. Phoenix stepped past him, climbing up the ladder toward the open air.

Dream is dying. Let her die in the light.

Phoenix shifted the camouflaging cover aside and looked around. Rubbed raw by almost twenty straight hours of constant peril, her every mutant sense was straining to assess any hint of danger before it occurred.

The sky was the color of gunmetal. A long false twilight bleached the ruins on the ground below to the color of old bones. Her surroundings looked like pictures of war zones on the six o'clock news: this was New York, but there was no landmark left to tell what part of New York it had been back when such distinctions mattered.

This is the land that all roads lead to. She couldn't get the Lila Cheney lyric out of her head. *This is the place where all things end.* It circled through her mind with an apocalyptic finality, the soundtrack for the end of the world.

Phoenix lifted herself out of the underground access and stepped back.

Scott. The accompanying mental picture told Cyclops everything he needed to know. He came up a moment later, carefully cradling Dream in his arms. His mind was closed, shutting even his wife and comrade out with the superhuman effort he was making not to react to the fact that Dream was dying in his arms.

He wanted to lay her down on the ground, but Dream clung to him, grimly forcing him to help her stand. She clung to his arm, her eyes bright and watchful, filled with hatred of her own body's failure.

And she saw them, as both Cyclops and Phoenix had known she must, even though it was a sight they had never wanted her to see.

Half a mile distant—in the direction the Tempometric Meter's signal had pointed—stood Sentinel Primes in row on row. The tallest thing in the landscape, their ranks went on and on, circling the Forbidden Zone.

Too many to count.

Far too many to fight.

"No . . ." All the remaining strength drained from Dream's body as her one hope died. Cyclops lowered her to the ground, still cradling her in his arms.

"It can't be for this, everything we did. All we've suffered. Not just for this." Dream's voice was thick with tears; all the suppressed grief, all the deferred sorrow of a lifetime of war came pouring out now. "I can't die now—not this way!"

Even now her voice was low, but the violence in it was like a strangled scream. She struggled weakly, trying to get to her feet once more. As she did, her efforts dislodged the makeshift bandage. It fell away, sodden with her life's blood.

"The Sentinels can't win," Dream sobbed, reaching with her last strength for something to use as a weapon, willing her shattered body to stand, to *fight.* . . .

In the distance, Phoenix saw one of the front-ranked Primes switch on its searchlight. All up and down the cordon, she could see watchlights wink to life on the giant mechanoids, as if the stars had chosen to come out early. *Scott—*

"Listen to me," Cyclops said to Dream, and in his voice was an intensity Phoenix had rarely heard. "I told you we were time travellers. Listen to me now. I've seen the future. The Sentinels are destined to be destroyed. This is the truth. I swear it, Dream."

The girl's bright gaze was fixed on Cyclops, as if through will alone she could see through the ruby quartz to the man beneath. In the distance, Phoenix could hear the whine of servos as the Sentinels began to move toward them.

"You're telling the truth," Dream said, her voice so faint that Phoenix would not have known the words without telepathy. "I *know* it."

And then her gaze became fixed, unseeing. Her hand relaxed in his, and Cyclops lowered her to the ground, as gently as if there were someone still there to feel it. As he got to his feet, he was already flipping open the cover of his TDR.

"Get ready to go," he said to Phoenix.

Phoenix opened the cover of her own device and prepared to trigger the recall that would return them to their own time and place.

"How could you . . . ?" she said hesitantly.

"Lie to her?" Cyclops asked. "I didn't." He pointed back the way they had come.

In the twilight sky, a wave of energy, darker than any night, was rolling across the sky, crushing the world beneath its weight.

Before the first Sentinel reached their location, the two X-Men were gone.

The universe soon followed. . . .

CHAPTER NINE

I t's all in the timing, Hank McCoy told himself. A moment ago he'd been at the mercy of two of Kang's enforcers—the white-skinned psychic succubus who called herself La Lunatica, and a speedster named Meanstreak who did his best to live up to his name. The third member of their team, a walking battery named Skullfire, had been giving Gambit a hard time. All three of the kids were out for blood and both the X-Men knew it; whoever they were, whoever they thought the X-Men were, they were playing for keeps.

The Beast's stamina kept him on his feet against Meanstreak's assault, but La Lunatica would be rejoining the fray almost momentarily, and The Beast was worried that Charles's shields wouldn't hold up as well against her second psionic assault.

"Look, folks, if you'd just—"

"Give up now," Meanstreak invited, stopping his flitting around so that the Beast could hear his words. "We aren't bargaining with anyone who works for Doom."

"Doom?" the Beast said. "Victor Von Doom? But this is 2099, surely he couldn't have—"

He broke off, springing back as a handful of charged cards exploded nearly beneath his feet. Gambit's fight was coming awfully close.

Incredibly, Meanstreak stopped to watch the other brawl. He was keeping a wary eye on the Beast, but his action once again confirmed Hank McCoy's deepest instincts: they were powerful, they were motivated, but they weren't as highly trained as someone whose high-school gym classes had taken place somewhere called the Danger Room. He kept a wary eye on Meanstreak and La Lunatica as he turned toward the other fight.

"Bad move, scumbag, when you know that anything you can generate, I can absorb," Skullfire taunted.

"Per'aps," Gambit agreed. "An' per'aps you were not the target, M'sieu Firefly." Gambit planted one end of his bo stick in the ground and used it as if it were a pole vault, slamming feetfirst into La Lunatica.

"Luna!" Skullfire shouted, dropping his guard as he prepared to charge up once more.

The albino succubus had been knocked off her feet; Gambit took an instant to blow her a kiss before signing her off more thoroughly with a charged playing card. The rest of the deck was in his hand, and he flung the cards away as though they'd offended him, too fast for the speedster to dodge. A flash, a yelp, and Meanstreak went flying.

Gambit glanced at the Beast; their eyes met, and in that moment a wordless council of war took place. There was no more time for attempts to explain why they were here to people who'd been tricked into fighting them with what must have been a really good story—not when the way to achieve their objective in this time was suddenly available.

Now that Gambit had taken out the Beast's opponents, Hank swung around toward Skullfire and delivered a punch that turned the supercharged mutant's lights right out. Without stopping, he turned back again and flung himself on Meanstreak.

Gambit ran—but not toward the remaining fight, nor even to make sure that the two unconscious combatants were likely to remain that way.

Gambit ran toward the aircar.

The slim silvery shape lay inert upon the grass at the edge of the water, just where the trio had parked it. If Gambit's next few minutes were successful, the X-Men would never know who these people were or why they'd jumped them the moment they'd seen them. Remy LeBeau was by profession and avocation a thief; he passed quickly through more lives than he could count, touching each of them only briefly. His life was full of such unanswered questions, and one more wouldn't hurt.

Gambit vaulted into the aircar and gazed down at the bank of unfamiliar instruments. There was no ignition key, and all the controls were labeled in Japanese or something that looked a lot like it.

But thieving was in Remy LeBeau's blood, and he'd learned his trade in a demanding school. A few moments after he got his hands on it, the power plant woke into life. He touched the controls experimentally, and to his ill-concealed glee the craft began to rise.

"*Bête!* We are leaving!" A Dead Man's Hand—aces and eights—fanned out almost reflexively between the fingers of Gambit's right hand and began to glow.

She wished they did not have to be enemies, but somehow that had been decided before the two of them had met. Storm flew higher, trying to get up-sun of her enemy, as all the British flyers did in the war movies Nightcrawler had liked—and forced her to watch when they had been teammates, before he moved on to Excalibur. Odd, in an academic sense, that he should make icons of his ancestors' enemies, but then Kurt Wagner's ancestors had been human, just as Ororo Munroe's had, and both of them were mutants, cast out from humanity, a third side in the eternal war between the wicked and the just.

Would it ever end? Humans, mutants in all their permutations—would there ever be a final peace? Or only a final war?

Her red-skinned enemy flew under the power of his great leathery wings—a predator in his natural element. But Storm had wind, not wings, to bear her aloft, and she used the advantage against him, stealing his element and sending him floundering through the air that had betrayed him.

Her body still ached from the effort of trying to control

the monsoon she had faced when she and Iceman had tried to stop Kang's Time Arrows. In other circumstances, there would have been a thousand ways for her to end this fight, but at the moment, her resources were too limited for her to engineer a quick flashy victory.

"Please!" she called down to him. "We mean you no harm. There's no need to fight." Unless he'd been sent to keep them from reaching the Time Platform. With the fate of all the universes riding upon it, she dared not take a chance on peace, no matter her own feelings.

"Leave now and there will be no quarrel between us!" Storm cried desperately.

"The quarrel was set before either of us was born, wind-witch!" the red-skinned flyer barked. "And Bloodhawk has sworn to defend those lands and their peoples too weak to save themselves from exploiters like you!"

Storm didn't know how Kang had gotten to Bloodhawk first, but realized sadly she did not have time to argue with his artful propaganda. With a wave of her hand she made a hole in the air beneath Bloodhawk, a vacuum into which he dropped, broad wings furling about him as if he were a discarded umbrella. Below both of them Storm could feel the spiralling tightness of Earth's energies coiling to release themselves in destruction. Though she knew she would see nothing, she looked behind her, toward the mainland, wishing she knew where Gambit and the Beast might be and how they fared.

Earthbound. Trapped on the mainland with whoever else had been in that aircar she'd seen. If Bloodhawk only wanted to keep her away from the Time Platform, she could return to the mainland—help the others, who were just as exhausted from their previous battles as she was.

But Bloodhawk had called her an exploiter, as if he saw her as a threat to the Savage Land itself. She did not know what story Bloodhawk had been told: if he had been told to smash the Time Platform as well as the X-Men. . . .

She looked for Bloodhawk, but he was no longer below her.

In the last instant, grinding hours of training in the Danger Room paid off. Storm reacted without thought, rolling in the air and lashing out against an attack she did not consciously expect.

The red-skinned transmorph stooped past her, his gleaming talons outstretched. They would have buried themselves in her back and seized her beating heart. With her evasion, all that Bloodhawk had was some scraps of her black costume. The lightning that crackled from her fingertips went wide by intention; Storm would rather warn off than hurt, rather hurt than kill. Because killing was forever, and when forever came, each person was trapped alone in the dark.

But her mercy was misplaced. Bloodhawk turned, pirouetting with the grace of a shark in the clear air. His leathery wings grabbed great sailsful of air and flung it behind them as he raged upward with terrifying speed to where Storm hung in the sky.

Go away, she wanted to tell him. *Go home. Forgo your master's madness.*

But she did not speak the words aloud.

The sun gleamed upon his talons. The scraps of her costume fluttered toward the surface of the sea.

Storm gathered the lighting in her hand and flung it—a fat ball of *ignis fatuus*, round as a child's snowball. It spattered against Bloodhawk's shoulder, spending its fat spark, and he cried out—in anger, in shock—and for a moment lost his hold upon the air and became an insect crushed by the cruel fist of gravity.

For an instant Storm pitied him, but only for that instant, because her nameless assailant was the predator that he was, and in a heartbeat he had converted an uncontrolled fall into a leap skyward, borne up by the same winds that held Storm aloft.

Clouds had gathered while Storm and Bloodhawk fought, and now the sky was no longer a placid lake for the two combatants to sail upon. Suddenly both of them were caught in the grip of the tempest, thrust back and forth by the squalls in the heart of the thunderheads.

It was a situation Storm was familiar with, both at work and play, but it seemed to catch Bloodhawk completely by surprise. He floundered amid the buffets of cold wet air, his lips pulled back in a snarling rictus of savagery. In that moment he looked far less human even than Wolverine.

But brute fury, it seemed, could do what skilled finesse could not. Where Storm allowed the tempest to dictate to her, Bloodhawk forced himself grimly through the aerial galleries, intent on his prey. A pocket of still air was all he needed, and then Bloodhawk was above her, and this time he would not spend that advantage in a single slashing attack.

Like the bird of prey he so much resembled, Bloodhawk harried Storm through the sky as she turned and twisted to escape him, forcing her always closer to the water as the storm raged around them.

Gambit had set them up nicely for him, but it was still two against one and even if they didn't have muscles in Colossus's class, Meanstreak and Skullfire—who, surprisingly enough, had gotten up after the Beast's first punch—both knew how to hit.

But when punch came to crunch, both of them were talented amateurs, and Henry P. McCoy was a top professional.

Meanstreak was still sluggish after having been peppered by Gambit's explosive cards, and La Lunatica wasn't even back in the fight. Skullfire—he of the ver-

dant electrical blasts—was operating at decidedly reduced power, but the punches still hurt, and the Beast
worried, somewhere in the back of his mind, that one of
the energy pulses would tag the recall device he wore,
and trigger or break it. Either would be disastrous.

So he sparred. Usually the Beast preferred a running
battle, but he didn't dare move too far away from the
coastline. Where was Storm? She should have been back
from her reconnaissance by now.

Then La Lunatica pulled a pistol.

There should have been no place for it in the tight
gunmetal-colored uniform that she wore, but there was.
The object itself was a thing of beauty—all green glass
and neutron fire—and it seemed as if time stopped while
she drew it, allowing Hank the time to remember the
long-ago time when he'd first become what the news me-
dia in those quaint old days had called a "costumed
adventurer." When it was tacitly understood—along with
the fact that lethal force would not be used and that the
opposition had the right to try to beat you face-to-face—
that you stood or fell on the powers that nature or nurture
had given you, and that to carry such irrelevant things as
a gun was a vote of no confidence in yourself and what
the world had made you.

But times had changed, even in this small segment
covered by the Beast's adult lifetime. Now the villains
played for keeps, attacked on every front, ferreted out
political hatchet-men to clip your wings long distance—
and killed. And the so-called good guys did the same
thing. And when there was no difference between them
at all in their methods, and only one goal—victory at any
price—what would be left of all the hopes and ideals all
of them had cherished in the morning of the world?

Gone, all gone. Dead and dust and ashes—gone with
the Best and the Brightest and the New Frontier.

"Tim—move!" the crazy woman shrilled.

Hank McCoy looked into her eyes and saw the future—her future, his future, a future that had no place in it for kindness or mercy or second chances. A world of scarcity and threat, where the chance to make a friend was the chance to lose to an enemy as well. But still she'd hesitated that heartbeat that might let him escape, because she did not want to shoot a friend.

Perhaps there was that much hope.

"Allez-oup, mon brave!"

Gambit's shout came from above him, just as La Lunatica fired. The Beast struggled free of Meanstreak and sprang blindly upward, hoping there was something there to grab.

Something hit him in the chest just as he leapt, stunning him, but despite that his fingers closed on slippery metal/ceramic and clung hard. A flight of charged cards flew by his head to sow confusion among the enemy. The Beast scrambled aboard.

A thin bright light ripped past them—once, twice. The aircar responded beneath Gambit's hands as if it were a live thing, slipping left, right, left, and away. Toward the island.

The Beast drew a deep breath, congratulating himself and Gambit on being alive and free. And when he did, the straps of the TDR slid free, and the charred and useless Recall Device slid free to land in his lap, still smoking.

"Oh, my stars and garters," Hank McCoy said, very faintly.

"Our ride! They're jacking our ride! Oh . . . shock," Skullfire finished inadequately. He lashed out at the aircar with all the reserves he had left (which weren't much), then had to sit down quickly as the world around him grayed out.

Luna snapped off a couple of shots with her hideout

pistol before giving up as well. She sat down beside Skullfire and put an arm around his shoulders.

"Don't worry, lover. The way that thing flies, they'll be lucky to make it home alive."

"If they're working for Doom, why didn't they take their *own* ride?" Meanstreak asked plaintively. "And come to that, where's Hawk?" he added, knowing the answer wasn't likely to be forthcoming.

The squall line that had been hanging out to sea all morning began to drift landward. In a few moments it would be raining here.

"Maybe," Skullfire said slowly, "maybe they didn't have one. There was something about those guys . . . maybe they weren't working for Doom at all. Maybe we played this one all wrong from the start."

"Cheer up, Fitz," Meanstreak replied with bleak cheer. "It wouldn't be the first time. You know what they've said about the X-Teams for the last hundred years: we're the hard-luck Harrys of the super hero trade."

"Yeah." Skullfire sighed, resigning himself to a long walk home. He got to his feet just as the first few raindrops struck the ground.

"What's a super hero?" La Lunatica asked absently.

Gambit kept the aircar flying as high as he could, to give himself more time to recover if the untrustworthy little future machine decided to stop flying. The aircar couldn't have brought the others any distance at all; it had little reserves, and was so underpowered that the Beast had been forced to ride in the back in order to balance out the weight distribution.

The squall-line lay ahead like a dark curtain of rain; a waterfall from the sky, but even now the outliers spit water at them on the wings of the wind, and one of the things this aircar seemed to lack was a roof of any kind.

He knew he didn't understand the controls as well as he might; and when they started flying into the rain he could wish all he liked for a canopy to keep the rain off but he didn't dare try to invoke one.

Behind him, the Beast sat absently brushing the last of the burned fur from his chest. The slagged TDR lay at his feet. Hank McCoy had lost his ticket home.

It wasn't as bad as it seemed. So long as he was in proximity to one of the others when the TDR was triggered, the bioelectric circuit would extend enough to pull both of them back in time. But one level of their failsafes had been removed, and they didn't dare be split up now for any reason, lest McCoy be marooned somewhere in the future.

Still, this was the least of their problems at the moment.

"I don' like to upset you unduly, *mon brave*," Gambit drawled slowly, "but 'ave you noticed dat our destination is sinking, it?"

The little aircar bucked frantically as it tried to make way against the storm. Both Gambit and the Beast were pretty well soaked by now. The Cajun's chestnut hair had darkened almost to black, and was swept straight back from his face by the wind. The Beast's fur was silvered with the beaded moisture, fluffed out around him in a futile attempt at protection and body-heat conservation.

"Sinking?" McCoy said.

Gambit waved him forward to the driver's seat so that he could see for himself.

"It could just be the fog," the Beast said. The boundary between Earth and air was becoming more vague by the moment, making it hard to be sure they were even moving. Only the island was still visible, an emerald jewel set in a silver sea.

"An' so Gambit t'inks at firs', but den he takes a landmark—which is not dere no more, no."

The Beast looked down at the Tempometric Meter in his hand. The tiny blue spark still pointed westward, toward the island. They'd reach it in only a few minutes more.

"You know," Gambit observed, apparently at random, "it would do dis ol' Cajun's heart good to get a sight of Stormy, jus' about now."

"Mine too," Hank McCoy muttered. "Mine too."

When two experts are matched against each other, the victory is won through the tiniest things, by the smallest margins. For minutes that seemed hours, the two adversaries had stalked each other through the mansions of the air, the smallest inattention of each being rewarded by the drawing of blood.

Storm bled freely from a dozen tiny wounds caused by the near misses of Bloodhawk's claws. Bloodhawk, named himself an X-Man, but she dared not care for that. He opposed what she had come here to do, and therefore she had to stop him, but each time she tried for the blow that would disable without killing, he evaded her. And time was on his side, not hers. To win—though he might not know it—all he had to do was to delay her. To lose, all she had to do was allow him to.

He'd forced her ever lower, trying to make her ditch over the water, but in the muddled air currents near the island she'd managed to slip free, summon an updraft, and shoot skyward over the island, losing Bloodhawk for a few moments.

The rain beat down on her face. She had to end things here, and quickly. Storm summoned the rain and the lightnings, even though it was dangerous, even though a strike against the earth could destroy Kang's Time Platform or trigger the quake that could cast it to the ocean bed in an instant. Despite the danger, she needed them now.

She watched as Bloodhawk soared, wings outstretched, gaining the height to attack her again. The rain trickled from both their bodies. Her small lightning did not hurt him, and Storm hesitated to strike with all her force. It would kill him, and she did not wish to kill. But now she had him where she wanted him.

It was not an easy thing she planned. Summoning all her strength, Storm seized the clouds and rent them asunder from sea level to thirty thousand feet. Arctic air from the very edge of space fell thousands of angels in an instant, pouring into the gap. Cold struck like a brutal behemoth's fist, and in a moment the rain in Storm's immediate vicinity had turned to sleet, to hail, to snow.

To ice.

And in that same instant, before he could shake off what she had done, Storm struck once, with surgical precision, and allowed the lightning to melt the ice on Bloodhawk's body, only to refreeze it harder, stronger— until Bloodhawk hung stunned but frozen, an animate hang-glider whom Storm could direct along the wind as she chose.

"It's snowing," Gambit pointed out, as he climbed out of the aircar. He spared a fleeting wish that there were some way for him to return it to *les enfants*, but banished the idea as impractical. He was just glad to be back on solid ground.

Still, the deed would have had a certain style.

"Merry Christmas," the Beast said absently, bounding over the side of the aircar and landing lightly on the frosted turf below. In his hand, the locator burned on unwinking.

"Why do you t'ink it does dat?" Gambit persisted, lighting a cigarette as he spoke. The snow was falling in big fluffy white flakes—he remembered how delighted, how *impressed*, he'd been the first time he'd seen snow—

and melting as it reached the ground. Gambit shivered, even inside his insulated battlesuit and leather duster. It was *cold* out here.

"Stop playing around, Remy," the Beast said, not bothering to answer the question about the weather. His voice was tense with suppressed excitement. "We've found it."

Where's Storm? Gambit didn't ask aloud. He knew that the Beast was as worried as he was about their missing teammate. Gambit scrambled through the underbrush to join him, and saw the Time Platform for the first time.

It lay a little canted to one side, as if it were a giant child's toy that had been flung away out of boredom. Like such a toy, it was brightly colored in shades of yellow and plum, glittering and expensive, like a Fabergé clockwork rejected by its intended owner.

"Does it work?" Gambit asked, moving cautiously closer. McCoy was crouched over the control panel, peering at the dials and buttons with a focus that banished the outside world—snow, sleet, dinosaurs—entirely.

"I don't know yet. Give me your recall device. I need some of the parts."

Gambit hesitated, his hand over the small mechanism, strapped to his chest, that was his only sure way home. What if Storm's had been destroyed too? For a moment, with a longing bordering on pain, he thought of Rogue's white skin, of burning coffee laced with chicory and bourbon, of the scent of the river from the levee at dawn.

He didn't have to give it up. He could use it now. Get home, tell any story he wanted to the others and be long gone before they figured out different. With Kang making things so hot for them, why should the X-Men bother to go chasing off after one little thief?

He could do that.

Gambit's hands shook only slightly as he unbuckled the straps and handed his recall device over to the Beast.

McCoy turned away, using his nails to pop open the casing and expose the delicate innards. Snow skirled through the air, looking oddly out of place on broad-leafed jungle plants. The huge golden flowers Gambit had noticed before were withering, dying in the cold. Would they all be dead before the whole island had sunk beneath the surface? Gambit hunched his shoulders against the biting wind and groped for another cigarette.

The earth quivered slightly beneath his feet—was it something the Time Platform had done, or just his imagination? He glanced behind him. Snow thickened on the Beast's fur, melting and freezing again until his shoulders were covered with an icy crust.

And where was Storm? He felt better about her survival than he had a moment before. She had to be alive, or else the snow would have dissipated by now. This weather was her work—unless the kids had brought a weathermonger with them—but where was she? He could use some sunshine just now, if anyone was interested.

"I think . . . I can make it work," the Beast said in tones of wonder. "At heart, this is just a simple teleport mechanism working on the same principles as Blaquesmith's Time Displacement Core. So I think," he finished, "that pressing this button this will bring us right into the heart of Kang's stronghold."

Suddenly the ground shuddered again—more strongly this time. Gambit staggered. The Beast, crouching, put one hand to the ground for balance.

And then the snow stopped, as abruptly as if it had been called away on other business. The clouds rolled back, letting through a torrent of hot tropical sunlight; its sudden brightness making Gambit wince. The snow that had collected in tiny pockets around the landscape—and frozen in Gambit's hair—melted almost instantly, and steam began to rise from the earth.

Storm landed beside the two of them, one flickering glance taking in the absence of the gleaming recall devices against the Beast's blue fur and Gambit's gaudy battlesuit. She ruffled Remy's hair, sending a shower of droplets in every direction.

Even tattered and bedraggled and weary as she was, Storm looked magnificent.

"Poor Gambit," she said, a faint note of amusement in her voice, "I know how little you like the cold. Believe me, if there had been any other way to defeat this Bloodhawk, I would have taken it."

"Dat who he say he is? So long as he join de rest of de juvenile delinquents, I don' mind, Stormy," Gambit said honestly. "But how come de groun' shaking like dis? Dis island, she sinking. You do dat too?"

"The quakes will only increase in force until at last they destroy the island utterly," she answered.

"Which is why we should be long gone from here before that happens, Ororo," the Beast said absently, continuing to make fine adjustments to the mechanism of the Time Platform. "Fortunately, Kang's technology in this instance does not seem to be that far distanced from our friend Cable's, and so—"

"You *t'ink* it'll work," Gambit finished sarcastically, his mood darkening suddenly. "What if it don't?"

The ground rocked again, harder this time, and Storm and Gambit clutched at each other for support. The TDR she still wore scraped against his chest. At least one of them still had a ride home.

McCoy shrugged, responding to Gambit's question. "If it doesn't work, then we'll find out what the heart of the sun looks like," he said. He straightened up and climbed onto the platform's tilting xanthic surface.

Storm was looking at him, Gambit knew it. Reluctantly, the Cajun climbed up beside the Beast onto the

Time Platform's slick, tilting surface, clutching at the railing to find his balance.

This would get them to Kang. Gambit concentrated on that. And it had better get them somewhere, because now Storm was the only one of the three of them with a recall device that worked, and nothing he'd seen persuaded Gambit that right here was a future he wanted to live in.

Storm mounted the platform last of all, and put a companionable hand on Gambit's shoulder. He turned toward her. The expression on her face was strained, distant. He just had time to notice that she was wounded—shallow scrapes that had already stopped bleeding—when McCoy pushed the button.

Just as he did, the biggest quake of all hit.

And the universe turned itself inside out.

The platform was rising up through them, cutting them painlessly in half like the glowing golden blade of a star-fire guillotine. . . .

No. That belonged to the past. This was the present.

And it wasn't the heart of the sun.

Hank McCoy blinked, not unsure whether or not he should be relieved that his juryrigging had actually worked. Everything around the platform was featureless and gray. He could not tell how far away the horizon was: it could be miles, or it could be less than an arm's length. He stretched out his hand, groping, but his fingers encountered nothing. There was not even the play of wind upon his face—as if this grayness were in fact his shroud.

"Are we here?" Gambit asked nervously. "Is dis Limbo?"

"I'm not sure," the Beast said, wishing he could give his teammate a more concrete answer. He knew of Limbo from the Avengers' files, but none of the trips Earth's Mightiest Heroes had taken there occurred during the

Beast's tenure with the team, and the descriptions were maddeningly vague. The only thing he knew for sure was that they'd arrived at the place the Time Platform had come from, wherever that might be.

"Ah, *no* . . ." he heard Storm moan. She turned toward him, her eyes gray-pale and staring. "There is *nothing*—"

She took a step backward, her steps as unsteady as a newborn colt's. Storm controlled the weather, and the Beast had seen the reciprocal effect time and again: Storm controlled the weather, and the weather affected her in turn.

What would the effect on a weather elemental be, then, in a place with no weather at all?

Gambit had turned toward her, but the Beast could see from the bewilderment on Remy's face that he was distracted by the strangeness of the place they had come to and had no idea of what was going on.

"Storm!" The Beast said urgently, hoping his voice would get through to her.

She reached out for him—blindly—color spilling back into her eyes as she fought for control.

"I am . . . all right, Henry," she said slowly, though her expression said that she was not all right, no, not all right at all.

"Stormy?" Gambit asked. The cigarette he'd lit before they'd left 2099 still burned, the smoke drifting upward in a thin unperturbed line, as if it burned in a sealed room.

"There is nothing here," Storm said to Gambit in a low voice. "No air. No weather. No . . . life."

"Dere's dat," Gambit offered, pointing. He shrugged. "Does dat help?"

In the distance there was a . . . something.

"Well," the Beast said, forcing a light tone, "since

there's no place like that place anywhere around the place this must be the place." *I hope*.

Feigning a confidence he was far from feeling, the Beast bounded into the strange unreal ground of Limbo. To his relief it was solid beneath his feet; firm and faintly springy, neither cold nor hot, like the Danger Room with all the holomasking turned off. A nullity, a waiting stage.

All the world's a stage, and all the X-Men's members merely players, Hank McCoy misquoted to himself. A disjointed blur of memories, suddenly vivid, flitted through his mind: wassail punch and Christmas Revels, the smell of new-cut grass, of sandy hot-dogs at the beach. As if his memory were trying to provide the vividness, the sensorium, that this place so completely lacked.

"Come on, folks," McCoy said encouragingly. Storm was the X-Men's other field leader, but he was the science geek. He'd gotten them here; that was as far as his writ ran. It was up to Storm to make the decisions that would allow the X-Men, one more time, to snatch victory from the jaws of nothing at all.

Beware the Jabberwock, my son! The jaws that bite, the claws that catch. . . .

Behind him, Storm shook her head, rousing herself as if from a trance. She shrugged her shoulders, bracing herself against what might come. "Stay close, both of you. We dare not become separated here."

"Gambit seconds dat emotion," Gambit said. He flung his cigarette away from him and waved Storm forward with an exaggerated courtesy that made them both smile. When you were staring armageddon in the face, sometimes the only thing to do was to play the fool.

"Oh, we're off to see the Wizard," the Beast sang, beneath his breath. Storm passed him and strode confidently forward into the nothingness. Her back was straight and her head held high, as if she had never felt a moment's fear.

"At last, my faithful lackey, all is in readiness—all!" Kang said in delight.

Lireeb watched, his own delight better concealed, as Kang rubbed his hands together, the very picture of a bully gloating over his victim's misfortune. Kang seemed oblivious to his own appearance as he raced from display to display in Tenebrae's control room, making everything ready for his masterstroke.

Yet when the moment came, a conqueror's habits remained: Kang did not act himself, but gave the order to his only remaining henchman.

"Send the Force Shield Generator to Ravonna's timeline!" Kang said grandly. "Let Kang's rich gift of existence itself go before him to announce his arrival—and to say to all the multiverse that this is the woman who has gained Kang's love, who is worthy of the conqueror of galaxies—"

"Who can understand a man who continually refers to himself in the third person," Lireeb muttered. He'd tuned most of the gloating out, his attention (even when he was not looking at it) focused on the viewscreen his body shielded, the one that was fixed on Limbo itself. The one that showed the Force Shield Generator.

And showed the three newly arrived X-Men journeying toward it.

"The great lord Kang knows, of course, that to teleport such an item as the Force Shield Generator must affect a great deal of the surrounding area?" Lireeb asked helpfully.

"Why do you tell me these things, albino?" Kang demanded. "Can you conceive—can you truly believe—that Kang the Conqueror cares whether this or that piece of Limbo is wrenched from its moorings and cast across the timestream? Let a thousand *leagues* of Limbo vanish with the teleport—let the realm itself be torn asunder, and it will make no difference at all to Kang!'' The small man in the gleaming green-and-violet armor raised his trembling fists, as though he would fell Lireeb with one savage blow.

"Then I may take it that you wish me to press the teleport button—now—and transport the generator and everything surrounding it to the continuum of the lovely Princess Ravonna?'' Lireeb asked. He had the faintly injured air of one attempting to be completely clear on what his orders were.

A silence, broken only by Kang's harsh furious breathing, was Lireeb's reply.

"Oh, very well,'' the albino said. He turned toward the console and pressed the button that stood beside the viewscreen. The picture was replaced with a tracking grid, a countdown as the teleport energy built to maximum. There was a beep as the reality-cracking energy dispersed, and then the view of Limbo was restored to the screen.

The generator and the three X-Men were all gone.

"The operation is complete,'' Lireeb assured his master. "The generator has reached its destination, as well as any—''

"Silence.'' Kang's voice was a strangled hiss. "You have done my bidding, albino—beware lest you do more than that.''

"Be assured, Master,'' Lireeb said smoothly. "All that I have done has been precisely in accordance with Kang the Conqueror's commands.''

CHAPTER TEN

They were known as the Midnight Wreckers, and they were, purely and simply, the best there was at what they did. They and others like them were the stainless steel rats in the walls of the global megacorporations. In their time they'd been called vandals, terrorists, and worse, all for the unspeakable crime of providing so-called forbidden technology to the people whom the megacorps didn't want to have it. Economic pirates, heroes of the consumer revolt—those were things the future might name them. Among themselves they were simply the Wreckers, spiritual descendants of the computer hackers of the bad old twentieth century. Any technology, any process, any access, the Midnight Wreckers could obtain it—at a price.

Providing, of course, that they liked you.

The four Midnight Wreckers and their companion stood on the tracks of one of the old-time subway lines (which had stopped running about the time most of them were born) and looked at the rubble.

"Whole thing's going to come down for sure, Hassle," Brain said, inspecting the bulging, overstressed ceiling.

He was dressed in a fashion from the turn of not the last century but the one before it, dressed in tweeds and knickers and stout oxblood broughams. The small round archaic glasses beneath the soft newsboy cap he wore made his cherubic blond good looks seem even more harmless and ineffectual. Which was why he did it, of course.

"It's already come down," Hassle snapped, gesturing at the rubble slide before her. Hassle's costume conveyed a Graustarkian air, from her slung-back hussar's pelisse to the gleaming jackboots she wore—but the Webley-Vickers in her hand was the very latest model and her short-cropped hair was a vivid shade of grass-green. "Now we have to get whoever's underneath it out."

At the edge of the rubble, Swift poked at the fallen slab with a salvaged length of metal. She was small and sprite slender, her head shaved except for a long ponytail of brown hair. Though none of the Wreckers—even Brain—lacked for bravery, Swift transcended them all. The willowy acrobat did not seem to even know the meaning of the word *fear*.

"Why?" Slick asked. "You know me, Hassle; I've been tight from the beginning of the Wreckers. It's a real giggle to crack Stark-Fujikawa coded transmissions in order to, like, know the enemy and get a ringside seat, but why risk our necks for a curve and two bots who might already be history?"

Slick was a burly giant of a man, dressed in the olive drab fatigues that were Subsidized Issue these days. But implants gleamed against his shaven head, and his face was painted in outlawed tribal images.

"Because—" Hassle began at the same time the newest member of the Wrecker pack did. She stopped.

"Because it's the right thing to do," Machine Man said steadily. "Because they might still be alive under there. And because anyone that Arno Stark has spent that much time and money to hunt is someone we want to know more about."

"But why—did he, I mean? Hunt them?" Brain asked. "We're in *Queens*. That's Spider-Girl's territory. Nothing happens in Queens, anyway."

"Yeah," Swift contributed. "This isn't anywhere near Baintronics's Fire Island dumping grounds—Queens is all holdfasts and arcologies."

"Maybe they'll still be alive to ask, once we get them out," Slick said. He picked up a long crowbar and began to pry at the face of the rubble. In a moment, Machine

Man was beside him, his extensible robot arms flexing as he slowly worked at dismantling the avalanche.

He didn't want to wake up. He knew if he woke up he'd probably be in a world of hurt, and would probably remember a lot of things he didn't want to remember.

On the other hand, maybe some of them would be worth remembering.

Spider-Man opened his eyes.

Nope.

He was lying on his side in a tiny pocket of space created by two slabs of prestressed concrete that had fallen angled against each other and now groaned with the weight of tons of rock above. It was a claustrophobic recess barely long enough to contain him. He wiggled his toes, relieved that he could do that much. He was all in one piece, anyway. Slowly he moved his hand up to touch the recall device strapped to his back. It was still intact. At worst, he could just undo the safety catch and slingshot himself back to the lab in Rosendale.

Assuming, of course, that the timeline he'd come from was still there.

And what about Cable and Aliya? Had they taken the easy out? Or were they dead? Or were they lying elsewhere in the rubble, trying to decide the same thing about him?

The last thing Spider-Man remembered, the other two had been several yards up the track, under what was probably now several tons of Queens. And if they were still alive he had to find them, free them, get on with things.

He heard a scraping sound.

Spider-Man froze, but his spider-sense signalled no warning. Whatever was making the sound wasn't an enemy, then—but if whoever it was brought down the roof with their digging, it wouldn't matter how well disposed toward him they were.

There was a grinding sound as of heavy slabs of rock shifting, and a hail of pebbles filtered down over his face. Reflexively Spider-Man covered his face with his hands— though the fine grit couldn't penetrate his mask—but as he did, something long and thin and slithery snaked through the rubble and seized him by the arm.

"You've got him!" Swift cried excitedly, as Machine Man pulled the last of the figures from the rubble.

Her red-and-silver companion was not human, though he had a human form: decades ago he had been manufactured by a man called Abel Stack as a prototype homiform artificial intelligence. His designer had done all he could to make Prototype X-51 human . . . and had succeeded too well, so that when Stack was ordered to destroy his prototype AI, he could not, and gave his life so that his creation might live.

There had been days of glory and sorrow after that, as the newly autonomous robot avenged his creator and waged a lone war against the forces of injustice—even finding such love as a metal man might with Jocasta, creation of the robot lunatic Ultron. But four decades ago, Machine Man had lost an important battle, and spent two score years as a spoil of war, his mechanical body reduced to its component parts and stored in the warehouse of robotics tycoon Sunset Bain. Only a fluke of inventory control had rescued him from that endless unlife, thrusting him into the company of these . . . strange attractors.

Brain. Hassle. Slick. Swift. They, along with his old friend Gears Garvin—still alive after all these years— had become not only his family, but a sort of moral compass in this strange, relativistic future. Their enemies were his enemies.

And his friends were theirs.

By now Slick had dug his way through to the third of the trapped survivors. With only a thought, Machine Man extended his arm in a long tube to pull the trapped victim free. The red-and-blue suit was familiar . . . too familiar.

"Spider . . . *Man*?" Machine Man said, with an odd hesitation in his speech. He was a machine, an artificial intelligence; emotion should not have roughened his voice, but it did.

"Who?" Hassle demanded suspiciously. "Not that bim—"

"No. Spider-Man. He's . . . an old friend."

Spider-Man struggled weakly in the metal grasp, disoriented. Behind the eye shields of his mask he squinted against the brightness of the lights, and then focused on the figure of his rescuer.

Right yet wrong, like everything else in this stupid decade. The shape was familiar, but the hero he remembered had been gunmetal blue and lacquered violet, skin that was armor for a man who was also a machine.

"Machine Man?" Spider-Man asked uncertainly. *I gotta stop eating those forty-inch pizzas before time travelling.*

The flexible composite of Machine Man's face stretched into a smile. "So you do remember me, Spider-Man."

"The paint job's different but the voice is the same," Spider-Man said, eyeing the red-and-silver figure before him cautiously. Suddenly, more recent memory intervened. "My friends! Are they—?"

"They're right here," Machine Man said, gesturing to where Cable and Aliya sat on the tracks, sipping from steaming paper cups and regarding their rescuers warily. "But how are you here? The Wreckers told me you were—"

Spider-Man held up his hand. Whatever they knew

about his future, he didn't want to know it. "It's a long story involving time machines, MM. A day or so ago, for me, it was 1998." *And before that it was 1867, but what's a few centuries between friends?* "But . . . ?"

"Oh, I reached this century—it's 2020, in case you were wondering—in the usual way," Machine Man said. "By living through all the years before it. If, of course, you can call suspended animation living. But let me introduce my companions. . . ."

Introductions were quickly made, and to Spider-Man's surprise, Cable held back and let him make the explanations for who they were and what they were doing here. He played it light, the way he always did: an Easter-egg hunt through time, with Kang the Conqueror as one of the players and he and the X-Men as the other.

He did mention, of course, the fact that Kang seemed to be cheating by hiring local help at something less than minimum wage.

"I'm not sure who the Iron Man knockoff was, but he doesn't seem to like Wreckers very much," Spider-Man finished. "That'd be you guys, right?"

Hassle smiled coolly without answering. Brain had poured him a cup of something from a vacuum flask, and Spider-Man had found the cup even more interesting than the coffee: it was thin enough that he had to hold it carefully to keep from bending it, but it was cool to the touch, despite the fact that it was filled with steaming coffee. It took nonconductivity to new heights.

Maybe—if they could steal a few hours here—he could take the chance to whip up a new batch of web-fluid. The stuff he'd made in Aliya's timeline was of inferior quality, and unstable besides. If things went wrong—and when didn't things go wrong?—he could find himself shooting web-flavored Kool-Aid at a bunch of killer androids from the future. Not a pretty thought.

"Iron Man doesn't like Wreckers because he works

for the corporations . . . and we don't,'' the woman Machine Man had identified as Hassle said. She looked like she could probably live up to her name, and then some.

"But that isn't what's important right now," Brain said. His bifocals flashed in the dim light. "Not if this Kang guy's hired hands beat you to the salvage."

Close enough to the truth, Spider-Man decided.

"Kang . . . didn't I hear about him in an old *Star Trek* episode?" Swift wondered aloud.

"You think you heard about everything in an old *Star Trek* episode," Slick told her mockingly. Swift snorted and popped a quick handstand.

"Is everyone able to travel?" Machine Man asked. "Iron Man has the best technology blood money can buy. Unfortunately, there's no chance he won't pick up your life signs as soon as you're on the move."

"The Tempometric Meter is still functioning," Aliya announced, getting to her feet. She had a new scrape on her cheekbone, and dried blood smeared along her jaw. But her blazing eyes were stubbornly indomitable.

Behind her, Cable stood like one of the less interpersonal cliffs. He gazed down at Aliya, and the desperate need to keep her safe that blazed from his one good eye made Spider-Man's stomach hurt. Because the business they were in was not safe, and the people you loved usually suffered most of all. Spider-Man had learned that lesson the hard way more times than he cared to count.

"Then let's saddle up and ride," Hassle said. Behind her, the rest of the Midnight Wreckers fell into line.

One moment Storm, Gambit, and the Beast had been in the universe's coat closet. The next . . .

In the distance, gleaming multi-colored towers rose skyward like premium office space in the Marvelous Land of Oz. The air smelled clean and freshly rain-washed. The Beast heard Storm suck air into her lungs in a ragged gasp of relief.

"Thank the Goddess!" the wind-rider whispered fervently.

"I do hope so," the Beast said, regarding the alien generator with concern. First it was there, surrounded by ominous mists . . . now it—and they—were here. But if this was not the dimension of their arrival, it was doubly not the dimension where the Time Arrows had their origin.

So where the triple-milled sandalwood-scented heck were they?

"Heads up," Gambit said quickly.

Imagine a world where everyone is perfect. Where war, disease, sickness, and hereditary illness have been eliminated so long ago that nobody even knows they ever existed. Where cosmetic surgery no longer exists as a medical specialty because the human genome has been so lovingly polished through the generations that everybody looks like they stepped out of a big-budget Hollywood movie from the day they were born.

For a moment the three time travellers were paralyzed by the sheer improbability of six men looking that glowingly well groomed and stress free outside of a Disney feature.

The feeling of disorientation lasted precisely as long as it took for the one wearing the most gold braid on his shoulders to open his mouth and speak.

"Intruders, you are under arrest," the leader said.

Why do guys from the future always have such lousy fashion sense? Hank McCoy asked himself. The six of them could have stepped right out of any *Buck Rogers* comic strip from the thirties: tight, shiny, candy-apple-red costumes, close-fitting cowl-type helmets with gleaming golden crests, and flared shoulder pads not found in nature. There wasn't a hand-weapon or even a swagger stick in sight, but when three more stepped forward behind their leader, holding out sets of gleaming shackles, they seemed to have no doubt that the intruders they'd stumbled over would tamely submit to detention.

Instinctively, the X-Men prepared to resist.

"Nom du chien!" Gambit swore, staring down at his hand. The cards in his hands were only that—not charged with the unique biokinetic energy that was Gambit's distinct mutant signature. He flung the useless cardboard away from him almost by reflex, in the instant before two of the guards seized him and began forcing his hands into the shackles.

Two of the other red-shirts had grabbed Storm. The wind she had summoned to whisk her aloft had failed her, but the mutant wind-rider was more than the sum of her elemental ability to control the weather. She slashed out at one with a chopping motion that left his arm dangling numbly at his side, and cleared his partner away from her with a roundhouse kick.

"Storm! Gambit! Stop!" the Beast said quickly. He was still untouched, his fearsome appearance making the soldiers think twice about closing with him. "There's obviously some sort of damping field here that subverts parapsionic powers. I think it's better if we go quietly."

Gambit shot him a look of utter disgust. Both the guards who had tried to seize him were down, but he followed the Beast's recommendation and stood quietly while two others came forward and shackled him. Two others dragged a ruffled but now unresisting Storm forward, while the remaining gaudily costumed guardsmen advanced on Hank McCoy.

"Dis better work out for de best," Gambit grumbled mutinously.

Better than getting into another fight where we don't know the ground rules, the Beast thought unhappily. Every instinct told him that these comic-opera troops were merely innocent bystanders—victims of more of Kang's gamesmanship—but what if he was wrong? What if by going with them now three of them were playing into Kang's hands, just as they had when they'd charged and detonated the Time Arrows?

There was no answer to that—at least not one that the Beast could know in advance—and as the gleaming golden shackles closed around his own wrists, Dr. Henry P. McCoy could only hope he hadn't just made a terrible mistake.

"Eh . . . If you don' mind, where we goin', *cher*?" Gambit asked breezily of his nearest captor. His temporary pique seemed to have vanished, and as a matter of fact, he looked very natural with his wrists shackled behind his back.

"Silence, Outlander!" the Buck Rogers Rockette answered. "You are to be conveyed to the Presence Chamber of Princess Ravonna. *She* will judge you."

"How very comforting," the Beast murmured to himself. He tried not to dwell on the fact that Storm now had the only working TDR unit among the three of them. The red-shirt's words had made it easy. *Ravonna. Isn't that the name of Kang's lost ladyfriend? Methinks our path and the conqueror's are about to intersect.*

"Those are X-Men!" In his fury, Kang's voice had become very nearly shrill. From the crow's nest of space-time he stared down upon a doll's version of Ravonna's jewelled city, to where three aircars—baroque and fantastic toys at this distance—conveyed three X-Men and Kang's own Force Shield Generator into the heart of the largest cluster of buildings. "How can there be X-Men there—how?" Kang demanded. "I sent the Force Shield Generator to that timeline—I didn't send them!"

"Perhaps they came with the generator," Lireeb suggested innocently.

Kang turned a gaze of incandescent bloodshot quivering fury upon his bland albino servitor.

"The . . . generator?" he said, very softly. " 'Perhaps they came with the generator'? "

"As my reverend and esteemed master the conqueror was undoubtedly aware when he gave the order to teleport the generator and all that surrounded it to the timeline he had chosen after all those hours of brooding over it . . . these things happen," Lireeb said, waving his hands airily. "Perhaps the mutants arrived in Limbo just at the very moment I pressed the button. Yes. That would make a good explanation, wouldn't it?"

Kang didn't answer. He'd used the transtemporascope to zoom in on the captives in the first car.

"The Avengers . . . always it is they who stand in the path of Kang's destiny," he murmured dreamily, as if to himself.

"Independent observation would suggest that it is the X-Men who are doing the standing on this occasion, Master of Time." Lireeb peered into the viewscreen. "I don't see any Avengers."

"Fool! You see but you do not perceive! That blue-furred helot is the X-Man—formerly the *Avenger*—known as the Beast. It does not matter to whom he swears his fleeting allegiance: I know it is the hand of the soi-disant Mighty Avengers reaching out to meddle in my grand design. Somehow, no matter what I do, no matter what vistas of time and space separate us, my destiny is intertwined with that of Earth's Mightiest Heroes, as if it had been fated from the very beginning of time. . . ."

"I daresay you'll show them, eh, sir?" Lireeb said heartily.

Kang glared. "I must go to Princess Ravonna at once—and yet, I cannot leave until I have finished the preparations to trigger the timequake and safeguard Tenebrae from all intruders. Normally, I would entrust those preparations to you, witless one, save for the fact that you had not the intelligence to note that interlopers had arrived within the purview of the teleport beam.''

''I suppose I did not,'' Lireeb said, as if the possibility had only just occurred to him.

It hadn't, of course.

CHAPTER ELEVEN

"Well, here it is," Brain said lamely. "That thing you were looking for."

For the last fifteen minutes, the Wreckers had led Spider-Man, Aliya, and Cable through the twisted maze of scavenger-created passageways that made a separate city beneath Queens. They didn't need to consult Cable's Tempometric Meter, though the big mutant kept a watchful eye on it; Spider-Man had the awful feeling they already knew where they were going. His worst suspicions (and he was a past master of really depressing suspicions) were confirmed when they stopped.

The thing that just had to be Kang's discarded Time Platform stood pressed up against a wall that still had most of its white institutional tile left intact. Against that backdrop, the alien metal gleamed, purple as a bruise.

It looked as if it had seen better days.

"This is it? This is all that's left?" Cable demanded.

Even Spider-Man could see that the Time-Platform wasn't all that it had once been. Pieces of the casing had been removed, exposing gaping interior spaces where components had once rested. In fact, it didn't look as if much was left of the original.

"We didn't find it until a couple of weeks ago, and by then, there wasn't anything left that we wanted," Brain said feebly.

"Another pack of Wreckers got to it first," Slick added. "I guess." His normal bravado was muted in the presence of Cable's disappointment and rage.

The four Wreckers looked at each other. While it was plain that they'd wanted to get to the salvage first, it was equally clear that they weren't quite sure why the three time travellers were so upset. In the Wreckers' world, parts were parts: sometimes scarce, but never irreplaceable.

"We might be able to trade for the components—get them back," Brain said hopefully. "If we can figure out who took them, I mean."

"Anything you can do with it, big guy?" Spider-Man asked Cable. If there wasn't, they could all push their red buttons right now and go home . . . assuming there was still a home left to go to.

And if there wasn't? What if the other three teams had failed and were counting on them? How could they know when they'd won . . . or lost . . . given the confusing nature of time?

His brain hurt. Come to that, Spider-Man reflected, everything else hurt too. In the space of the last subjective week he'd been catapulted back in time to 1867, fought a robot wagon train, spent a brutal sabbatical in an alternate 1998 that wasn't there anymore, watched his counterpart in that timeline die, taken a side trip into *Blade Runner: The Next Generation*, met Iron Man's evil twin and a young lady he had a sinking suspicion he knew, had a subway tunnel dropped on his head, and now found out that he'd done it all for nothing. Every muscle hurt, and as for his mind, he though it had gone numb a few decades back, right around the time his sense of wonder broke.

What did they do now? And where did they do it?

"Let me see." Cable shouldered through the others and approached the Time Platform, as warily as if it might lash out at him. He dropped to his knees in front of it, like a man entering a shrine of his faith.

"How long do we have before Iron Man and Spider-Girl find us again?" Aliya asked practically, swinging her rifle down into an attack position and backing up in Cable's direction. Once again Spider-Man was reminded of how close Cable and Aliya were—like two halves of one superb machine.

How did you go on living your life after half of you

had been ripped away? And what did you do when you thought you might get your missing half back? Spider-Man thought back to a young woman he'd loved very much thrown off the Brooklyn Bridge by a man in a goblin costume, and tried to delude himself into thinking he knew the answer.

"Minutes," Hassle said, looking at a chronometer the size of a bagel that she wore on her wrist.

"Then it's time for you to go," Cable said, without looking at them. He crawled forward, until he was kneeling on the Time Platform, crouching as he looked into its innards. His silver hair gleamed in the dim light of the station, and, with his metallic arm, he looked as if he were almost a part of the Time Platform himself.

"The Time Platform is disabled, but perhaps it is not completely useless," Cable said meditatively. "I may be able to find the coordinates from which it was sent, if there's enough time before we have to disengage. But you need to leave now. We have the means to escape our enemies through time, and you don't."

The Wreckers looked unimpressed.

"Yeah. Escape. Look how well your escape plan worked the last time," Hassle said mockingly.

She's got a point, Spider-Man thought. If the three of them were buried alive again, if they lost their recall units or they were damaged, if Kang had already won . . .

That's why you get the big bucks, web-head, Spider-Man told himself. *For taking on the most hopeless causes in sight, armed with nothing but a couple of web-shooters and a line of snappy patter.*

"This is our fight—not yours," Cable said, this time turning to look at them. "Leave now while you still have the time." His bionic eye glowed in the dimness, giving him a baleful piebald aspect.

For a moment Spider-Man thought that Aliya would object to losing their allies. He'd known her long enough to realize that she was a cold-blooded pragmatist who would sacrifice anything to achieve a worthy end. She'd already spent herself—years of her life, all that she had—to achieve Magneto's Power Liberation Front goals, only to see her entire reality wiped out seconds later by Kang's mad whim.

That had to have some kind of effect on a person.

But Aliya stood in the dim amber glow of the Midnight Wreckers' work lights looking as if she'd been carved from purest alabaster; a battle-goddess crafted of harsh necessity, pure and merciless. She said nothing. She didn't even look at Cable.

Time to get out of here, web-head. Whatever there is in this air, you've definitely been breathing it too long.

"Yes," Aliya said reluctantly, when the tense silence had stretched to breaking point. "Cable's right. This isn't your fight, Wreckers. You'd better go."

"You can't win," Machine Man told the time travellers earnestly. "Iron Man has all the vast resources of Stark-Fujikawa behind him. I won't leave you to defy him alone. Hassle, Slick, Swift, Brain—you go. I'll stay here until Cable's mission is complete, and meet you back at Sanctuary."

"No!" several different voices chorused at once.

Spider-Man glanced at the four Wreckers, each of whom looked horrified in his own particular way at the thought of leaving Machine Man to face Iron Man and his hordes without them. Aliya's mouth quirked in an expression of grim humor.

"Look, MM, it isn't that we don't think it's a great idea—" Brain began earnestly.

It's just that we don't, Spider-Man supplied silently.

"It's just that it wouldn't be fair for you to have all the fun," Swift added.

"And we've already seen some of what they're throwing against them. I wouldn't be surprised if he had a C-28

Death-Dealer with him. Fun's fun, buddy, but this just doesn't scan,'' Slick said.

"If Machine Man stays, then so do I," Hassle said. "Wreckers don't run out on each other."

"News to me," muttered Slick.

"Go on," Spider-Man urged his old friend. "Go with them. They're right, chrome-dome. This isn't anything to do with you." *At least, it isn't if we stop Kang.*

"They're coming," Swift said. She sounded excited by the thought of the fight, gazing eagerly back the way they'd come.

"I won't leave you to face him yourselves," Machine Man said stubbornly.

"Look at it this way," Spider-Man said. "If you leave now, you can go on annoying ShellHead and his little iron buddies for years to come. Just think of yourself as the gift that keeps on giving."

A reluctant smile tugged at the corner of Machine Man's face. "You're as recklessly brave as ever, old friend."

Spider-Man smiled, though he knew it couldn't be seen beneath his mask. He raised his hand and waggled his fingers in a good-bye wave. "Here's your hat, what's your hurry? Don't forget to write, MM."

"Farewell, then, Spider-Man," Machine Man said gravely.

"Come *on*, if we're going," Hassle snapped. She gestured with her Webley-Vickers in the direction of the exit.

"Gotta go," Swift said, favoring Spider-Man and Aliya with a last sweet smile.

And the Midnight Wreckers melted into the shadows as silently as they'd come. Only the work lights they'd left behind gave any evidence that they'd ever been there, but Spider-Man's spider-sense was already tingling. The

Wreckers had been right: the intermission was over, and the second half was just about to start.

"Cable?" Aliya said, staring into the gloom as if she could make Iron Man appear through sheer will alone.

"I need more time," came the emotionless reply.

"And we need more fighting room," Spider-Man said. "C'mon, Aliya. If Cabe needs more time, we can hold them better at the mouth of the tunnel."

Aliya shot him a glance of surprised approval. "Come on, then." She smiled: an expression that Spider-Man actually found rather chilling. "We'll go out to meet them."

Her name was May Parker, and once upon a time she'd thought she'd known what she was doing. Her father had been a super hero, and a famous one. Only a few years after his death he was turning into a legend, and some people whispered that he hadn't died at all.

She could tell them the truth. She'd been at his funeral—most of the people there hadn't known it was him, or, rather, hadn't known that the Peter Parker they mourned was also the amazing Spider-Man. The chaste marker over his grave told the world nothing save the dates of his birth and death. His true identity had been a secret until the end, as hers still was. Would Iron Man have been so careful of her sensibilities if he'd known she was a twentysomething page designer for Cadence Communications Corporation who still lived at home with her mother because of the housing crunch? Spider-Girl didn't think so. But he wasn't talking to May Parker. He was talking to Spider-Girl.

She couldn't remember a time when she hadn't known that her dad was Spider-Man. Mom had been so freaked out the first time she'd announced her decision—in her freshman year at high school—to go into the "family business," but May Parker had always known that she'd grow up to wear the webbed mask and the famous blue and scarlet garb. Mutated as a young man, her father's DNA had been irrevocably changed by the bite of the radioactive spider, so that his daughter, through genetic transference, had inherited the powers he'd gained. Her buccaneering career had been something that was meant to be.

But though Spider-Girl had known from her father's stories how hard the life of a masked adventurer would be, he hadn't been able to tell her how hard the choices she would have to make would seem when she reached the point where she had to make them. The world was a smaller, darker place than when Dad had been a boy. The choices weren't as clear anymore.

Take Iron Man, the legendary mercenary. Normally she'd have steered clear of him completely, but when he'd come to her with this tale about terrorists she'd had no hesitation allying herself with him in order to make sure that the best interests of the people she'd sworn to protect were served. She skittered along the wall beside the gleaming golden hulk, keeping a close eye on Iron Man as he strode purposefully along. Only, she hadn't known that one of the terrorists was impersonating her father. And she wasn't giving Iron Man a second chance to bury these terrorists under a rockslide before she'd had a chance to have a chat with one of them in particular.

Arno Stark wasn't happy. At noon today this had been a simple job: smash some Wreckers, collect the bounty. The tamper-proof signal in his gun cameras would provide more than enough evidence of their deaths for the Product Standardization Council. And it would be a better way to blow off steam than a few boring sets of handball at his skytop health club.

The only trouble was, the Wreckers hadn't cooperated by dying. He'd dropped an entire subway tunnel on them and according to his tracking devices, they were still up and moving.

And if they were the type to be able to climb out from under half the infra-structure of New Queens, they might be worth more to him alive than dead. There was a new company just listed on the NASDAQ. Something called Alchemax. And it proposed to take a very aggressive stance on what had so far been black-market bioshop technology. He wondered if Alchemax would like some experimental subjects. . . .

Sternly Iron Man forced his mind away from future profit. Only four of his Iron-Bots remained with him. He'd sent the rest of them home once the evening's entertainment started to get interesting. These four—Heyer, Austen, Brontë, and Wharton—should be more than enough to bring three Wreckers under control, no matter how well they were armed. And he could trust them to be discreet afterward.

Spider-Girl, on the other hand, showed a certain disturbing streak of idealism.

He thought she just might have to go.

"We've got them, sir," Austen said.

"Then what are we waiting for, gentlemen?" Arno Stark said. "Let's frag some Wreckers!"

"The first rule of war is to take the battle to the enemy," Aliya said.

"Just like Butch and Sundance," Spider-Man said. Aliya shot him a baffled uncomprehending look before moving out.

They reached the mouth of the tunnel and just as Spider-Man had thought, it was a good place for a last stand. Beyond it, the room opened out into another segment of subway platform, with white tile walls and yellow-striped concrete floor. *Cable should be able to work*

*undisturbed while the two of us hold off Iron Man,
Spider-Girl, and a horde of spear-carriers.*

Yeah, right.

Now all they had to do was wait.

He wished Cable would hurry.

Aliya was utterly still; he couldn't even hear her
breathing. As he strained his ears, the first thing Spider-
Man heard was the thin whine of bootjets echoing in the
confined space. Iron Man—or this twisted future version
of him, anyway—was on his way.

Either this Iron Man wasn't used to enemies who
fought back or he was just plain overconfident. He came
zipping down the tracks so fast that Spider-Man nearly
missed him. There was just enough time for Spider-Man
to tag the hurtling armored body with a web-line and then
reel him in with the proportionate strength of a spider.
Iron Man made an unscheduled right turn into the wall
with a sound like the impact of the Hulk's fist.

Aliya began shooting before the echoes had stopped.

"Tense? Irritable? Don't take it out on your children,"
Spider-Man cooed to the fallen titan. "S'matter, Chuck-
les; cat got your tongue? Upsy-daisy, fella—it's time to
rock 'n' roll!"

Iron Man reared back and took a clumsy roundhouse
swipe at the taunting figure.

"Aw, c'mon, IM, this isn't what I'd expect from a
thug of your calibre. Copyright infringement's a serious
thing, you know: what if the *real* Iron Man found out
what you're doing?" Spider-Man hardly paid attention
to his own words. The whole point of the snappy patter
was to drive the other guy crazy and distract yourself
from the utter imbecility of taking on somebody who
could probably use you for toothpaste.

And it was amazing how often it worked.

"*I am Iron Man!*" Stark roared, running the suit's
speakers full blast as he grabbed for Spider-Man.

The wall-crawler nimbly skipped back and forth, out of range; Road Runner to IM's Wile E. Coyote. The Xerox copy didn't seem to have brought as many reinforcements with him this time: Spider-Man didn't hear nearly enough gunfire for that.

He hoped Aliya was having as much fun as he was.

They couldn't possibly win—that was, if you defined winning as neutralizing every member of the enemy forces once and for all. Fortunately, Aliya mused to herself, they didn't have to do that. All they had to do was hold Iron Man and his allies here long enough for Cable to strip what information he could from the already vandalized Time Platform. Then they could retreat. And then she and Nathan could be together, and his death would only be a bad dream, a false start that would fade beneath the reality of the many years they would have together.

These thoughts only took up a small part of her mind, however. The majority of it was occupied with doing what Aliya had been trained to do, and doing it superbly well.

A red-and-blue figure advanced up the tunnel in bounding leaps; Aliya bracketed it with a short burst of rifle fire. Aliya would have shot it dead center if she could—the flaunting red hair was a giveaway that this wasn't Spider-Man, just another of the multitudinous reflections of the Park that the timestream seemed to have cast up—but not even Aliya was fast enough for that.

The spider-girl landed on Aliya feetfirst, driving her out of cover. Aliya got the rifle up in time to block the first punch but not the second. The dimly lit chamber dissolved for a moment into bright stars.

''Spider-Girl!''

The distortingly overamplified voice yammered off the walls of the room.

"Leave the woman to me! Get him! *Get him!*" Iron Man shouted.

Spider-Girl hesitated, and the hesitation was enough to give Aliya her chance. She swept her legs out, toppling the other woman, and then swept the air blindly with plasma-blasts. That bought her the instant she needed to clear her head, to see that Spider-Girl had abandoned her to focus on Spider-Man.

Fine.

All she and Spider-Man had to do was hold Spider-Girl and Iron Man here. That was all.

CHAPTER TWELVE

C able shut his mind to the sounds of battle that echoed through the underground complex. He had no illusions that the enemies Spider-Man and Aliya faced would show them any mercy at all. The Iron Man of this time was out to kill, much as the minions of Apocalypse in his own time had been.

His own time. Could he say with any certainty when that really was? If he had been left to grow to adulthood from the year of his birth without any intervening time travel, he'd be in his thirties in 2020. Somewhere—some *when*—there was undoubtedly a Nathan Summers for which this was true. Maybe even a Nathan Summers who wasn't a mutant.

Cable regarded the thought with a dour mix of amusement and distaste. The concept was so alien to his entire experience that he'd never even wished for it. At first his life had been a struggle just to survive upon a dying Earth. Later, he'd been driven by a need to act out against a society that appalled him even before he had words and concepts to describe his feelings. At last he had become a warrior, and in doing so had found the only measure of peace he was likely ever to know because, to a warrior, all battlefields were endlessly, inevitably alike.

Carefully, he levered the case off of the Tempometric Meter to expose what was left of the inner works. His next task would be a delicate piece of work, if it could even be accomplished at all.

Fortunately the Time Platform really did seem to rely on basic technology very close to that of Cable's own time—which meant that Kang's Time Platform would incorporate a hologramatic redundancy principle in its power and navigation chips.

The chips themselves were gone, along with anything else that had looked to the scavengers of this period as though it had possessed value. This Time Platform would never work again. But that didn't matter, so long as the interface was still here.

With infinite care, Cable pried the small ceramic wafer loose from the housing. It had only looked like a bit of insulation to the looters, and so they'd left it behind. But like a computer disk, it contained a copy of all the information that had passed through it—and one of those bits of information was the instruction on how to reach this location in the multiverse.

Once he'd read it—if he could read it—all he needed to do would be to reverse its information, and the X-Men would have the coordinates to Kang's base of operations.

The underground complex shook. Cable froze until the vibrations had subsided, then resumed his painstakingly delicate task.

He tried not to think about what Aliya and Spider-Man were facing.

The real Iron Man—Spider-Man couldn't stop thinking of the man he faced as some sort of impostor—would probably never have fallen for it, but overconfidence seemed to be this guy's middle name.

Or maybe he just got a secret thrill knowing that the enemy was gazing right into his baby browns just as he finished them off. And the trick had worked earlier to-day—*earlier today?*—with the evil alternate-world version of the Beast. At any rate, a faceful of webbing squirted right through the open eye-slits had been enough to discourage him, at least temporarily.

However, now Spider-Man had other problems.

Over the years, a number of people had told him how unnerving the featureless, expressionless, full face mask he wore was, how it made him resemble a faceless, in-sectile automaton. He had a live update for them: it was much more unnerving when you could see your opponent's features twisted with hate.

Hate she was directing at you.

"I'm not the enemy!" he shouted at the woman who'd just taken several tiles off the wall with a venom blast and was looking forward to doing the same to him.

"Liar! *Thief!*" she cried.

Spider-Girl came with more firepower than the original model; he felt bits of rock spray against his face as another of her venom blasts hit the wall beside his head. She was coming after him with everything she had, not even giving him a moment's breathing space to web up Iron Man and buy Aliya—and Cable—a little time.

Almost automatically he led Spider-Girl away from the Iron-Bots and Aliya—*divide and conquer; sometimes a great notion*—and as he did, he realized how uncannily similar their fighting styles were. As if someone he knew—

—someone he *was*—

—had taught Spider-Girl everything she knew.

No. Forget it. It's too corny.

He knew who she was—secretly, he'd known from the moment he'd first seen her—and he knew what he had to do. *First Richard and Mary. Now her*. He didn't want to do it. It went against everything he was. But the stakes were too high. He and his opponent were too equally matched.

He had no choice.

"I surrender," Spider-Man said, dropping to the ground.

"Surrender? You wish!" Spider-Girl spat.

She crouched on the wall above him, drawing back her fist to deliver a venom blast that he had no doubt was intended to be lethal.

"May Parker!" Spider-Man said quickly. "Your name's May Parker—your mother's name is Mary Jane

Watson-Parker. You were named May for your father's aunt.'' He hesitated. She'd stopped.

"No one knows that,'' she said coldly. "And in another minute, you won't either.''

"Wait!'' Spider-Man said. Gritting his teeth, he reached up and yanked off his mask.

It felt like all those bad dreams where you found yourself walking naked down Broadway. His heartbeat was still racing—his body knew it was in the middle of battle—but here he was standing with his mask off, his greatest secret available for the taking.

"There's no need for us to fight,'' he said quickly. "I'm—I'm Peter Parker. But I'm not your father; I'm from a parallel past. No matter what you've been told or who you've been told it by, there's no need for us to fight. All we want to do is take our toys and go home, May. I swear it. Nobody needs to get hurt—''

But she wasn't listening to him.

"Daddy?'' Spider-Girl said. "You're alive?'' The hope in her voice nearly broke his heart.

She dropped from the wall and advanced on him, muscles still tense with menace.

"I'm from the past,'' Spider-Man repeated carefully. "A past that runs parallel to yours.'' *But it might be the same one. Couldn't it be? This could be my daughter, all grown up. . . .*

She was close enough to touch, gazing intently at him in the dim light. He couldn't see her eyes, but she had MJ's jaw, and the same stubborn set to it. He saw it harden, the harsh lines around it deepening, as she made up her mind.

"Sorry, 'bot. No prize,'' she said, raising her venom blast.

A long moment passed.

Spider-Girl sighed, dropping her hand. "You're so

young,'' she said plaintively. *I can't do it*, her voice and body language told him.

"Sorry," Spider-Man said. He shrugged. "Do you mind if I put the mask back on?"

She gestured assent. "If you aren't—" she began, her voice harsh and husky with suppressed emotion. "How did you know who I was?"

"I'm married to . . . your mother," Spider-Man said awkwardly. "We're planning to name our first child after Aunt May." *Someday. And she'll inherit my powers—is that something I really want to know? MJ and I have wondered about that, but . . .*

"Kind of tough on him if he's a boy," Spider-Girl said, with a ghost of his own bravado. "Okay. Dad said this kind of thing happened sometimes."

She used the past tense. So I'm already dead, here. No wonder she was so furious when she saw me.

"Why are you helping them?" Spider-Girl asked. "They're terrorists—Wreckers—Iron Man showed me the EuroS.H.I.E.L.D. file on them."

"And that was good enough?" Spider-Man shot back. "You need to find out the truth for yourself before you fight. With great power comes great responsibility. A great man once told me that."

"Uncle Ben," Spider-Girl said, hanging her head in shame.

"We're from the past—all three of us," Spider-Man said quickly, wishing there were some way he could make this easier for her. "And all we want to do is go back there, once we've got what we've come for."

"And that is?" Spider-Girl asked, glaring at him again.

"Just some information. Then all three of us will disappear, and you'll never see us again." *And I'll never know what happens to you. Whether Kang succeeds in snuffing out this timeline along with all the others, or—*

"All right," Spider-Girl said, coming to a decision. "Go on. Go." She stepped back, waving him away.

It was all in the timing, Aliya told herself. Every battle had a rhythm, and so did every opponent. And what she had was an ion cannon.

It was a fairly common weapon where she and Cable had come from: a microminiaturized nuclear reactor capable of delivering ionized pulse energy in forms from a diamond-cutter beam to a street-sweeper blast. A side-effect of the weapon was the high-frequency harmonics and EMP waste that effectively scrambled an opponent's technology. In short, the ion cannon was a weapon made for its own time and enemies.

But it worked pretty well wherever she went, actually.

Spider-Man had blinded the armored berserker before the tide of battle had swept him from her sight, but the impediment hadn't lasted long. Its residual effect kept the armored avenger from firing any of his beam weapons—probably he couldn't see the heads-up displays inside his armor.

Her good luck.

And the respite had lasted just long enough for Aliya to reconfigure her weapon to a setting Cable had once called *leave no evidence*: as piercing as the armor-cutter setting, with as much raw power as the street-sweeper adjustment. Once it had powered up, the ion cannon would deliver one blast that should be powerful enough to punch a hole from here to the sun through anything in its path.

All it needed was the time to charge. She just hoped Iron Man was going to give it to her.

Aliya flung herself out of the way of a gleaming armored fist. She didn't have the resources to trade punches with Iron Man or to take even one hit. The moment her acrobatics failed her was the moment she died. She dropped to the ground and rolled, and as she did, a high *ping!* from her weapon told her it was fully charged.

Aliya whipped onto her back and fired, closing her eyes tightly as she pulled the trigger. There was a thunderclap of sound so loud it could not be dissected into its component parts.

Aliya released her weapon the moment it discharged, but in that instant it had already become hot enough to raise blisters on her hands. She hoped it still worked. Even through her closed eyelids she could see a galaxy of colored lights.

She sat up.

Iron Man was embedded like a frog in a thickly-iced birthday cake in the remains of the wall that had been behind him. Everything that could be melted down or blown loose from the front of his armor had been. The cherry-red enamel and the gold heat-diffusion coating had both melted away—along with the top several microns of the armored surface—and were now a wide corona of black vapor on the tiled wall around him. His force field must have survived long enough for it to protect him because, frankly, she hadn't expected him to still be there at all.

His armor made faint pinging sounds as it cooled.

Aliya swung the rifle to cover the four Iron Bots. She didn't have another charge available and might even have melted her gun, but they didn't have to know that. She smiled at them.

Slowly, all four of them got to their feet, stepped out of cover, and raised their hands.

Against the wall, the unconscious form of Iron Man sagged, beginning to pull slowly loose from the crater he had made, like pennies slowly being pulled free of hot tar on a sunny day. There was a crash like a falling piano as he fell facefirst onto the floor.

Cable stepped out of the corridor. His expression

didn't tell Aliya whether they'd won or lost.

"We're ready to go," he said.

He flipped open the cover on the TDR that he wore, and then he smiled. "We have everything that we need to take the war to the enemy."

Spider-Man moved to stand between Aliya and Cable, flipping open the safety cover on his TDR as he did so. A sense of relief filled him. At last they were going home—it might be to the biggest fight of all, but at least it was away from these haunting vistas of what might have been . . . or yet could be. "I feel like the Ghost of Christmas Present," he muttered to himself.

"Let's go," Cable said.

"Well, what are you waiting for? Pick him up and let's go."

Spider-Girl walked past the three time travellers as though none of them existed and stood in front of the four surviving Iron-Bots. She pointed at Iron Man's insensible body. "You're on my turf just now, 'bots, remember? So let's go."

And though their total firepower probably exceeded hers, the Iron-Bots moved to obey her; slowly at first, and then faster as they realized that compliance would take them safely away from the smiling madwoman holding the gun that had so thoroughly felled their employer.

In a few moments they had lifted the unconscious armored body, much in the manner of pallbearers carrying a coffin.

"Go on," Spider-Girl said encouragingly.

"Wait!" Spider-Man called after the retreating figure of Spider-Girl. She stopped, looking back at him, her face expressionless. "Just tell me one thing," Spider-Man called after her. She stopped. "Why Spider-*Girl?*"

Amazingly, the question made the tall redhead laugh. "I started doing this when I was fourteen, 'bot. It would

have been pretty stupid to call myself Spider-Woman before I was old enough to drive. I just never got around
to changing it." She waved—almost jauntily—and
turned again to follow the retreating Iron-Bots.

"And now," Cable said, "it's payback time, people.
Activate."

"It's time? You're really going to do it? Finally? You're
not just toying with my foolish heart, are you, Kang
dear?" Lireeb said.

"Silence, fool," Kang snapped. He hesitated over the
main control panel of his Time Displacement Core like
a gourmand selecting a particular delicacy from an opu-
lent box of chocolates. "With one stroke I shall detonate
the pods that store the energy that the X-Men have so
kindly provided to my Time Arrows. Thereafter, an explosion will discharge, causing the crucial timequake."

Lireeb waited expectantly as Kang pressed the button.
Nothing happened, though neither being had really expected to see immediate results.

"And now," Kang said grandly, "Kang the Conqueror goes to greet his happy bride. Have you made the
security arrangements for Limbo while I am gone?"

"Oh, well, Limbo doesn't need that much. . . ." Lireeb
began obsequiously. Then, seeing the expression on his
master's face, Lireeb decided that discretion was perhaps
the better part of humor. "Yes, of course. A little surprise
plucked from the annals of your own adventures in the
Age of Heroes, guaranteed to stop any interloper. If it's
worked on gods, why meddle, say I."

"And so you should, hapless wight," Kang responded
sulkily. He seemed to feel that the moment called for
something more than it was providing, but after an instant, he shrugged and turned to walk toward the teleport
chamber.

"Don't touch anything while I'm gone," Kang com-manded, positioning himself on the teleport plate.

Lireeb bowed. Kang vanished.

Lireeb straightened, stretching as if his back hurt, and heaved a deep and grateful sigh.

"Well, thank Limbo *that's* over with. Now, providing those scatterbrained mutants do their part, all should be well. Finally."

"Why do all these secret super-villain sanctuaries look alike?" Spider-Man asked.

Reality filled itself in around him and Cable. The two of them stood inside something that looked like the Euro-Disney version of a haunted castle. If it had a name, only Dr. Strange knew it. All Spider-Man knew was that he was farther from home and on weirder ground than he'd ever been in all his young career, and it gave him the creeps.

Aliya was not with them. Their recall devices had taken the three of them back to Blaquesmith's lab in Rosendale, but they'd stopped there only long enough for Cable to leave a copy of the coordinates gleaned from the Time Platform behind with Aliya, and then he and Spider-Man had followed those same coordinates here, while Aliya gathered their reinforcements.

They hoped. Spider-Man and Cable had come on ahead to keep Kang too busy to interfere—or to destroy their home timeline—but at the moment it looked as if they'd wasted their time. The castle seemed deserted.

"What, no welcoming committee?" Spider-Man wisecracked. From all he knew about Kang, he'd have shown up in a New York minute to gloat over their helplessness and throw a couple of squads of androids at them.

"Don't borrow trouble," Cable rumbled. He swept the Tempometric Meter around himself in a wide arc: he'd recalibrated it back in Rosendale, but Spider-Man hadn't yet had time to ask for what.

"Why should I? You get so much of it free."

Spider-Man took a cautious step away from his arrival point . . . and sprang instinctively to the wall as his spider-sense jangled at the same time something came moving toward them down the curving corridor.

It was about the size of a large rat—a large *green* rat—but a moment later, Spider-Man saw that it was actually a tiny mechanical doll.

"Intruders: halt in the name of the Master!" it piped in a high fluting voice.

Cable swung his rifle down.

"Don't shoot!" Spider-Man yelped, but it was too late.

The blast batted the thing back out of the way, but the form that Cable had fired at was gone in the first instant of impact. What slid back down the corridor was already the size of a child . . . and there was another one following it.

"Intruders: halt in the name of the Master!" the two homunculi chorused an octave apart.

"I feel stupid running away from a couple of Cabbage Patch Dolls," Spider-Man complained. He spread a net of webbing to tangle them in, but the Terrible Twins simply forged through it as though it were cotton candy. *I gotta whip up a better batch of this before Ralph Nader comes after me for having defective webbing.*

"Running," Cable suggested, "might be a good idea right now. Those creatures seem to take any force directed against them and use it to increase their size—and they're already big enough to cause trouble."

He turned, jogging in a businesslike fashion away from the deadly dolls. Spider-Man took one glance behind him and followed along the wall.

"Halt!" squeaked the two green androids.

"Now, this just isn't *fair*," Spider-Man complained a moment later.

The curving corridor that he and Cable had first found themselves in ended at a staircase that led downward, and standing at its edge were two more of the tiny doll-like creatures. The first two—one child sized, one the size of the new pair—had almost reached Cable; in the moment that he hesitated the child-sized creature and its partner flung themselves on Cable with thin, high-pitched war-cries.

He flung them off easily, of course. And the blow he struck added several inches to their heights. Of course.

"I can see where this is going and I don't like it," Spider-Man grumbled from his vantage point on the wall. He webbed the two tiny homunculi at the head of the stairs into one large sticky cocoon, and then swung it— by the still-attached web-line—high against the wall. The impact made them grow, and in a few moments they would have freed themselves, but for now the stairs were clear.

"Cable—come on!" he shouted, bounding forward.

The two supermarionettes that had attacked Cable were already the size of grown men . . . and Spider-Man had the sinking feeling that it wasn't going to stop there. Cable thrust them away once more and ran for the stairs.

I'd be really worried if we didn't have reinforcements coming, Spider-Man thought as he bounded after the mutant time warrior. A sudden horrible thought made him hesitate. *You jerk. What if they're already here?*

The Growing Men flung themselves after the fleeing heroes, shouting in chorus: "Intruders: halt in the name of the Master!" They were highly sophisticated android mechanisms, created by Kang himself to provide elementary policing wherever the master of time might require it, and they were capable of a nearly sentient range of verbal response.

On the other hand, the last person who'd had access

to their programming was the albino Lireeb, who'd felt that the endless repetition of that single statement might be nearly as effective a weapon as the Stimuloids' brute physical strength.

The four Stimuloids bounced down the curving staircase like a cascade of rubber balls, each impact making them larger. Now the two largest were nearly eight feet tall, and the two smaller fully half their size.

"Rats," Spider-Man observed succinctly.

The stairs opened into a hall the size of the flight deck of an aircraft carrier. There were three archways at the opposite end, about half a mile away. Other than those three, there was no exit from the vaulting chamber. It was empty of furniture; he wondered what Kang used it for, then dismissed the question to think about some other time. Of more concern to him than the decor was the fact that the ceiling was a mass of spindly spiky things. He could hang from a web-line anchored between them, but he couldn't run across it. Reluctantly, Spider-Man dropped from the wall to the floor.

Cable raised his weapon and pointed it back up the stairs, and then lowered it again. Spider-Man could almost guess what he was thinking: while he might be able to bring the roof down and bury the Growing Men, he might bury the two of them as well. And the memory of their last entombment was too fresh for either Cable or Spider-Man to want to risk something like that except as an absolute last-ditch measure.

So they ran.

Unfortunately, the Growing Men ran faster.

His spider-sense gave him a scant second's warning; enough for Spider-Man to be able to spring aside as one of the homunculi jumped at him from behind. It was one of the smaller ones, but even as it hit the ground, the force of the impact made it larger. He supposed the force of a punch would be even worse.

Stopping to think had been a mistake. Another of the Growing Men flung itself onto his shoulders and closed its fingers around his throat. As Spider-Man struggled to free himself, he could see Cable duking it out with the two giant economy-size models. Cable's ion gun lay on the ground, abandoned, and one eye blazed with more than human fire.

But Spider-Man had problems of his own.

"Intruders: halt in the name of the Master!" all four Growing men chanted in harmony.

So he did. Spider-Man went completely limp in his shorter-but-stronger opponent's grasp, falling to the floor with the Growing Man still perched on his back like an unholy incubus. And as he'd hoped, it let go.

He knew it was for only a brief instant, that the Growing Man had released him only in order to get a better grip, but the tiny respite was enough to allow Spider-Man to spring from its grasp, and leap to the wall high above its head.

Now. A little elementary engineering, maestro. . . .

"Cable! Catch!"

The web-line he had fired struck Cable on the shoulder, but the time warrior managed to free his hand and grasp it. Against the increasing might of his attackers, the brawny figure of the timeswept mutant appeared almost childlike now, but Cable was still substantial enough to make Spider-Man grunt with effort as he hauled back on the other end of his web-line.

Spider-Man was only twenty feet up a wall that ran for at least forty more, but the length of mutable adhesive cord in his hand fed through another loop glued firmly to the ceiling. It acted as a pulley—when he hauled back, Cable was pulled upward until he swung free of the floor . . . and his attackers. They jumped up and down beneath him, raging impotently.

"What do you suggest we do now?" Cable asked calmly. "I could blast them, but they'd grow. That would just bring me within reach." Though Cable's rifle lay below him on the floor, Spider-Man had no doubt that Cable was still multiply armed.

Down below the Growing Men, cheated of their prey, had begun hammering the wall upon which Spider-Man perched, hoping to jar him loose. He only hoped they wouldn't think of forming a human pyramid to reach him.

"Intruders: halt in the name of the Master!" the Stimuloids carolled as they rhythmically battered at the wall.

Spider-Man shook his head to clear it. "We've got to get out of here without hitting any of them." *And without getting hit by them either. Why is it always me who ends up facing homicidal androids from the future?*

"And you suggest?" Cable demanded.

"Start swinging."

Spider-Man's muscles strained. His whole being was concentrated on holding on to the strand of webbing and his place on the wall while Cable swung back and forth at the other end of the web. He just hoped the Brand-X web-line wouldn't dissolve until he was through with it.

The Growing Men had quickly figured out what Cable was up to: using his own momentum to swing out of their reach to freedom. They'd stopped battering the wall and had taken up posts beside both the stairs and the other three exits from the room.

But there were only four of them, and some of them had to be wrong.

In fact, they all were.

• • •

As soon as they'd spread out around the walls, Cable judged his moment. He reached the lowest point in his swing—directly beneath his original position—and let go of the web-line. As Spider-Man skittered away along the wall with a disturbingly insectile motion, Cable lunged for the dropped ion cannon.

He'd had an idea.

In the few seconds he had before they reached him, Cable trained his weapon on the Growing Man that was guarding the center exit and hit it with everything he had.

"Uh, Cabe?" he heard Spider-Man say.

It doubled in size, then doubled again. And again. It crouched beneath the ceiling, looking like an illustration out of the Tenniel *Alice*.

Cable nodded with grim satisfaction, and began to run toward it.

It was a simple strategy. If there was a condition the enemy could not control, exploit it. These things grew when they were hit, and so far Cable had noticed no upper limit to their growth.

Fine. Increase its size until its size trapped it.

The Growing Man began to realize its plight. It flexed its muscles, attempting to stand. A tracery of cracks appeared in the ceiling, but apparently there was enough masonry above it to slow even something with its superhuman strength. It groped toward Cable with clumsy fingers the size of Greyhound buses, its awkward motions making it chillingly reminiscent of the mutant-hunting Sentinels.

Cable didn't know if the things could reverse their growth, and he didn't intend to wait around to find out. There was a flash of blue and scarlet as Spider-Man cleared the gap between the Growing Man's enormous elbow and the doorway. Cable reached the same place a moment later, vaulting through the gap and folding in midair to fire behind him at the Growing Man's enormous verdant thigh.

There was a faint wail of frustration from the creature as its size doubled again.

"Come on," Cable said. He consulted the Tempometric Meter and gestured. "This way."

"What are we looking for, by the way?" Spider-Man asked a few minutes later. *Other than trouble, and that we've found.*

"Those," Cable said, and pointed.

The building shook as the gigantic Growing Man they'd left trapped behind them struggled to free itself. They'd been on the run for the last five minutes, slowing only long enough to put obstacles in the path of their pursuers: sealed doors, furniture barricades, anything that would buy them some time. They'd passed through Kang's black museum, where the furnaces of Auschwitz roared eternally and the *Titanic* slid beneath the icy North Atlantic sea; where machine-gun fire echoed through Belleau Wood and the *Challenger* made a bright second dawn in the sky.

Neither Spider-Man nor Cable had seen anyone else as they fled through the castle, and if Kang were here, he ought to have shown up by now. Although—if this was Limbo—how much did time matter here?

Never mind.

Their last turn had taken them into an enormous Command Ops chamber, and the tingling of his spider-sense warned Spider-Man that they'd nearly used up their lead. He and Cable were going to have to make a last stand soon. He wasn't sure they could pull off any of their previous tricks again, and neither of them was in a class to take on multiple Terminators in a slugfest.

But Cable seemed to think this was nearly as important as surviving, so Spider-Man glanced around.

The Command Ops center was something that would make Tom Clancy turn green with envy. The huge chamber held every sort of display, readout, and meter.

It also held the four Energy Pods that Kang had sent the Time Arrows into the past to fuel.

They looked a little like chrome-purple torpedoes, and for some reason, though he'd never seen them before, Spider-Man had no doubt of what they were. Thick cables snaked away from each to the machines along the wall, possibly to funnel their energy out of Limbo and across the multiverse. The gauge on each was prominently displayed, with a bright green needle sliding upward through a brilliant fuchsia bar graph as bright blue dots rippled beneath.

"They've almost reached critical mass," Cable said quietly. "When they do, they'll explode."

And when the Time Bombs exploded, everything Spider-Man or any of them had ever known would cease to be—not only their own timelines and every dear familiar face in them (and at the moment, Spider-Man was even willing to consider Venom a dear familiar face), but every parallel time line that might at least contain some familiar referent.

"We've got to disarm them," Spider-Man said.

The building shuddered again, and a black webbing of cracks appeared in the floor with the suddenness of a lightning bolt. If Kang had left these guys here to watch the place while he was gone, he wasn't going to be very happy when he got back.

But if Kang wasn't here, where was he?

"I don't think we have enough time," Cable answered slowly.

CHAPTER THIRTEEN

The caravan brought the Beast, Storm, Gambit, and Kang's generator to the palace that dominated the city's central plaza. At any other time, the view would have been worth the trip. Everything they passed seemed to have been created by intellects that held beauty to be as important as usefulness and did not feel that color was for wimps. The buildings, the floating walkways, the landscaping that filled every curve and corner of the dreaming city, all seemed to have been hatched whole from some beautiful Winsor McCay future in which Nature and Technology at last walked hand-in-hand.

It was too bad that none of the three X-Men was in the mood to appreciate this once-in-a-lifetime opportunity to see the future that resulted when all the right choices were made. Even shackled, they could have escaped a thousand times. Both Storm and Gambit had long years of experience picking locks. But where would they escape to? If they didn't confront—and stop—Kang the Conqueror, no victory was possible.

The convoy took them to the tallest building in the city. Outside its gleaming emerald walls, the X-Men had been forced at gunpoint to exchange their shackles for heavier bonds attached to chains as thick as the Beast's arm. Each set of these chains were attached to a long floating crossbar that hung in the air. A control box held by the captain of the guard adjusted each crossbar to a height that left its prisoner dangling uncomfortably on his or her tiptoes, enveloped in a stasis field that did not allow any of them to move even a muscle. When they were safely secured, the captain entered the building with them—and the generator that had come with them—in tow.

From there they had been wheeled into the Throne

Room itself, to wait in the corner as the captain first conferred with the court chamberlain, then approached the throne itself. After a moment he beckoned, and the three X-Men were wheeled forward, stopping at the foot of the Throne.

The throne room was vast (it would hardly do to call it futuristic) and might have intimidated any other prisoners than the X-Men. But the three mutants who had been brought before the judgment of the Princess Ravonna had seen too much, been too many places, to really be impressed.

That didn't mean they weren't worried.

Ravonna was a tiny woman—the Beast imagined the top of her head would barely reach Kang's shoulder, and Kang the Conqueror was not a tall man. Her skin was a creamy pale color that cosmetics companies would have killed for the ability to reproduce, and her eyes were colored the true tiger-green. Her long raven-black hair fell in curls about her shoulders, and she was dressed in the same type of comic-opera Lurex and Saran Wrap couture as her guardsmen, with an odd sort of tiara and veil upon her head and a long purple cape about her shoulders.

But no matter how ludicrous her costume appeared to twentieth-century eyes, Ravonna was every inch a princess.

"Highness," the captain of the guard said, sweeping into a deep obeisance at Ravonna's feet, "we apprehended these miscreants in the greenbelt park. They brought with them this device—" he gestured toward the generator, which hulked like a sullen violet ranid in the corner "—and if not for the damping field, they would surely have offered us harm through the supernormal abilities that they possess."

Who are these people? The Science Police? the Beast wondered. He cleared his throat.

"Your, ah, Highness. If I might interpose a few words?"

Nobody shot him, though Ravonna, her guards, and the rest of the fantastically garbed courtiers all turned to stare as though a statue had suddenly been given voice.

"Never will I let it be said that any who petition the Princess Ravonna for a chance to speak will be turned away without a hearing," the princess said imperiously. "Speak, outlander, and know that Ravonna hears your words."

A lead-in like that was enough to make any extempore filibusterer dry up, but the Beast was made of sterner stuff. He had to be glib enough to win not only the X-Men's freedom, but the survival of the multiverse.

"First of all, let me apologize for our purely unintentional trespasses against your customs. My name is Dr. Henry McCoy—though some call me the Beast—and these are my companions, Storm and Gambit. We're X-Men, from the Earth of the twentieth century, and we mean you and your people no harm. In fact, we didn't intend to come to your dimension at all." He paused.

"Didn't you?" Ravonna interjected mockingly.

A tough audience. But the Beast had faced tougher. And he was counting on the fact that he was telling the truth and could keep his temper while doing it. He knew Kang; like all too many megalomaniacal villains, Kang had a big mouth, a short fuse, and a total inability to bluff.

"No, Your Highness. In fact, we were looking for a chap that calls himself Kang the Conqueror someplace else entirely—that's his tollywocket over there, not ours—and—"

"Heed them not!"

The outcry came from the entrance to the throne room, about a football field away. Though all of the X-Men struggled in their shackles, they couldn't see the source of the noise, nor what action Ravonna's guards took in response—but in seconds the shouting had been overtaken by the sounds of brutal fighting, followed by a blinding flash of energy that filled the room.

Whatever damping field is short-circuiting our inbred mutant powers doesn't seem to be doing much to stop whoever this is, the Beast thought to himself.

The brightly dressed courtiers drew back against the walls in horror, and now the X-Men could clearly see the scene at the back of the room. A small man in gleaming green-and-purple armor was struggling against half-a-dozen red-garbed guards . . . and winning.

Gambit said in a low voice. "Dat Kang, he know how to make an entrance."

"Henry, Remy—can either of you break free?" Storm asked.

The Beast's only response was to sigh. Gambit winked at her.

"Dey turn down de volume, Stormy, but dey ain' turn off de radio," Gambit said. "I t'ink maybe I give dem a surprise in a while." He smiled sunnily at Hank, his whole expression indicating that he had nothing more stressful on his mind than a fast game of softball.

"Do what you can," the Beast said. If he'd been able to, he would have crossed his fingers for luck.

Kang flung off the last of the guards and strode the last few paces to Ravonna's throne with something of his customary swagger. Here was his generator, here were his enemies in chains, and here was the woman he loved. And best of all, the bioenergetic damping field with which this dimension's Ravonna had surrounded her principality rendered the meddling mutants powerless but had no effect on his armor's powerful arsenal.

"Ravonna—beloved—" he cried, flinging himself to one knee before her. "Long have I loved you from afar—

sought you through time's dark pavilions and the dust of galaxies! And at last I reach your side—barely in time to save you from these duplicitous invaders!''

At a gesture from Ravonna, the scarlet-clad guards fell back, to Kang's secret delight. They wouldn't have been particularly successful in restraining Kang in any event.

''Invaders?'' Ravonna said. ''If you will forgive my bluntness, stranger, it seems to me that both you and they are invaders here.'' Her tone was cool, regal. Its very disdain caused Kang's heart to beat faster. Here was his love. They could begin again.

''The cursed X-Men and I may both equally be invaders, but *I* have come to save you, Ravonna—from them!'' Kang said.

The three X-Men stared at Kang the Conqueror in horror.

Spider-Man stared at the Energy Pods in horror. He thought he'd adjusted to knowing that they were playing for all the marbles this time, but the disoriented sinking feeling of absolute despair that turned his stomach to a queasy lump of ice told him he'd just been kidding himself. He hadn't been prepared for defeat. Nobody could be. Not with the stakes so high.

''You mean . . . we've lost?'' Spider-Man asked. His voice cracked with emotion, even as what MJ liked to call his indomitable fighting spirit rallied. There *had* to be a way!

''Not yet!'' Aliya cried.

Spider-Man's head whipped around in the direction of her voice. Aliya had rejoined them . . . and she hadn't come alone.

Behind her stood Cyclops and Phoenix, and with them Bishop, Iceman, and Wolverine. All of them looked battered. Bishop and Wolverine were burned, their uniforms shredded. Iceman showed no visible effects, but he seemed a touch wobbly. Cyclops and Phoenix just looked furious, their expressions enough to make even their strongest enemy think twice about facing off with them. They were hurting and exhausted from the battering they'd taken, disoriented from the intertemporal version of jet lag. Each of them had seen too much—futures that were all different, but all equally dark. They had bidden farewell to children who might never be born, seen societies that were the ruin of all of humanity's hopes. And still they fought on, in mute defiance of Kang's lust for victory. Because they were heroes.

"Glad you could make it," Spider-Man called gaily.

"Wouldn't miss it for the world," Iceman shouted back.

Cable drew breath to fill them in on what he and Spider-Man had discovered here in Limbo.

And the wall of the Ops Center exploded.

The event seemed to happen in slow motion. At first it almost looked as if the stones would stretch. Powdered mortar sifted down the wall behind the video screens like smoke, and the cyclopean blocks seemed to ripple like water. Then the illusion shattered as the stones began to pop free under the intolerable strain, caroming into the room as if they were kernels of popcorn escaping from some mad giant's microwave.

And then the wall was gone, and the largest of Kang's Growing Men was reaching through the gap as his brethren climbed over the rubble.

Inevitably, it cried, "Intruders: halt in the name of the Master!"

"Not a chance!" Cyclops shouted furiously. There was a flare at the front of his visor as it began to rise to unleash his deadly optic beams at the intruder.

"No, wait!" Spider-Man shouted, just as Cyclops's optic blast connected with the lead Growing Man. "They grow when you hit them," the wall-crawler added weakly.

But Cyclops had already figured that out. Spider-Man could tell from the set of his mouth.

Spider-Man. It's Phoenix. Let me psi-link to you: we need to know how to fight these things.

The stakes were high enough that it was only long afterward that Spider-Man realized he would normally have hesitated before opening his mind to anyone, even someone as trustworthy as the telepathic X-Man Phoenix. But right now the Doomsday Clock was ticking at one minute to midnight, and he didn't even think twice. He felt her riffle through his experiences of the last hour in the space between two heartbeats; felt the psionic equivalent of a kiss on the cheek as she withdrew.

Thanks, web-head.

Anytime, Red, Spider-Man thought giddily. There was something about a redhead. . . .

"X-Men, go get 'em!" Cyclops shouted, though it was hardly necessary.

And battle was joined.

"It is very simple, Princess. I am a man of deeds, not words, but words are all I have to offer you now." Kang spread his hands in their mailed gauntlets disarmingly as he stood before the throne of Princess Ravonna. "I have come to warn you of a great peril. Your entire existence—all this sceptered realm—is merely one of many. One among a myriad of different times, all existing intangibly side by side in the timestream."

"Our scientists are not unfamiliar with this concept," Ravonna said briefly. "Please continue, Lord Kang." The expression on her face was of curiosity, almost of wonder, as though in gazing upon Kang's face she was also gazing upon the answer to a riddle that had bewildered her for all her life.

"She don' be fallin' for him, her?" Gambit whispered in disbelief.

"Be quiet," the Beast whispered back.

"I am an explorer and conserver of alternate realities," Kang said fulsomely. "For many years I have walked among their trackless shadows, seeing all manner of creatures and civilizations. Yet never did I encounter the face of true evil until I looked upon the face of these three invaders—the X-Men. It is they who are destroying every timeline in existence!"

With his last sentence Kang raised his voice, turning upon the X-Men and gesturing to them with all the bravado of a top-seeded trial lawyer.

"Alas," he said, lowering his voice and turning his soulful gaze back on the princess, "by the time I became aware of the scope of their extinction agenda, it was too late for me to stop their vile plans. I can only save one time line now by means of this generator—which my enemies attempted to steal from me, as you have seen. It was no easy decision to choose from among all the different realities which one could survive. But I have chosen this one, Princess . . . for love of you," Kang finished, eyes downcast in feigned humility.

Ravonna recoiled in startled surprise, though she concealed it well. But her dark eyes flickered as she glanced from the bound X-Men to the free—and armed—Kang.

"Your words are bold, stranger," Ravonna said, obviously playing for time.

"Eh, Princess, dat Kang's some love-talker, eh—for a murderer?" Gambit smiled lazily at the Princess, as though the two of them were the only people in the room.

"Silence, insolent cur!" Kang snapped at the Cajun X-Man. "I have come bringing the Princess Ravonna the greatest gift of all—surely that is proof that my intentions are pure?"

" 'Timeo Danaos et dona ferentes.' I beware the

Greeks, even when they bring gifts,'' the Beast said quietly.

But it was Storm who spoke directly to the ruler of this land. ''Princess Ravonna!'' the wind-rider cried. ''You must be strong—judge between our cases carefully, for the sake of all your people. The danger may be greater than you think.''

Ravonna smiled faintly. ''The danger is always greater than one thinks, Storm. But I am my people's ruler, and the burden of caring for them is one I have shouldered since my girlhood. Be sure that you shall both receive a fair hearing of your claims, and my decision shall be that which is best for my people.''

She is very lovely, Gambit thought, looking at the princess as though he hoped to memorize every curve of her face. *But in the eyes of love, Rogue is more beautiful, and Remy wants nothing more than to tell her so.*

He only hoped he'd get the chance once this day was over. He could feel the energy trickling from his fingertips, charging his fetters. He'd been working carefully on them almost since he'd been captured; eventually they'd have taken enough of a charge to explode.

He hoped eventually came soon.

And didn't take his hands with it.

For a moment Spider-Man wondered if there'd be enough fighting room—even in a space as big as Kang's Ops Center—but an instant later he realized he needn't have worried.

Phoenix levitated upward from the floor, her body surrounded by a red-gold nimbus of ionized energy. The largest of the Growing Men had doubled in size when Cyclops hit it; the palm of the hand with which it reached for Phoenix was more than twelve feet across. If the Growing Man got any larger it wouldn't need to do anything to defeat all eight of them except sit down.

Phoenix grabbed it telekinetically and flung it backward with every ounce of power at her command. Its Brobdingnagian form punched through the outer wall of the labyrinthine castle as if it were a human cannonball, and disappeared into the curling gray fog of Limbo beyond. Phoenix followed it, her body gleaming like a star.

Now there were only three of them to defeat.

Through the psi-link, Phoenix had told each of the X-Men what Spider-Man and Cable already knew: that any offensive force would be transformed by the Growing Men into increased size and strength. They had to find some way to use that against their enemy—and fast. There was nowhere to run, the Time Bombs were ticking, and of the seven of them, only Phoenix could fly.

To succeed against superior force, do the unexpected. The years he had spent training—not only in combat techniques, but in strategy and tactics as well—stood Cyclops in good stead now. These Growing Men knew that the X-Men were aware of their power to transmute force to size. They would be expecting evasion, flight.

What they wouldn't be expecting was a frontal assault.

The nearest of the Growing Men was fifteen feet tall. Cyclops turned to face it and opened his visor wide. The full power of Cyclops's deadly optic blast hit the thing square in the chest, knocking it back through the hole its brother had recently made and out onto the misty plane of Limbo.

"Cable!" Cyclops shouted. "Hit it with everything you've got!" As he spoke, Cyclops ran forward, keeping his force-beam trained on the Growing Man.

Cyclops stopped as he reached the edge of the rubble. Wisps of Limbo stuff were already curling into the building through the shattered wall, and, though he could not be certain of what he was seeing, he thought that the hole itself was closing, as if the building were an organic thing that had the capacity to heal.

Cable and Aliya joined Cyclops at the opening. The Growing Man was almost doll sized with distance, but Cyclops's optic beams were still trained on their target, and slowly the distant figure was clambering to its feet.

"The ion cannons don't seem to have any destructive effect on it," Cable said. There was an undertone of worry in his voice.

"We don't have to destroy it if we can overload it," Cyclops said with more confidence than he actually felt. "My guess is, that android isn't designed to grow indefinitely."

"You hope," Aliya said, swinging her ion cannon down into firing position. Next to her, Cable did likewise.

"I hope," Cyclops said under his breath.

There was a roar as Cable and Aliya both fired.

"Don't hit it," Spider-Man cautioned Iceman, as the unstoppable android—only the size of a human, but no less formidable for that—lurched toward them.

Iceman zipped up out of its way on an ice slide made from the frozen moisture in the air. There was a faint crackling sound—like a static, or a hard frost—as his icy body cracked, melted, and refroze a thousand times each second. The Growing Man raised its fists and shattered the slide, sending chunks of ice flying in all directions. Even such a slight impact caused Kang's android to increase in size by a few inches.

Iceman quickly froze himself a new ride. Out of the corner of his eye he could see the fourth and last of the Growing Men closing with Bishop and Wolverine, its massive fists clenched.

The Growing Man shattered the new slide, then lunged upward and seized Iceman by the ankle. Swinging the cryomorphic X-Man around its head, the Growing Man launched Iceman at the nearest available wall. The sound the impact of Iceman's body made was that of an ax hitting wood, and Spider-Man winced in sympathy, even as he sprang out of the way of the Growing Man's renewed attack.

The trouble was, Spider-Man reflected, as he bounded back and forth, remaining tantalizingly just out of reach of the now-silent android, that, even exhausted, he could do this for hours. And it wouldn't bring them any closer to defeating Kang and saving the universe.

Bound. Whump.

"Intruder: halt in the name of the Master," the Growing Man said.

Bound. Whump. Iceman wasn't moving.

"Aw, c'mon, buddy—give it a rest, why don'cha?" Spider-Man urged.

Bound. Whump. Spider-Man was starting to suspect that Kink Kong there had enough patience to keep this up until he made a mistake—and hey, presto: wall-crawler roadkill.

Bound. Whump. He steeled himself not to look in Iceman's direction. There was nothing he could do for the ice-laden X-Man, other than keep tall, green, and single-minded here out of Iceman's way. At least he had the android's full attention, which made it one less homicidal android from the future for the X-Men to deal with.

Bound. Whump.

And was it his imagination, or were its outlines starting to blur?

No. Spider-Man blinked hard beneath his mask. The Growing Man wasn't starting to blur. It was being covered with frost.

Across the room, Iceman had gotten unsteadily to his feet. His head still rang with the force of the blow, and he had a headache that even his natural icepack wouldn't touch. He still ached from Yondu's arrow. But Iceman was a pro. He had his target, and Priority One was to drop the target.

Silently he blessed the wall-crawler for his seemingly inexhaustible font of acrobatics. An ordinary foe might have given up by now, but Spider-Man was working tantalizingly close to the monster's armored fists, like a toreador working close to the horns of the bull, encouraging it to think that if it could only move just a bit faster . . .

Not on my watch, Mister, Bobby Drake vowed. *Maybe I can't hit it hard enough to bring it down, but let's see how happy it is at minus a thousand degrees Celsius.*

Normally Iceman used his mutant ability simply to make ice by freezing the moisture in the air, but icemaking wasn't his power, just a useful side effect of it. Iceman's power was to make *cold*, not ice.

The operation he planned would call for the most delicate control. Iceman wanted to neutralize the Growing Man by superchilling it, but Spider-Man couldn't survive even a hundred-degree temperature drop. He had to keep his cold-field focussed directly around the android itself. It would take all his concentration. He could not spare one iota of attention to watch out for enemy attacks. He would be defenseless.

So be it.

Iceman set to work, blocking out everything in his surroundings, concentrating on the mad dance of atoms that signified heat and cold on the material plane. Every erg of his consciousness was focused on slowing their whirling motion into the slow sleep of entropy and the endless arctic cold of stasis.

His smooth icy form grew jagged and monstrous as he worked, turning the dense intransigent blue of polar ice. His fingers grew spikes of ice. Spines multiplied along his arms and legs. A forbidding razor-sharp mane of ice crystals cascaded down his spine. A patch of ice spread beneath his feet as his body radiated cold down into the very rock of Kang's castle.

Stay sharp, Drake. Lose control of the local weather and you do Kang's work for him.

This was what had always frightened him about his power, deep down inside. It was the same thing that Scott and even Logan lived with every day of their lives: lose control of your mutant power and you would kill. Snowballs were one thing. He was comfortable with that. But a cryofield of the sort he was working with now could turn a live, warm body into a dead popsicle in the space between heartbeats. That was a responsibility Bobby Drake didn't want. Let him stay the X-Men's clown, a snowman pretending to be a hero, not a mutant who rode into battle with death in his hands. He didn't want that. He'd never wanted that.

But everything he'd ever believed in was at stake, and just now Iceman had no choice. Cold was something the Growing Man had no defense against. It wasn't force. A drop in the temperature wouldn't trigger its defensive growing ability. But it might stop it.

How cold could he go?

What temperature would stop it?

Down, down, down . . . The air around him began to darken as Iceman's own body temperature dropped lower than it ever had before. He'd always assumed his mutant gift came with a natural firewall that would keep him from killing himself, but at the moment he wasn't so sure.

But that wasn't the point. The point was to win. At any cost.

Bobby Drake concentrated. And the Growing Man began to freeze. Its metal skin turned cold enough to burn an unprotected touch; cold enough to suck the moisture out of the fog of Limbo and cover itself with a dew of ice crystals. Its body began to smoke, generating the same fog that dry ice—frozen nitrogen—did, and for the same reason.

Cold.

Spider-Man realized what Iceman was doing almost as soon as the cryomorph began dropping the temperature— there were some advantages to having been a science geek, after all. He knew what his role in the play was: keep the Growing Man distracted, keep it thinking that it had time to take him out first before smashing Iceman.

Bound. Whump. Didn't that thing ever get bored?

And was it his imagination, or was it moving just a bit slower?

Fair or not, Spider-Man had always considered Iceman something of a lightweight in the super hero sweepstakes, but as the seconds passed, he wasn't so sure. The air around the Growing Man shimmered as first the water, then the noble gases, were sucked out of it by sheer cold . . . and it hadn't grown an inch. Spider-Man didn't even want to think about what temperature the Growing Man's skin was right now, but he bet it would make Pluto look like Club Med.

Bound. Whump.

It was slowing. Then it stopped, looking almost confused, just as a human hypothermia victim might. Slowly it turned away from the wall-crawler, in the direction of its true tormenter.

It was time for Spider-Man to earn his keep. But if he touched it, the touch would hurt him, even through the gloves of his insulated costume, a lot worse than it would hurt the Growing Man. Quickly Spider-Man turned his web-shooters on himself, webbing both fists in a protective cocoon of his densest weave.

Then he hit the Growing Man with all his might.

Spider-Man was stronger than he looked. He might not be able to trade punches with the Hulk, but he could certainly survive one, and lesser foes had had many occasions to rue their dismissive assessment of his deceptive leanness. He knew there'd be no second chances and no round two. Spider-Man's roundhouse punch came up from the floor and it had every ounce of force he could muster behind it.

The webbing-gloves froze the instant he touched the Growing Man, and shattered like glass with the force of a punch that sent red lightning bolts of pain throughout his entire body.

The Growing Man's head snapped back. Was it Spider-Man's imagination, or did the android's beady eyes open wide with indignant surprise?

Kee-ripes! I think I broke my hand! Spider-Man mourned silently.

The Growing Man staggered backward, jerky and uncoordinated, limbs twitching spastically as it fell to the floor, thrashing as though it were having some sort of mechanoid seizure. By all the laws of its design imperative, it should grow now.

Holding his hand and sucking air through his teeth to keep from groaning aloud, Spider-Man heard the sharp sound of breaking that seemed to come from somewhere within the Growing Man's chest—as if somewhere inside its robot body, things tried to move that had been frozen into glassy immobility.

Fyunch(clik), the Growing Man said.

And stopped.

Spider-Man looked across the chamber, just in time to see Iceman drop to the floor again, ice crystals crusting his body like mad fractals. The unleashed cold radiated from his body like waves.

He wasn't moving.

Wolverine and the Growing Man circled each other warily. The armored green mechanoid was twice Wolverine's size, and the contrast would have been ludicrous save for the six gleaming claws jutting from the backs of Wolverine's hands.

He'd sliced up tin men before, from the mutant-hunting Sentinels to the Nimrods his own organization (in his pre-X-Men days) had once sent into the field to force him back into the clutches of Project X. If there was one thing Wolverine knew how to do superlatively, it was smash androids.

Smashing this one would just take a little extra planning.

"I hope you've got a plan," Bishop called to him.

Only minutes before, Bishop, Wolverine, and Iceman had been on a space station in the middle of nowhere facing down an insurmountable horde of acid-spitting slugs in a habitat that was about to explode. They'd returned to Cable's Rosendale lab only to find Aliya waiting for them to bring them to the place all four time-travelling teams had been searching for all along: Kang's base of operations.

They'd been eager to finish the job, but that didn't mean they weren't hurting. Bishop's dark skin was patched and welted with acid burns. The black M scar on his face stood out lividly against skin that had the gray undertone of fatigue, and his bright blue-and-yellow combat suit was tattered, the nearly indestructible unstable molecule fabric rotted away in patches from its exposure to acidic alien slug slime.

But if there was one quality that defined Bishop, it was his stubbornness. Like Eeyore, he saw the worst in every situation—and kept on fighting.

"Relax. I been shellin' these armored lobsters since before you was a gleam in your daddy's eye," Wolverine said to him.

Bishop smiled grimly at the thought. "Long before,"

he agreed. "Although they tell me there's no time in Limbo."

"Then we got all the time we need," Wolverine said, speaking almost absently as he waited for his moment, "t'do all we need t'do."

His plan was simple, woven from desperation and necessity combined. It didn't matter how fast one of these things grew, as long as it could be cut.

They'd have to find out.

Wolverine had been stringing it along, letting it think he was getting tired. Encouraging it to take its best shot. From the capsule briefing Jeannie had been able to feed them, Wolverine didn't think these things had any offensive capabilities other than their fists; and for sure it hadn't taken any of the openings he'd offered it to cut him down from a distance.

Time to take it up on its invitation to the dance.

As it swung at him, Wolverine ducked under the blow and struck back with all his strength. It was a brutal upward blow, and if the Growing Man had been a human being Wolverine's gleaming claws would have punched through its heart and come out through its back.

But it wasn't.

Wolverine's needle-sharp claws sheered through the android's carapace with a grinding squeal. Normally, the Canadian mutant's next move should be to pull his right fist free and follow up with a left-right-left combination of slashes that would probably cut his opponent right in half.

But Wolverine didn't pull his claws free. He couldn't.

Somehow the monster had managed to trap Wolverine's claws within its body. And as he struggled, the Growing Man—more than a foot taller from the force of Wolverine's first blow—wrapped its massive arms around him and began to squeeze.

Bishop was already running toward his teammate. His

mutant power enabled him to harmlessly siphon away energy directed at him into his own body and return it as blasts of overwhelming force. The only problem with his mutant power at the moment was that nobody was shooting at him.

Wolverine's left hand was placed palm-flat against the Growing Man's chest, its gleaming adamantium claws fully splayed and extended as he strained with all his might to resist the Growing Man's crushing hug. Its arms were wrapped around his shoulders in an obscene parody of affection, and its face wore a bland archaic smile. Wolverine's adamantium-plated bones would not break, but enough pressure would crush his heart, and he knew it. The Growing Man could make him die almost as easily as if he were a normal human being.

Almost.

Bishop leapt to the creature's back. If he could distract it, Wolverine might have a chance to slip free. Ignoring the pain of his own unhealed burns, Bishop grabbed the android beneath the chin and began attempting to pull its head back.

He might as well have been trying to bend a bronze statue. Except for the fact that Bishop could feel its body vibrating with energy, the android might as well have been an inert and lifeless thing, unyielding as the earth itself. He could feel its power plant raging just out of reach, its energy inaccessible to him.

Or was it? He'd never tried to siphon the energy from a passive system before. But there was no time like the present to try.

Bishop strained, dragging at the Growing Man's head with all his might. His thighs were clasped around its torso, and through them he could feel its mechanical pulse.

The Growing Man reacted to his efforts, and began to grow.

Bishop absorbed the growing energy.

The Growing Man stayed the same size. It did not grow at all. Its turretlike head swiveled to regard its new tormentor.

"Attaboy, Bishop," Wolverine gasped. "You an' me, we'll double-team this sucker."

Grunting with the effort, Wolverine coiled his body, bringing his feet up against the android's chest. The awkward position gave him the leverage he needed to rip his claws—and himself—free of the Growing Man while it was distracted by Bishop. He bounded backward with the momentum of his thrust, but before the android could return its attention to Bishop, Wolverine had closed with it again, claws slashing.

He didn't make the mistake again of attempting to skewer the creature. As Bishop—again and again—drained the Growing Man's energy before it could use it to increase its size, Wolverine slashed at it repeatedly, slowly stripping away its armored carapace piece by piece.

The open chest cavity revealed strange alien circuitry, its multicolored lights playing over the Canadian X-Man's grim intent face. Wolverine darted in under its flailing fists, striking and bounding away, his attacks distracting it and keeping it away from the walls.

But despite the damage Wolverine had already done, the Growing Man's strength—if not its size—seemed unabated. It whirled and danced like a dervish, trying to throw Bishop from its shoulders or at least smash him into one of the nearby walls. Bishop's body hummed with the energy he was drawing from the mechanoid. His earlier weariness and pain were gone; he was filled with vitality and power.

"Wolverine!" he shouted. "I'm going to try something!"

"Go wild," his teammate responded. "A guy could

get old tryin'a unwrap this package.'' As he spoke, Wolverine slashed at the Growing Man again, but the android seemed to have some mechanical equivalent of his own accelerated healing factor. Even with Bishop's mutant interference with its enlarging powers, it still retained enough moxie to stand up to Wolverine's assault.

Bishop clasped the Growing Man's head in his two massive hands and let the power that had been building in him cascade back into the Growing Man's body.

The android responded to the energy blast by attempting to increase its size.

Bishop siphoned away that energy, drawing it back into himself before the Growing Man could convert it to increased size and power.

Charged with even more energy, Bishop blasted the android again.

It tried to grow.

Failed.

Bishop blasted it.

The cycle repeated, each time faster, until the Growing Man's straining body seemed to flicker and blur and there was a nimbus of eldritch energy surrounding Bishop like a radioactive fog. Any sensible person would have hung back to see what would happen, but no one in his right mind would ever have called Wolverine sensible. And he figured it was about time the fight went his way. He waded into the fray once more, conscious only of the need to win, a small part of his mind focused on the necessity to remember that Bishop was there, in the line of fire, and vulnerable to a slash from Wolverine's claws.

The android's body seemed to shimmer beneath his blows, as if—instead of becoming larger—it were becoming more insubstantial with each passing moment. Its metal eyes rolled wildly in its alloy skull as the message of its own destruction slowly began to penetrate its inanimate consciousness.

And then the fight was over. Wolverine reached with both hands into the opening he had made, seized whatever he could grasp, and pulled with all his might. There was a shower of sparks. A pinging sound. And suddenly the head that Bishop was hauling on with all his might came loose easily, as if it were a ball-and-socket joint on a fashion doll.

Bishop sprang back, dropping to the floor in a shoulder roll as the Growing Man android fell to the floor in three separate pieces.

Wolverine was already looking around for fresh targets. But of the four Stimuloids they'd begun with, one was in three pieces; one was lying on the floor smoking with cold; one lay motionless outside the castle on the Limbo plain, its body engorged to fantastic size on the power of Cyclops's optic blasts and Cable and Aliya's cannonfire.

And one was absent.

"Where's Jeannie?" Wolverine asked into the silence. His voice had a rusty sound, as if from long disuse.

In the distance, through the Limbo mists, a bright spark could be seen, the only thing of warmth and color in all that sere gray vista. Slowly it came closer, as if journeying from an unimaginable distance, taking on form and shape as it neared.

Phoenix drifted gently to the floor just inside the opening.

The Growing Man she had fought was nowhere in sight.

"I found the off button," Phoenix said, opening her hand. On her palm, a three-inch-tall Growing Man raged impotently.

Scott Summers smiled one of his rare smiles. "Terrific," he said. "Now all we have to do is stop the explosion of Kang's Time Bombs."

"That may be harder than you think, Cyclops," Cable

said. "The Energy Pods are primed to explode. There is very little time left. And the one thing that could contain that explosion here in Limbo and keep it from ravaging the timestream isn't here."

The seven heroes looked at each other in exasperated exhaustion—had they done all they had done, suffered what they'd suffered, only to lose now?

But Cable wasn't finished speaking.

"Kang has a force field generator of some sort strong enough to withstand the blast—it is the means by which he intends to save one dimension from the destruction. He must already have taken it with him to his destination, but I believe I can use his command center to retrieve and configure the device."

"Then what are you waiting for?" Cyclops snapped. "Do what you have to do, Cable."

Limbo was not a country for sane men, and as the heat of battle faded, Spider-Man and the X-Men realized this more with every second. Even the mock-medieval walls of Kang's stronghold did not seem to fit together in any normal fashion.

"It's a good thing Storm isn't here to see this," Bobby Drake muttered woozily under his breath. He moved slowly, like a fighter still groggy from the punches he'd taken. All of his teammates looked the next thing to dead on their feet—but they still looked ready to fight. More than ready.

Cable began walking slowly past the banks of alien machines, looking for a familiar starting place. Each of the remaining monitors in Limbo's Ops Center was focused upon a different shifting reality, and the X-Men couldn't keep from staring.

There were worlds where the skyline of New York City was strangely altered, worlds where a dirigible was moored at the top of the Empire State Building, and the monitor lingered upon a tall bronze-skinned man with a close-cut skullcap of nearly metallic hair as he clung to the running board of an automobile like none they'd ever seen.

Worlds where a masked man in a gray-and-black costume, its cape braced and scalloped so that it resembled the wings of an enormous bat, stalked the rooftops of an unfamiliar fog-shrouded Gothic cityscape beneath an enormous skull-white moon.

Worlds where the sun burned low and red upon the horizon, overlooking a desert stripped of all life.

Where there was nothing left but the place where a city had once been, where gleaming skeletal robots stalked through the wreckage, mad red eyes gleaming.

Where the sun shone on a New York much like their own, save for the fact that its colors were so intolerably bright.

Infinite possibility. Infinite peril.

"I've found it," Cable announced, turning away from the console he had been working at. "As soon as the Time Platform can lock on to the generator it can bring it here to this place. Once the force shield is up and running, it will circumvent the explosion by bottling it up inside the generator field. Everything it contains will be destroyed, but everything outside—such as time—will be safe, because no force in all of existence can penetrate the field it will generate."

"Finally," Iceman said with the relief of a man who finally understood what was going on. "So you do this, and we all go home?"

"I don't think you got it quite figured out, Drake," Wolverine said with slow realization.

"Someone has to stay," Aliya whispered harshly. "To activate the force shield from the inside—and die in the explosion."

The others fell silent, each trying to find some way out of the deadly paradox.

"If Hank . . ." Phoenix began, and fell silent. Hank McCoy and the X-Men who had gone with him to 2099—Storm and Gambit—had not returned to Rosendale in time for Aliya to find and bring them to Limbo.

"Someone has to die to make this work," Cable said inexorably. His tone was patient, almost reasonable . . . but then, he'd known the price he was being asked to pay almost from the very beginning. "I'm the only one here with the technical knowledge to do this. It has to be me."

"It isn't fair," Spider-Man said quietly.

"Haven't you heard?" Iceman asked bitterly. "Life sucks, then you die. It seems like we're always leaving our friends on battlefields."

Cyclops raised a hand, silencing his teammate. Cable was more than a teammate to the X-Man's leader. Cable was his son. And Cyclops was going to be forced to do something few fathers ever faced. He was going to have to watch his son die twice.

"It's time to go," Cable said to Cyclops, silently acknowledging the unspoken bond between them. Phoenix put her hand on her husband's arm, her expression grim.

Cyclops drew a deep, painful breath. "Okay. Everybody check your TDRs—there are not going to be any second chances this time. Spider-Man, Iceman—go."

Both of them popped back the rigid caps on their TDRs, and pressed the buttons. Iceman's image wavered for a moment, his unit still recovering from the subarcturian cold to which he'd exposed it, and then he vanished from Limbo.

"Bishop, Wolverine."

Their faces were expressionless as they triggered their own recalls. Neither of them liked sacrificing a comrade. Both of them had buried too many friends.

"Jean." Scott's tone plainly said that this was no time for discussion. Phoenix triggered her TDR and vanished from sight.

And then there were three.

CHAPTER FOURTEEN

"Tell me, Kang, what do you hope to gain from this offer?" Ravonna asked. "Kang the Conqueror," she mused, without giving him time to answer. "Truly a warlike sobriquet for one who claims to come in peace."

"It is but a souvenir of boyhood adventures," Kang said hastily. "But we are running out of time, Princess! You must allow me to activate my force shield at once— before the bomb that these vile X-Men and their allies have placed elsewhere in the continuum explodes, triggering the timequake that will destroy this world as well as all the others!"

I think it almost be worth dyin', not to hear that va-chon talk, Gambit mused. He could feel the faint tingle in his fingertips as the kinetic energy charge left his body, seeping into the metal shackles that held him.

How did he do it? Even Gambit wasn't entirely sure. It was an ability that was so much a part of the way he was . . . mysterious, mercurial, explosive . . . that how it worked was something that had never worried him.

His first reaction to discovering his mutant gift all those years ago, was of how much *fun* it was. Firecrackers you didn't have to pay for. A hotfoot no one could expect. A hole card for a man with the beat of Mardi Gras in his veins, a man who liked to gamble. Who liked dangerous parties, the wilder the better. The perfect gift for a thief and a player, a bayou knight-errant who lived on the edge of the blade.

But in all his checkered career, Remy LeBeau had never tilted closer to ultimate disaster than he did now.

Kang was still talking, urging Ravonna to let him turn on his machine. The explosion he had planned must be close to going off, and if Gambit was sure of nothing else in this whole mad caper, he was sure of the fact that

Kang loved his own skin. So while Gambit would have bet that he could charm Ravonna and outtalk Kang any day of the week, he didn't have time to test his theory. The Time Bomb must be just about ready to go off. And Gambit was betting that if Kang couldn't turn on his force field, he'd bolt back to Limbo to stop it somehow. At any cost, Gambit had to stop Kang from either triggering that force shield generator or escaping with it.

It was time to trigger his blast. While he'd never injured himself with the biokinetic charges he was capable of placing on any inanimate object, that didn't mean Gambit was immune to his own power's effect. And blowing the shackles off his wrists was shaving the barber pretty close. . . .

But there was no time like the present to find out if it would work. With the innate optimistic recklessness that was his hallmark, Gambit shoved his bound wrists back against the charged cuffs as hard as he could.

The reaction was immediate and electrifying. The force of the explosion—a small one, all things considered—not only sprang the clasps around his wrists, but short-circuited whatever mechanism was powering the rest of the restraints. The crossbar fell from the air with a crash. With a leap, Gambit was a free man.

His mutant powers were still suppressed by Ravonna's damping field, but Gambit's reflexes and agility owed nothing to the fact that the enigmatic Cajun had been born a mutant—which was just as well. The moment Gambit began to move, Kang spun away from Ravonna and pulled a blaster from somewhere within the depths of his armor. Kang's teeth were bared in a grimace of fury more frightening than the weapon itself as the conqueror of centuries fired upon Gambit's colorful dodging figure without regard for the innocent courtiers his weapon endangered.

"Always you attempt to thwart Kang!" he shouted.

"Now, insignificant flea, see what it is to have angered Kang, founder of dynasties! Kang, the unstoppable! Kang, conqueror of worlds!" As the furious conqueror shrieked, he fired as if to punctuate his words.

"Kang—who talk too dam' much!" Gambit shouted back.

Where it hit, Kang's weapon's fire left blackened melting craters, and Gambit had no desire to find out what it would do if it hit one only lightly armored mutant thief.

"Stop! *Stop!* Guards! Arrest this man!" Princess Ravonna cried. She sprang to her feet, fearless indignation upon her lovely features, and started down the steps of her throne as though she would subdue Kang herself.

There was a near riot in Ravonna's throne room as opulently dressed court functionaries fought to reach the doors, balking the efforts of the palace guards to come to the aid of their mistress. The red-suited security officers were having all they could handle to enforce an orderly exodus from the room, and for a few fatal seconds their attention was entirely upon that task.

Gambit continued bounding away from Kang like a mountebank. He dared not lead Kang's fire anywhere near his comrades; Kang would gun them down without a thought. Yet he had to reach them—his only hope was to trigger the TDR Storm wore and let Cable's Time Displacement Core whisk them away from a fight they'd already lost.

Though it was only a fight, and not the war.

Apparently dissatisfied with its performance, Kang flung his weapon aside and prepared to attack Gambit with his armor's inbuilt weaponry.

In that instant's lull, Gambit lunged for his imprisoned comrades.

And Kang, seeing only a blur of motion, fired.

"*No!*" Gambit screamed, stopping and falling to his knees.

And Ravonna crumpled to the ground.

We'll always have Paris, the old tag ran. To Remy LeBeau, Paris was blood and pain in the dirty shadows of Notre Dame while a girl named Genevieve died in his arms, killed by the murdering monster called Sabretooth because Gambit had been . . . clever.

Gambit lunged for the dying woman. He reached her an instant before Kang did, but the master of time batted him aside like an insect and Gambit went flying, his body passing through the space that Kang's generator had occupied only a moment before.

As for Kang, the conqueror had only time enough to lift Ravonna's slender form in his arms before Princess Ravonna—the only woman Kang the Conqueror ever had, ever would, love—was dead.

Again.

In a castle in Limbo, Scott Summers stood facing his son.

"We always seem to be saying good-bye," he managed to say.

Cable smiled faintly. "There will be better days, Scott Summers," he said.

Scott shook his head, his mouth tightening into grim lines of pain. There would be no better days for him and Cable. Nor for Dream, the almost-grandchild already slain on the altar of Kang's ambition. Friends, lovers, children . . . in his life as an X-Man, Scott Summers had suffered so many losses. It ought to make one more easier to bear, but somehow it did not.

Scott glanced at Aliya. Her sorrows made his seem insignificant. She'd lost the man she loved, lost her whole world and everyone she had known in both the future and the past, and now she was about to lose Cable once more. Yet her face remained smoothly impassive, implacable as a machine.

"Better days," Cyclops said aloud. Cable raised his hand in a half-salute.

Scott raised his hand in turn, jerking open the cover of the TDR strapped to his chest and striking the trigger. In an instant he was gone.

Cable turned to Aliya.

"You have to leave as well," he said. "Once I flip the activation switch on the force shield, not even the fundamental particles of time will be able to escape its field."

"I know," Aliya said. "It was kind of Summers to leave us our moment. Because if I am truly never to see you again, Nathan Dayspring Summers, I need you to kiss me good-bye."

She set the stock of her ion cannon against the floor and reached out for Cable with both hands.

An expression of pain greater than any man should have to endure flickered across Cable's features as if it were summer lightning. Without speaking, Cable took the woman he loved into his arms, and set his mouth upon hers as though he were sealing a covenant that must last until the end of time.

And Aliya's hand came up from her side with all the force and strength at her command. She grabbed her ion cannon by the barrel and wielded it with the whipcrack force of a bludgeon against the side of Cable's head.

Cable dropped without a sound.

"Here's something you never knew about me, my love," Aliya said to the unconscious man at her feet. "I'm a coward. Don't you see? Without you, there's nothing left for me, and I can't bear that. I'm not strong enough. Go back to your friends and your family, my love, Askani'son. But remember me."

She knelt beside him, her fingers fumbling for a moment as they found the catch and the trigger for Cable's TDR. She pressed the button.

Then he was gone, as safe in his past as she could make him. Aliya turned to the Force Shield Generator.

The only sound in all the echoing chamber was the sound of weeping. Kang cradled Ravonna's dead body in his arms, crooning to her through his sobs as though she were a sleeping child.

"There, my pretty, there. You must open your eyes, you know, for Kang commands it, and Kang has conquered galaxies, all to lay at your feet. . . ."

Gambit struggled upright, wishing he did not have to hear the sound of Kang's voice. He'd feel the shock of this moment later, he knew; it would be one of those that kept him awake nights and haunted the small insomniac hours of the cold predawn. But now Gambit had to pretend that he felt nothing; he had to keep moving, keep *doing*.

And not stop to hope that the generator's disappearance meant that somewhere, some*when*, one of the other teams had done the job successfully.

Gambit started toward Storm and the Beast, but one of the guards waved a weapon at him and he stopped. Storm was the only one with a TDR. It would be too easy for all three of them to be lost in time, marooned in this candy-colored tangerine-flake future. He had to plan his next move very carefully.

Gambit watched as four of the red-clad guardsmen approached Kang, carrying gleaming metal shackles in their hands. The slayer of universes did not seem even to notice as they pulled him away from their murdered monarch and bound his wrists in cuffs that glittered malignantly as they damped the power from his armor.

"You. Outlander." Tears of grief for his slain princess coursed down the guard-captain's face, but his demeanor was grim and businesslike as he gestured at Gambit.

Reflexively, Gambit raised his hands over his head.

Old habits died hard, and the captain had so much of the air of *les flics* about him.

"All four of you are guilty of the foul murder of our liege lady and princess, and the moment a tribunal can be convened you will answer for it. Rejoin your comrades, outlander."

This was his only chance.

"Wit' pleasure, *cochon*," Gambit sneered. The guard was expecting him to walk; Gambit flung his body into a forward layout that took him to the platform on which Storm and the Beast still stood imprisoned. He said a quick prayer for luck as he pressed the button on the TDR Storm wore, then clutched both his teammates tightly as he felt his body begin to fade out of existence.

It occurred to Aliya that she was tired, and that she had been tired for a very long time, almost longer than she could remember. But soon she could rest. There was only one last thing she had to do.

She left her weapon on the floor and strode over to the Force Shield Generator. It was not so very different from others she had seen. She brought its external sensors online and waited for the self-diagnostic to run as she programmed in the area of affect for the shield, watching as the tiny holograph rotated above its display platform, the radius displayed in universal binary code. Its metal surface hummed as she tapped her fingers on it, impatient for it to be ready for use.

And then it was, and she pulled down the three switches that brought the power source online; felt the crackling static over her skin as the shield swelled to encompass the entire castle, growing stronger with each heartbeat.

There. Now I can—

And then there was light, light enough for the morning of the world.

EPILOGUE

C yclops looked around Cable's laboratory, trying to orient himself. The Rosendale lab looked strange, as if it, too, had somehow changed while they were gone.

Or perhaps they had not returned to the place from which they had left?

No. Don't think that. Those thoughts could drive a man mad, lost in the maelstrom of what might be.

Beside him, Phoenix touched his arm, sharing his thoughts through the bond of long comradeship. Shaking his head mutely, Cyclops stepped down from the platform.

Spider-Man crouched atop one of the huge machines, silent for once. Wolverine, Bishop, Iceman . . .

As he and Phoenix stepped down from the platform, Storm, Gambit, and the Beast appeared. Gambit looked around wildly, his face breaking into a grin of relief when he realized they'd come home. "We made it!" he said.

Storm shrugged off the recall device and Gambit grabbed it out of her hand. It glowed orange at his touch, and then he flung it away from him as hard as he could. It exploded in an empty corner, shaking loose dustmotes that sparkled in the late afternoon sunlight.

No one said a word. All of them shared Gambit's feelings, actually.

"Kang seems to have been neutralized as a problem," the Beast said cautiously. He glanced around the lab as he spoke, counting heads. It was an automatic habit they'd all developed: the head count that would tell the X-Men whether their side had truly won or lost—a victory or defeat each one of them measured in the lives of the X-Men left to share it.

"In his arrogance, Kang slew the woman he loved," Storm added. "I pity him."

"Well, I don't," Gambit said roundly. He ran a hand through his shaggy hair and then began looking in his duster for a cigarette. "Hey, where Cable and Aliya?" he asked innocently. "Dey get back early?"

"Cable ain't—" Wolverine began, and stopped. Aliya should have returned by now, even if Cable wasn't going to make it home this time.

"She couldn't have chosen to stay with him," Phoenix said in horror. "He wouldn't let her."

"The Time Platform signals incoming traffic," Blaquesmith said in his thin inhuman voice.

A moment later, Cable's unconscious body appeared on the Time Platform. The Beast bounded over to him, feeling for a pulse.

"He's alive," Dr. McCoy announced. "But from the size of that lump, he's going to have one heck of a headache when he wakes up."

"I hate to ask the obvious question," Spider-Man said from his perch high above them, "but if Cable's here, who's minding the bomb?"

"Aliya," Jean Grey said with grim certainty. "She came from the same future, more or less. She had the same technical knowledge that Cable did. She could activate the force shield as well as he could."

"An' she didn't want ta be the survivor," Wolverine said with surprising empathy. "Not twice."

There was a moment of silence. None of them was quite able to believe it was over, that they'd won.

Assuming, of course, you could call this winning.

"All right, X-Men," Cyclops said briskly. "This one's over. Let's go home."

Home to lick their wounds, and grieve, and live to fight another day. And no one else on Earth would ever know what the eleven of them had done here today. And no one would thank them for their anguish.

"Great," Spider-Man said, bounding from the generator to the floor in one fluid move. "Anyplace around here I can get a cab? I think I'm late for dinner."

Elsewhere there is sunlight and flowers. Elsewhere gleaming towers rise toward the sun, and in them people live and work, the even tenor of their days undisturbed by threats of disease or war. In the center of their happy realm is the royal palace, where once a princess named Ravonna lived, beloved of her subjects and loving them in her turn. Now she lies in state, her body preserved in stasis just as it was in the moment of her death; her samite-draped bier the goal of all her grief-stricken subjects' pilgrimage.

But the palace that was once Ravonna's home continues to hum with activity. It is the seat of the bureaucracy, as well as its monarch's home. It is the nexus of law and of justice, and its work goes on. Here are the chambers of judgment, of punishment, of execution, where the lawful justice of this realm is served.

Law and justice . . . and retribution.

The palace's levels extend deep into the bedrock, and beneath them all there is a cell.

Only one.

Those who built this palace in centuries gone did not think there would be many in the land for whom no punishment could be great enough, for whom execution would be too swift and merciful a fate. They hoped there would never be any. For centuries this lone, almost-forgotten cell has gone unoccupied, as the prayers of its long-ago designers came true.

It is occupied now.

The cell is not a large one, and it is very far away from sunlight and the free air above. For most of the hours of each day it is in darkness, but it is a cell of punishment, so for a few brief hours in each day one thin shaft of sunlight—or of light, at least—filters down through a crack in the chill cyclopean stone to fall upon the face of its prisoner.

His conqueror's armor with its weapons and defenses is gone: his gloves, his gauntlets, his swirling cape, the high boots in which he used to strut arrogantly before his universe-conquering armies. A thousand universes away his armies wait for him in vain, not knowing how close they came to extinction at their master's whim. They wait in vain, for Kang will not be back.

Naked, powerless, he lies curled, oblivious upon the bare stone in this cell deep beneath the throne of the woman he has loved longer and more madly than any man has ever loved.

The woman he has slain.

Even now, should he turn his mind to it, escape would not be impossible, but that effort is not one Kang cares to make. In his mind, the moment of Ravonna's death is all he sees; the moment when her heart stopped and his joy in life was extinguished like a spent candle. Nothing can matter now. All his passions are dead, cold as the cinder of a star, and nothing survives in their wake.

Since he was a young man, Kang's obsession had been conquest. He had suffered setbacks, even defeats, but always they were temporary, a moment's hinderance that would only serve to add lustre and glory to his legend in the inevitable moment when he triumphed.

No more. Kang, who always mocked the misfortunes of others, their failures, their defeats, has failed as no man has ever failed in all the history of time. Once he was the unwitting cause of his beloved's death. This time he has slain her himself. And in that moment Kang's fierce raptor gaze was turned inward, and he saw that all his passion and valor, his conquests and his dreams, were the evanescent nonsense of moments, a madman ranting in an empty room. He had always believed himself to be, very simply, the best there was in every field of endeavor.

Until now. When he failed. When victory was within his grasp and his own stupidity and arrogance prevented his triumph. When he—he and no other—slew the princess Ravonna.

He is not who he thought he was. He has failed. He will always be alone. In all the multiverse, there is no other Ravonna. He has slain his love and doomed himself. It is his own fault.

And nothing else matters.

Nothing else will matter.

Ever.

The stronghold and all it contained should have been vaporized when the timequake was triggered—but this is Limbo. Reality is only a matter of opinion here, and time doesn't exist at all. Like they say, it's always morning in America somewhere.

Lireeb walked through the castle, inspecting the damage. The temporal field had fallen with the destruction of the Time Bombs. The generator was gone. And time—everywhere but in Limbo—would continue as before.

"So it's over," Lireeb said aloud. "These our actors were but spirits, as they say. The tangle of timelines spawned by the Age of Heroes is significantly weeded—not gone, but tidied—and one more incarnation of Kang the Conqueror has been neutralized forever. A good day's work, I'd say."

Lireeb reached Kang's black museum and, with a wave of his hand, dismissed all the time-lost anomalies to their own times . . . or to the void. In moments, the chamber was cleared of the catalogue of pain and disaster that had given Tenebrae's last occupant so many hours of viewing pleasure.

The creature known to Kang as Lireeb did not take joy from others' pain. Neither did it sadden him.

He reached the control room, where Kang had spent

so many hours doing his work for him—where, in another fold of Limbo, Aliya had sacrificed her life so that Kang's greater design could be thwarted, leaving the man called Cable to mourn her once more. All here was as it should be, and if the castle's occupant was aware of the pain his game had inflicted, the number of lives he had stood by and watched Kang destroy, he did not show it.

As he crossed the threshold of his sanctum, his appearance changed. In place of the solemn black robes that Kang's cynical lackey had worn, the man now wore a short tunic and sturdy boots in royal purple. Upon his chest there was a round medallion, its device bearing an odd resemblance to a compass rose. Lireeb's hairless white skull vanished beneath a tall cylindrical headdress, and the cape that fell from his broad shoulders had a flaring collar that vaguely resembled a down-pointing arrow.

His skin had darkened, his hollow, wasted features becoming merely lean. The light of madness vanished from his now-dark eyes, and he stroked his short beard as he surveyed his domain.

He smiled harshly, though there was no one here to see. "I am Immortus, Ruler of Limbo, Keeper of Time, and my responsibilities place me above such petty concerns."

The barn and its underground laboratories were empty now, filling with twilight shadows as silently as if the events of the previous several hours had never happened. The vast futuristic machines soared into the darkness, throbbing faintly with the trickle of power that kept them functioning and ready for use. Here within this chamber was the philosopher's stone that poets and scientists alike had sought: not only a time machine, but a dimension machine as well.

Cable stood gazing at the Time Displacement Core, as

silent and immobile as one of his own machines. He'd
sent the others away and spent the last several hours
searching the multiverse, using his machines to sound its
intricate web of energies to find evidence of Kang's meddling. Storm, Gambit, and the Beast had each spoken of
tracing Kang to Limbo and then to the one timeline that
Kang had proposed to spare, the timeline of his long-lost
love. The woman Kang himself had—this time—slain.

Cable had searched, but found no evidence that Kang
had renewed his plot. The remaining parallel worlds were
safe, spared from destruction. In one of them, Aliya still
lived. Somewhere. He could find her if he searched.

Expressionlessly, Cable shut down power to the main
scanner, and watched its light dwindle into darkness. He
was alone again. He'd had time to grow used to the fact.

Alone. Now. Again. Always.

The power died, and Cable walked away from the machine. Never again would he search through the multiverse for a world in which he and Aliya lived happily
ever after. He no longer believed it existed.

He had lost her twice.

He could not bear to see her alive again.

It was better not to hope.

It was evening in Queens. He hadn't been late for dinner
after all, a felicity that Spider-Man was disinclined to
question. Let sleeping chronauts lie, as the Parker family
always said. Or should have said, in any case.

"Home sweet polluted overpriced high-crime home,"
Peter Parker murmured fervently. He was dressed in
street clothes, his bare feet firmly gripping the surface of
the steeply-pitched shingled roof.

He was thinking of dead and absent friends. Of his
other self, who'd died in the moment he'd achieved all
he'd fought for, leaving behind a wife as well as an Aunt
May and Uncle Ben who lived and grieved for him. In

some ways the Park had almost possessed the life Peter had always wished he'd been lucky enough to have: one where he'd made all the right choices, instead of so many wrong ones. In that world, Gwen Stacy had not died, his best friend was not revealed to be his most implacable foe, he'd never been stalked by clones, alien clothes, symbiotes with attitude, or even J. Jonah Jameson. And he'd died for a cause he believed in with all his heart.

But the Park hadn't been free. He'd never known the joy of web-swinging high above Manhattan traffic, through a spring twilight when the Big Apple almost seemed like the new Atlantis its boosters hoped it would be. The Park had never had the adventures Peter Parker had, met the people he'd met, found the friends he had.

Or the wife.

Peter turned as the bedroom window opened, and Mary Jane craned out. "Peter? Are you going to be up there all night?"

"Just admiring the view." He reached down. She took his hand, and he helped her climb up onto the roof. "It's a great sunset," he said, his arm around her waist.

"Sure." MJ was unconvinced.

The evening light gleamed on her red hair, and Peter was reminded of someone else he'd met among the time-streams: May Parker. His daughter.

Their daughter.

What would the future really be like? Cyclops had said the future they saw wasn't necessarily the future they'd get. Would his future be as bleak a place as the one he'd seen, where there weren't any good guys, just costumed gladiators stalking through an urban jungle? What sort of a life was that for his daughter? What sort of a life was it for anyone?

But the future wasn't fixed. There was still time to make it travel a different path. The whole mad adventure was starting to seem less real, the weirdness and terror all part of a highly colored dream. With enough time, memories of his meeting with his other self—with his daughter—would recede further, to become just another bizarre episode in Spider-Man's checkered career.

"Peter? Are you sure everything's all right?"

Despite his dark thoughts, Peter had to smile. If he'd suffered great losses in his life, he still had a lot to be thankful for—MJ, and their life together. And after all, the good guys had won again, more or less.

"C'mon, hon. Let's go inside."

He thought about Cable, and for just a moment Peter shuddered, clutching MJ tighter. He was lucky, and he swore he'd never forget it. It wasn't always true, but just sometimes, against all the odds, true love did win out in the end.

TOM DeFALCO entered the comic book industry in the summer of 1972 as an editorial assistant for Archie Comics. Learning his trade from the ground up, he pasted down character logos, proofread stories, and even served time as an occasional colorist. Within a few months, Tom sold the first of what would eventually become an avalanche of stories. Over the years, Tom has written for such diverse comic book titles as *Jughead's Jokes, The Flintstones, Scooby Doo*, and *Superman Family*. He joined the editorial staff of Marvel Comics during the early 1980s and eventually became the company's Editor in Chief. Tom has recently returned to full-time writing. He currently supervises Marvel's new MC-2 line, for which he writes *Avengers Next, J2*, and *Spider-Girl* (a variation on the character who appears in these pages). He also coauthored a novella with Stan Lee for *The Ultimate Silver Surfer*, and wrote short stories for *The Ultimate Super-Villains* and *Untold Tales of Spider-Man*.

ELUKI BES SHAHAR also writes as Rosemary Edghill, and is the author of over twenty books, like eluki's Hellflower series and her X-Men novel *Smoke and Mirrors*, and Rosemary's Bast novels, plus the occasional short story in places like *The Ultimate X-Men, Alien Pregnant by Elvis*, and *Urban Nightmares*. From earliest infancy she has suspected mutagenic influences in her environment, and bought *Uncanny X-Men* #1 off the stands, thereby changing the entire course of her life. She thinks Scott and Jean should have gotten married *years* ago, and has always thought the green costume with the skirt was silly. She is presently hard at work on a new X-Men novel.

TOM GRUMMETT started doing commercial illustration while working for the Saskatoon Board of Education's printing department. His first comics work appeared in the 1980 *Captain Canuck Summer Special*, and he went on to work on *The Privateers* and *The Shadowalker Chronicles*. In 1989, he started doing fill-in work for DC Comics, including issues of *Animal Man, Secret Origins, Action Comics*, and *Wonder Woman*. He has served as the regular penciller on *The New Titans, The Adventures of Superman, Robin, Superboy*, and, for Marvel, *Generation X*. Tom presently lives in Saskatoon, Saskatchewan, Canada, where he resides with his wife, Nancy, and their two children.

DOUG HAZLEWOOD has been inking professionally since 1985. After winning the inking category of the "Official Marvel Try-Out Contest" in 1986, he plunged into comic books full time. He has enjoyed stints on the critically acclaimed *Animal Man*, and was a part of the death and resurrection of Superman on *Adventures of Superman*. Doug currently is the inker on *Superboy* for DC Comics. A native Texan, he lives in Victoria, Texas, with his wife and two children.

CHRONOLOGY TO THE MARVEL NOVELS AND ANTHOLOGIES

What follows is a guide to the order in which the Marvel novels and short stories published by Byron Preiss Multimedia Company and Berkley Boulevard Books take place in relation to each other. Please note that this is not a hard and fast chronology, but a guideline that is subject to change at authorial or editorial whim. This list covers all the novels and anthologies published from October 1994–October 1998.

The short stories are each given an abbreviation to indicate which anthology the story appeared in. USM=*The Ultimate Spider-Man*, USS=*The Ultimate Silver Surfer*, USV=*The Ultimate Super-Villains*, UXM=*The Ultimate X-Men*, and UTS=*Untold Tales of Spider-Man*.

If you have any questions or comments regarding this chronology, please write us.

Snail mail: Keith R. A. DeCandido
             Marvel Novels Editor
             Byron Preiss Multimedia Company, Inc.
             24 West 25th Street
             New York, New York, 10010-2710

E-mail: KRAD@IX.NETCOM.COM

                —Keith R. A. DeCandido, Editor

"The Silver Surfer" [flashback]
by Tom DeFalco & Stan Lee [USS]
     The Silver Surfer's origin. The early parts of this flashback start several decades, possibly several centuries, ago, and continue to a point just prior to "To See Heaven in a Wild Flower."

"Spider-Man"
by Stan Lee & Peter David [USM]
     A retelling of Spider-Man's origin.

"Side by Side with the Astonishing Ant-Man!"
by Will Murray [UTS]
"Suits"
by Tom De Haven & Dean Wesley Smith [USM]
"After the First Death . . ."
by Tom DeFalco [UTS]
"Celebrity"
by Christopher Golden & José R. Nieto [UTS]
"Better Looting Through Modern Chemistry"
by John Garcia & Pierce Askegren [UTS]
     These stories take place very early in Spider-Man's career.

"To the Victor"
by Richard Lee Byers [USV]
     Most of this story takes place in an alternate timeline, but the jumping-off point is here.

"To See Heaven in a Wild Flower"
by Ann Tonsor Zeddies [USS]
"Point of View"
by Len Wein [USS]
     These stories take place shortly after the end of the flashback portion of "The Silver Surfer."

"Identity Crisis"
by Michael Jan Friedman [UTS]
"The Liar"
by Ann Nocenti [UTS]
"The Doctor's Dilemma"
by Danny Fingeroth [UTS]
"Moving Day"
by John S. Drew [UTS]

"Deadly Force"
by Richard Lee Byers [UTS]
"Improper Procedure"
by Keith R. A. DeCandido [USS]
"Poison in the Soul"
by Glenn Greenberg [UTS]
"The Ballad of Fancy Dan"
by Ken Grobe & Steven A. Roman [UTS]
"Do You Dream in Silver?"
by James Dawson [USS]
"Livewires"
by Steve Lyons [UTS]
"Arms and the Man"
by Keith R. A. DeCandido [UTS]
"Incident on a Skyscraper"
by Dave Smeds [USS]

    These all take place at various and sundry points in the careers of Spider-Man and the Silver Surfer, after their origins, but before Spider-Man married and the Silver Surfer ended his exile on Earth.

"Cool"
by Lawrence Watt-Evans [USM]
"Blindspot"
by Ann Nocenti [USM]
"Tinker, Tailor, Soldier, Courier"
by Robert L. Washington III [USM]
"Thunder on the Mountain"
by Richard Lee Byers [USM]
"The Stalking of John Doe"
by Adam-Troy Castro [UTS]

    These all take place just prior to Peter Parker's marriage to Mary Jane Watson.

"On the Beach"
by John J. Ordover [USS]

    This story takes place just prior to the Silver Surfer's release from imprisonment on Earth.

Daredevil: Predator's Smile
by Christopher Golden

"Disturb Not Her Dream"
by Steve Rasnic Tem [USS]

"My Enemy, My Savior"
by Eric Fein [UTS]
"Kraven the Hunter Is Dead, Alas"
by Craig Shaw Gardner [USM]
"The Broken Land"
by Pierce Askegren [USS]
"Radically Both"
by Christopher Golden [USM]
"Godhood's End"
by Sharman DiVono [USS]
"Scoop!"
by David Michelinie [USM]
"Sambatyon"
by David M. Honigsberg [USS]
"Cold Blood"
by Greg Cox [USM]
"The Tarnished Soul"
by Katherine Lawrence [USS]
"The Silver Surfer" [framing sequence]
by Tom DeFalco & Stan Lee [USS]
    These all take place shortly after Peter Parker's marriage to Mary Jane Watson and shortly after the Silver Surfer attained his freedom from imprisonment on Earth.

"The Deviant Ones"
by Glenn Greenberg [USV]
"An Evening in the Bronx with Venom"
by John Gregory Betancourt & Keith R. A. DeCandido [USM]
    These two stories take place one after the other, and a few months prior to The Venom Factor.

The Incredible Hulk: What Savage Beast
by Peter David
    This novel takes place over a one-year period, starting here and ending just prior to Rampage.

"On the Air"
by Glenn Hauman [UXM]
"Connect the Dots"
by Adam-Troy Castro [USV]
"Summer Breeze"
by Jenn Saint-John & Tammy Lynne Dunn [UXM]

"Out of Place"
by Dave Smeds [UXM]
  These stories all take place prior to the Mutant Empire *trilogy.*

X-Men: Mutant Empire Book 1: **Siege**
by Christopher Golden
X-Men: Mutant Empire Book 2: **Sanctuary**
by Christopher Golden
X-Men: Mutant Empire Book 3: **Salvation**
by Christopher Golden
  These three novels take place within a three-day period.

Fantastic Four: To Free Atlantis
by Nancy A. Collins
"If Wishes Were Horses"
by Tony Isabella & Bob Ingersoll [USV]
"The Love of Death or the Death of Love"
by Craig Shaw Gardner [USS]
"Firetrap"
by Michael Jan Friedman [USV]
"What's Yer Poison?"
by Christopher Golden & José R. Nieto [USS]
"Sins of the Flesh"
by Steve Lyons [USV]
"Doom²"
by Joey Cavalieri [USV]
"Child's Play"
by Robert L. Washington III [USV]
"A Game of the Apocalypse"
by Dan Persons [USS]
"All Creatures Great and Skrull"
by Greg Cox [USV]
"Ripples"
by José R. Nieto [USV]
"Who Do You Want Me to Be?"
by Ann Nocenti [USV]
"One for the Road"
by James Dawson [USV]
  These stories are more or less simultaneous, with "Doom²" taking place shortly after To Free Atlantis, *"Child's Play" taking place shortly after "What's Yer Poison?" and "A Game of the Apocalypse" taking place shortly after "The Love of Death or the Death of Love."*

"Five Minutes"
by Peter David [USM]
This takes place on Peter Parker and Mary Jane Watson-Parker's first anniversary.

Spider-Man: The Venom Factor
by Diane Duane
Spider-Man: The Lizard Sanction
by Diane Duane
Spider-Man: The Octopus Agenda
by Diane Duane
These three novels take place within a six-week period.

"The Night I Almost Saved Silver Sable"
by Tom DeFalco [USV]
"Traps"
by Ken Grobe [USV]
These stories take place one right after the other.

Iron Man: The Armor Trap
by Greg Cox
Iron Man: Operation A.I.M.
by Greg Cox
"Private Exhibition"
by Pierce Askegren [USV]
Fantastic Four: Redemption of the Silver Surfer
by Michael Jan Friedman
Spider-Man & The Incredible Hulk: Rampage (Doom's Day Book 1)
by Danny Fingeroth & Eric Fein
Spider-Man & Iron Man: Sabotage (Doom's Day Book 2)
by Pierce Askegren & Danny Fingeroth
Spider-Man & Fantastic Four: Wreckage (Doom's Day Book 3)
by Eric Fein & Pierce Askegren
The Incredible Hulk: Abominations
by Jason Henderson
Operation A.I.M. takes place about two weeks after The Armor Trap. The "Doom's Day" trilogy takes place within a three-month period. The events of Operation A.I.M., "Private Exhibition," Redemption of the Silver Surfer, and Rampage

happen more or less simultaneously. Wreckage *is only a few months after* The Octopus Agenda. Abominations *takes place shortly after the end of* Wreckage.

"It's a Wonderful Life"
by eluki bes shahar [UXM]
"Gift of the Silver Fox"
by Ashley McConnell [UXM]
"Stillborn in the Mist"
by Dean Wesley Smith [UXM]
"Order from Chaos"
by Evan Skolnick [UXM]
 These stories take place simultaneously.

"X-Presso"
by Ken Grobe [UXM]
"Life Is But a Dream"
by Stan Timmons [UXM]
"Four Angry Mutants"
by Andy Lane & Rebecca Levene [UXM]
"Hostages"
by J. Steven York [UXM]
 These stories take place one right after the other.

Spider-Man: Carnage in New York
by David Michelinie & Dean Wesley Smith
Spider-Man: Goblin's Revenge
by Dean Wesley Smith
 These novels take place one right after the other.

X-Men: Smoke and Mirrors
by eluki bes shahar
 This novel takes place three-and-a-half months after "It's a Wonderful Life."

Generation X
by Scott Lobdell & Elliot S! Maggin
X-Men: The Jewels of Cyttorak
by Dean Wesley Smith
X-Men: Empire's End
by Diane Duane
X-Men: Law of the Jungle
by Dave Smeds

X-Men: Prisoner X
by Ann Nocenti
>*These novels take place one right after the other.*

Fantastic Four: Countdown to Chaos
by Pierce Askegren

"Mayhem Party"
by Robert Sheckley [USV]
>*This story takes place after* Goblin's Revenge.

X-Men & Spider-Man: Time's Arrow Book 1: **The Past**
by Tom DeFalco & Jason Henderson
X-Men & Spider-Man: Time's Arrow Book 2: **The Present**
by Tom DeFalco & Adam-Troy Castro
X-Men & Spider-Man: Time's Arrow Book 3: **The Future**
by Tom DeFalco & eluki bes shahar
>*These novels take place within a twenty-four-hour period in the present, though it also involves travelling to various points in the past, to an alternate present, and to five different alternate futures.*

Spider-Man: Valley of the Lizard
by John Vornholt
Spider-Man: Venom's Wrath
by Keith R. A. DeCandido & José R. Nieto
Spider-Man: Wanted Dead or Alive
by Craig Shaw Gardner
>*These novels take place one right after the other.*

NOW AVAILABLE IN HARDCOVER
THE GRIPPING NEW THRILLER
SPIDER-MAN®
WANTED: DEAD OR ALIVE
BY NEW YORK TIMES BEST-SELLING AUTHOR
CRAIG SHAW GARDNER
PUTNAM